# *Darling*

BRAM STOKER AWARD®-WINNING AUTHOR

# MERCEDES M. YARDLEY

.

ISBN: 978-1-64548-119-5

Cover Design and Interior Formatting
by Qamber Designs and Media

Published by Black Spot Books,
An imprint of Vesuvian Media Group

For my children, who thus far remain unstolen.
Mama loves you always.

# Chapter One

CERISE ESCAPED THE claws of Darling, Louisiana at sixteen. She hopped into the passenger seat of her new husband's rusty Camaro and drove away, her puff of brown hair flying behind her.

"You will not marry that piece of trash, do you hear me?" Mama's white face had gone even whiter, but with spots of color riding high on her cheeks. "Ephraim is disgusting. Vile. He's got the blood of a monster in his veins. God will damn you forever, Cherry."

"I'm goin', Mama."

"You'll regret it."

Those were the last words her mama spoke to her before she left. Her head was high, and her voice was as cold as it ever was.

But her mama was wrong. Cherry didn't regret leaving at all. Not when she had her first child a few months later. Not when the baby refused to meet her gaze, or eat properly, or when the doctor told Cherry and E that something was wrong with their newborn son. Not when E left them, saying he wasn't going to play daddy to no retard. Not when she was cleaning houses with her new son strapped to her chest in order to make ends meet, or when she was forced to do things she didn't like to pay the rent, and not when those things resulted in her sweet baby Daisy.

She didn't regret leaving that evil little town for one second, a town where the very soil was steeped in something as old and wicked as the Earth itself. In Darling, she was just Cherry, Iris's pretty daughter, and there was nothing more to her than that. Until she became Cherry, Iris's troublemaker daughter who got pregnant in high school, that is.

And then one day the phone rang.

"Hello," the man on the phone said tentatively. "I'm looking for Cherry LaRouche." He had clear diction and a professional way about him. Cerise hoped he wasn't calling on the bills.

"This is Cerise. Hush, sweetie," she said to Daisy, who was playing on the floor with Cerise's slippers. Sliding them on her tiny toddler feet. Sliding them off. On. Off.

"Cherry?"

"Nobody calls me Cherry anymore. Who is this?"

The man cleared his throat. "I'm very sorry. This is John Holfield. I'm a lawyer from Darling. Perhaps … you remember me?"

"John Holfield? Johnny H? Don't tell me you're a lawyer now!" Cerise laughed, the first real laugh she'd experienced in a long time, and the sound of it was sweetness. She never thought anything from back home would make her laugh again, but the idea of that old bully Johnny H. being the neighborhood lawyer, well. That was something that would make the heavens themselves wipe tears from their eyes.

He chuckled back. "Yes, well. Things have changed since we were kids, Cherry. Er, Cerise. I haven't lit fire to anything in ages now." And then he was serious again, his voice the voice of a man with a Very Important Something to say, and not the freckled boy who spent more time grounded than not. "I hate to be the bearer of bad news, but your mother passed away last week."

He stopped, pausing awkwardly while he waited for the news to hit. Johnny H. had certainly learned some manners in the last few years, Cerise thought to herself vaguely. She bit her lip for a second before saying, "I'm sorry, Johnny, did I hear you right? Did you say my Mama …?" She couldn't finish. There was a feeling inside of her chest, something hard and out of place. Is it sorrow? Perhaps it is, but it feels something exquisitely close to hope.

"I'm sorry I didn't tell you earlier," he said hurriedly, "but it took me a while to track you down. You're not listed anywhere."

Cerise leaned against the counter, squinted at the new cobweb that had been spun during the night. "Sometimes things are better off not being found if you know what I mean. Mama's death isn't my concern." She felt dizzy, like the weight she had been carrying for years had lifted off her shoulders, and decided to press itself against her head instead. She grabbed a chipped mug the color of the sky and ran it under the faucet. After drinking it down, she held the cooling mug to her forehead.

"Ch— Cerise, we need to know what you want us to do with your mother's body."

"Put it in a box and shove it in the ground," she said. "That isn't my mama anymore. It's just something else."

"But," John said delicately, "there are other matters to attend to."

"Like what? Her stuff? Sell it all. I never want to see it again."

"The house," he said. "The house, Cherry. It belongs to you."

Cerise paused. Daisy pulled herself up on Cerise's leg, balancing awkwardly.

"Cherry? Are you there?"

"I'm here."

"About the house …"

"Sell it. I don't want nothin' to do with it."

John sighed. "I know that sounds like a good idea, but it just isn't possible. Your mother's will specifically states—"

Trust her mother to make everything difficult. Cerise closed her eyes and concentrated on breathing.

"I'm sorry, Johnny. What was that?"

His voice was spun together out of patience. He was a different man altogether from the boy she had known. This both pleased her and made her heart drop.

"I said you can't sell the house for five years after your mother's death. You can't rent it out, either."

"Mama always was particular about people touching her things."

She heard the smile in John's voice. "So I heard. It's empty, Cerise. If you want it."

"Thanks, but no."

"There's more."

"More?"

"Iris paid in advance for the lights. Phone, water, sewers. All of it. For the next five years."

"What?"

"House is running. Only thing missing is you."

"Why would she do that?"

"Maybe she wanted you to come home."

Cerise's world spun. She slammed a hand down on the counter to steady herself. She gagged. Caught her breath. Rinsed her mouth out in the kitchen sink.

"Cherry?"

"I said no, Johnny."

She hung up. Glanced around and saw the tattered human-colored wallpaper and moldy ceiling from the broken pipes above.

Her son, Jonah, crept from the next room. His arms and legs were made of too-thin bones and knobs. He flicked his hand at the phone and cringed.

Cerise fell to her knees and hugged her son. At seven, he was still as short and slight as a much younger child.

"Was the phone too loud? No more phone, sweetheart. It's time to go to work anyway. Want to bring your ball? You can bounce it on the stairs while I clean."

His blue eyes stopped roaming the room and drew back to her face. She kissed the top of his fuzzy blond head.

"All right, baby. Let me just grab your sister."

Cerise settled Daisy on her hip and grabbed her keys. She herded Jonah out and carefully locked the door behind them.

4

Into the car and across town. The children played and slept and snacked while Cerise scrubbed and vacuumed. Three houses today. Her body ached by the time she returned, feeling as though it belonged to a much older woman. Both children had fallen asleep in the car. Daisy clutched a doll that Cherry had clumsily but lovingly sewn together with scraps.

"Jonah," she whispered, shaking his shoulder gently. "I need you to get up. Time to go inside, baby."

"Kids sacked out, huh?"

Her landlord's voice startled her. Cerise gasped and jumped, hitting her elbow hard against the car door. She rubbed it, blinking away tears.

"You scared me," she said.

"Getting back pretty late tonight. You're usually home before dark."

"I picked up an extra house today, sir."

Her landlord barked.

"Sir," he said. "Oh, I think we're beyond that, don't you?"

The voice was thick as syrup and twice as sticky. Cerise kept her expression neutral, tried to add a little friendliness to it. Something that wasn't a smile but vaguely resembled one.

"What can I do for you? Rent isn't due for another couple of days."

"I know that. I just saw you drive up and wondered if you needed help, that's all."

"No, we're fine, thank you. Jonah, wake *up*."

"Want me to carry him in for you?"

"No!" She heard the panic in her voice. Saw his eyes narrow dangerously. Reminded herself she needed this apartment.

"No, thank you," she said again, kinder this time. She bared her teeth again, and he smiled back. "Although it's nice of you to offer."

Jonah moved, yawned, allowed Cerise to pull him to his feet. He staggered forward under her guiding hand. She grabbed sleeping Daisy and kicked the car door shut with her foot.

"See? Right as rain," she said, but the landlord continued to walk with her.

"Cerise. How is money this month?"

She nearly stopped walking.

"Excuse me?"

"I'm looking out for you. I wanted to see if you needed to ... work out a trade again. If you'd be short on the rent this month, is all."

Her mouth filled with a vile taste. She felt her lips twist and buried her face in Daisy's brown curls.

"I'll have the full amount this time, sir."

Her landlord rested his hand heavily on Cerise's shoulder.

"I want to help you, you know. Make sure the kids have enough to eat. If you ever need anything, any money or anything, I'm sure we can work something out."

Cerise made a sound deep in her throat. She coughed to hide it.

They reached her door. She scrabbled at it, pushing her key into the lock. Her hand was shaking, and she gritted her teeth, determined to steady it.

"Offer's always open."

The door opened, and she pushed Jonah inside, then slammed the door behind her.

She locked it. Wished there were four more locks to throw.

"Bedtime, darlings."

Daisy didn't move when Cerise put her in the old bed and kissed her goodnight. She helped Jonah change into his pajamas and then put him down beside his sister. She went to the chipped bathroom sink to splash her face with water. Dabbed at her face with a threadbare towel.

She was afraid to peek out of the window in case a dark silhouette still stood outside her front door.

It was late at night, but not too late. She called Johnny back.

"The house," she said quietly. "I'll take it. Thank you."

She set the phone carefully in its cradle.

For the first time in eight years, Cherry LaRouche was going home.

# Chapter Two

*T*HE HOUSE HAD always terrified her.

It was beautiful by anyone's standards. Set far off the main road of Darling, separated from sight by trees and a winding dirt and gravel path that made it seem grander, somehow. Three stories of gorgeous Southern architecture. The paint was always crisp and white, offset by dogwood and purple wisteria. Red and yellow roses climbed the trellis outside the large porch. Iris LaRouche had spent many hours tending to her garden, making the house look as stunning outside as it did inside.

But beauty is only skin-deep, as Cerise had learned early from her beautiful, beautiful mother.

The house was just like the town. It harbored something deep inside. Something dark. Something that roiled under the thin veneer of magnificence, something pulsing and veiny and ugly. Cerise always knew it. Always felt it. There were nights when she swore the hallway rose to trip her. Where she heard whispers coming from the walls, like gossiping neighbors. But if the house was neat enough, shone enough, if there was enough sparkle and paint and shine, maybe nobody else would know it. Maybe they wouldn't believe it. Perhaps that's why Iris was always planting and pruning and hiring teenage boys to keep the paint pristine. Perhaps that's why Darling always held parades and fairs and the Dogwood Festival. Hide the rot under something pretty and blooming. Hide the sickness. Don't let it show.

Her childhood home made her gasp now. The paint was

peeling terribly. Windows were broken. The garden was full of weeds.

Her mother was dead. It hit home suddenly, the only explanation for the house's decay. But there was more than that. Had she been ill? A tired, run-down woman at the end? Cerise couldn't picture her mother standing this level of deterioration. It would have struck right into the gut of her pride. Something must have been terribly wrong. She felt a split-second of guilt and then pushed it aside.

Jonah quickly crawled out of the car seat. He looked at the house and his face crumpled.

"It isn't that bad," Cerise promised him. Her eyes roamed over a large wasp's nest in the eaves, the paint rubbing off the wood in moldy patches.

"At least, it won't be that bad for you two." She squatted down and rubbed noses with her son. "We'll make it feel like home, won't we?"

She took Daisy under the arms and swung her to the ground.

"What do you think? See the house? This is where Mama lived when she was a little girl. Just like you."

Daisy tipped her head back, taking in the house and the dark trees that lined the lane. Tall trees with cruel, extending branches. They were the types of trees that terrified little girls.

*I'll cut them all down,* Cerise promised the kids silently. *If they scare you the tiniest little bit, I'll take an ax to them myself.*

It was a house of horrors. A house of nightmares.

Cerise took both of her children and shepherded them inside. Today was going to change everything.

She wasn't afraid anymore. She wasn't a child. She was a grown woman with responsibilities that would crush somebody younger or more fragile. She had come into her own and gone from Mama's Cherry to her own Cerise.

Except her heart beat hard against her chest and she started to sweat as soon as she stepped across the threshold. She let go of Jonah's hand and ran her palm against her forehead.

It hadn't changed inside, not in all the years she had been gone. The same hard green wallpaper hinted at something floral, but reminded Cerise more of something sinister and mean, like the gardens that inhabited her nightmares when she was a small girl. The sunny yellow kitchen had somehow managed to be stormy. The overstuffed chair sat in the corner of the living room, surveying the area with Mama's stern eye.

Cerise suddenly felt sick.

Jonah wrapped himself around her legs and whimpered. Daisy snuggled close as well, pointing at the old stuffed owl her mother had kept over the fireplace. Its face was twisted, cruel, and the bend of its body was unnatural.

"That was a barn owl," Cerise told her children. "Owls like to eat mice. What does an owl say, do you remember?"

But they didn't want to remember. They buried their faces against her jeans and Cerise closed her eyes. The old owl had terrified her as well when she was younger.

"Do you like it?" she asked too brightly. "Do you want to see my old room?"

Without waiting for an answer, she prodded them gently up the wooden stairs. Both kids held the handrail carefully.

"Good kids," Cerise said. "Look how careful you're being."

The second floor hadn't changed, either. The floorboard on the right still squeaked. Old family pictures of people Cerise had never recognized hung haphazardly on the walls. The back bedroom was full of dust and old odds and ends hidden under ragged blankets. Cerise smiled before she opened the door to her room.

"Here it is," she said and swung it open. "This is where I—"

Her words were cut short. The room was empty. Her bed, her dresser that she had bought with her own money, the full-length mirror she used to get ready in front of for school every morning.

It was all gone. The room was horrendously, heartbreakingly bare. She had been erased.

The kids looked inside, and uninterested, turned away.

Cerise half-listened to the giggling as the kids, forgetting their earlier fright, took turns stepping on the creaky board. She looked around her old room, her heart as bare and unkempt as the walls.

"Hello, Johnny. Yes, we arrived safely, thank you. Yes, the place still feels the same."

Cerise sat in the kitchen. The phone was older than she, a dial round that reminded her of secretaries in old movies. The kitchen, although hard, was still the most welcoming room in the house.

"How was your trip? And what do the kids think of the house?" John sounded a little less like John the Lawyer and more like the Johnny H. of her childhood. Cerise was grateful for this. It was a reminder that there were some things she had loved while growing up. He was one of them.

"They're all tuckered out. I put them up in the main bedroom. They're going to sleep with me tonight. I thought I'd get a few things unloaded while they're sleeping and not underfoot."

"Cherry, folks'll be out to help you in the morning. You don't have to do any of this yourself."

Cerise stopped toying with the phone cord. "Help me? You mean people know I'm coming back?"

He laughed. "You coming back to Darling is all anybody has been talking about of late. You know how it is. Any little thing that happens is fodder for the rest of them. Not much that happens here."

"Yes, I know exactly how it is." Cerise seldom heard her voice sound so ugly, but the chill started in her gut and spilled its way out. *That's why I left this place: people couldn't mind their own business. They didn't know where my life ended and where their lives started.* "I don't want their help, John. I'll do it myself."

She slammed the phone down firmly and buried her face in her hands. It was hard enough coming back to this horrible place, but knowing that people had been talking about her for weeks? What would they say about her children? What would they say about Cerise and her lack of a husband? She either had a husband when she ought not or didn't have one when he was supposed to be around. Whatever her choices were, the timing was always off.

Cerise uncovered her face and stood. She took the old, terrifying owl from over the fireplace and tossed it out of the front door, into the darkness. The wildlife scattered away, and it was satisfying. She was tired of running and wasn't a scared teenager anymore. No matter what the townspeople said about her, she was going to hold her head high. She was Cerise LaRouche, and that counted for something. She'd make it count for something.

# Chapter Three

CERISE WOKE UP suddenly. There was a sound, something sliding against the wood outside of her window. She lay still and silent, her children snuggled beside her in the bed.

There it was again.

Cerise slid out of bed and crept to the window. It was an animal of some kind, most likely. It sounded too substantial to merely be the wind, but what kind of animal could make it up to the third story of the old wooden house? She tried to remember if there were any trees close enough to scratch against the window, but her memory didn't stretch that far.

Scratch. Slide. Scrabble.

Cerise looked around for something to use as a weapon. She didn't want to be caught empty-handed if some diseased animal came crashing through the window at her. Though that was being silly, wasn't it? Such things didn't happen in real life.

Did they?

She picked up a heavy lamp from on top of her mama's chest of drawers and held it like a baseball bat. She peeked back at her children. Still sleeping with tearstains long dried on their cheeks. Today was a tough day for all of them.

Cerise walked softly on her bare feet, slowing the closer she got to the window.

*Please don't let there be spiders or, heaven forbid, snakes on this floor,* she prayed fervently. It would be more than she could stand. It would send her straight around the bend to crazy town.

She reached the window, took a deep breath, and gently rapped on the glass. There was a swift swirl of violent movement and a sound that made her scream in her throat. She fell back and swung the lamp at … nothing.

A quick glance at the kids. Still sleeping. Cerise froze, listening, but the scrabbling was gone. She stepped quickly to the window and peered out. A shadow ran through the trees, but whether it was a man or an animal or simply her imagination, she couldn't be sure.

It would be several hours before she could go back to sleep. The sun was already starting to brighten the treetops outside when she managed to crawl back under the covers and put her arms around her little sleeping ones.

"There," she whispered against Daisy's hair. "Our first night in the house. We survived."

It was such a little thing, but it seemed of the utmost importance to Cerise. She fell asleep even while the birds began to sing, a small smile on her face.

Again, Cerise awoke to a noise. This time it was hearty and bright. The sound of car doors slamming and heavy boots on the porch.

"Cherry! It's just me, darlin'. Joe Benson. Me 'n a coupla guys are here to haul your furniture on in."

The voice was friendly and jovial, floating up the stairs. Cerise sat up and automatically grabbed for her clothes.

"Oh, and we have the little 'uns. They came running downstairs a few minutes ago. They ain't causing no trouble, so don't worry about them none."

Cerise noticed the bed was empty and cursed under her breath. She'd talk to the kids later. Right now, she just needed to get downstairs.

She shimmied into her jeans and pulled on an old purple bra with a safety pin in the back. She put on the same shirt she wore the day before. She hadn't brought in any clean ones; they were all in Old Sal.

Running her hands over her dark hair, Cerise hurried down the stairs. When Joe saw her, he tipped his hat.

"Cherry. You have certainly grown."

"How have you been, Mr. Benson?"

"Real good," he said. "Two kids? They're cute ones, too. Are they both Ephraim's?"

The question socked the wind out of her.

"Jonah is E's. Daisy's daddy is different. Both were no account scum who didn't know how to be men." She looked Joe dead in the eyes and was a little surprised when he didn't look away.

"I'm not sayin' they were and I'm not sayin' they weren't. Ain't no business of mine what happened between you and the Lewis boy. I ain't got a beef with either of ya." His eyebrows pulled down and Cerise took a step back. "So, don't you be smacking me on the nose with no newspaper when all I did was ask, young lady. You were raised with better manners than that, and don't you forget it."

Cerise dropped her eyes to the floor.

"I'm sorry, sir."

He cleared his throat.

"Looks like your little 'uns are hungry. Why not rustle them up something for breakfast while we unload your stuff? Where's the moving truck?"

Cerise shifted uncomfortably.

"There isn't one. I ... don't have much."

Joe looked at her.

"Anything for us to move?"

She flushed but looked him in the eyes.

"I have some garbage bags in the back of the car. Clothes."

Joe nodded. "Well, this place has everything you need, doesn't it? Me and the boys will work on the outside for a bit, then. Clean some things up. Save you some trouble." He cleared his throat. "Lulu sent over some food for ya. Knew you wouldn't have time to go shopping what with the move and all."

Cerise's smile was forced. "Thank you."

Daisy ran into the room, her pigtails flying like banners. "Mama! Trucks!" She flew into Cerise's arms, and Cerise held her close.

"Sweetie, I need you to stay by Mama, all right? You and your brother can't be underfoot. Where is Jonah, anyway?"

Daisy pointed out the front door.

Cerise took Daisy's hand, nodded at Joe, and stepped onto the ratty wooden porch. "Jonah! Come inside for breakfast!"

She sounded like her mother. She never thought that would happen, but there it was. Standing on that old front porch and yelling for her kids. She strode toward the truck, Daisy running alongside as quickly as her legs would let her.

"Jonah. Breakfast. Now, I don't want you bothering …" The words died in Cerise's throat as she looked into the truck.

"Hiya, Cherry."

His youthful face had changed since she had last seen him. He'd filled out, his hard planes and angles had softened into the features of a man. He wore a beard now. She never thought she'd see this lanky youth with a beard.

"Hello, Mordachi. It's been a long time."

"It has."

"Mama! Jonah!" Daisy pointed at her brother, who was sitting in the driver's seat, steering the parked pickup truck happily.

"Cute boy you have here," Mordachi said. His eyes never left Cerise's.

"He's a good boy. Jonah, come on down. Let's get you some toast."

Jonah made a sound of protest, a sort of screaming cry, and Cerise sighed. "Sweetheart, let's go. Don't you want some peanut butter toast?"

She dropped Daisy's hand and reached up for her son. Mordachi leaned over, grabbed the boy, and lowered him down with a strong arm.

"Thanks," Cerise said. She walked the kids toward the house.

"Sure is nice to have you back, Cherry," Mordachi called after her.

"Wish I could say the same thing," Cerise answered in a grim tone. She went inside and sat the kids at the table. Opening the basket of food that Lulu had sent over, she made breakfast. Daisy ate. Jonah, not as much. She searched through the bag of treats she had stashed in the pantry the night before. The basics. Bread. Peanut butter. Apples. Grapes. Water bottles. She dropped the bread into the toaster and she and Jonah sat watching it while Daisy ate and chattered away in baby speak.

Cerise pulled Jonah on her lap. "Are we waiting for the toast?" she asked. He made a "huh" sound. "Are you excited, sweetheart? Will it be yummy?"

"Huh."

"And did you have fun in the truck? You were pretending to drive, weren't you?"

"Huh. Huh."

The toast popped up. Jonah flapped his arms in excitement and hooted happily. Cerise put the toast on the white kitchen dishes she had hated as a child. Pristine. Cold. Harsh. She carefully spread the peanut butter with a knife. Corner to corner. Jonah watched in fascination.

"Here, sweetie. This is for you. Go sit down."

A shadow fell across the table. Cerise looked up. Mordachi was standing in the doorway with a strange expression on his face.

"What do you want?" Cerise asked him. It came out harsher

than she intended, but she was too tired and flustered to do anything about it now.

Mordachi blinked slowly at her.

"What are their names?"

"What?"

"Their names. What are their names?"

His voice was so soft and gentle that it took Cerise back for a minute. What did she have to fear from Mordachi? This was the voice of the boy she remembered. Trailing along behind her on their way to school. Sitting on the back porch, cradling the broken body of a tiny stray cat that had run into the family's dogs. Watching from his window while she drove away with E.

Suddenly Cerise was ashamed of herself. Mordachi had done nothing but try to help her, and she was punishing him for sins not of his making. She could be gracious, this once.

"This is Jonah. He's seven. And this is Daisy. She's almost two. How many fingers is that?"

Daisy held up four pudgy fingers. Cerise gently pushed two of them down.

"I'm lots and lots of fingers," Mordachi said. He spoke slowly, just as he always had. It had irritated Cerise. More than once she had told him he should just spit it out, just hurry up and say whatever it was he had to say, that the world didn't have enough time for him to drawl everything out.

"So, Jonah is E's, huh?" Mordachi said. It wasn't a question. He gently ruffled Jonah's fuzzy hair.

"Don't do that, he doesn't like to be touched," Cerise said automatically. She reached her arms out for the boy, but he didn't squawk or scream. He didn't throw his toast down in terror and flee the room. He continued eating, unfazed by the heavy hand resting on top of his blond hair. Cerise looked at the hand in surprise. "He doesn't seem to mind you, Mordachi," she breathed in amazement.

Something moved in Mordachi's eyes, then, something hidden and a little angry. This was a change from the gentle man-boy she had known, and Cerise leaned back slightly.

"Think I'll hurt your boy, Cherry? Think I don't know how to handle a child? That maybe there's some bad blood running in my veins?"

Cerise grabbed his hand from Jonah's head and held it tightly in her own.

"No, it isn't that at all, Mordachi. It's just that he doesn't usually react well with strangers. Or even people he knows, for that matter. But you're doing fine, aren't you, sweet boy?" She turned her attention to Jonah. He looked at her and grinned, both eyes squinching closed like they did when he was genuinely happy. "You like your uncle Mordachi!"

"Uncle ... Mordachi?" The man said the words gently, letting them roll around in his mouth like candy. "I haven't thought about that for a long time." His brown eyes flicked to Cerise. "Why didn't ya let me meet them before? I thought lots about being an uncle, back when it first happened. I thought maybe you'd bring them home sometime. You or E."

Cerise sighed and let go of his hand. "I was never going to come back."

"So why are you here now?"

"I needed the house."

"That's it?"

"What do you mean, 'That's it'? Of course, that's it. What else is there?"

Mordachi ruffled Jonah's hair again, tugged gently on Daisy's pigtail, and stepped back. "Yeah, how could I even ask such a stupid question? What else would be here for you? Nothin', I guess. You sure left us in the dust quick enough."

The color rose in Cerise's face. "You have no right to come in here and—"

"I think I have lots of right, Cherry. You took my brother from me when you left. Think E ever came home after everything fell apart with you?"

Mordachi turned on his heel and left without a word. The busy sounds of sanding and hammering stopped suddenly. Cerise peeked her head out of the kitchen and saw a handful of local men standing there silently, staring at her.

Mordachi's truck started outside, and his spinning tires threw mud against the house before he drove away. It sounded very loud in the uncomfortable silence.

Cerise stood there. Her children, noticing the change in atmosphere, huddled up to her side.

"I'm sorry," she said. "I just ..." She put her arms protectively around her children and blinked rapidly to keep the tears out of her eyes. One of the men shifted, looking uncomfortable, and Cerise cleared her throat again.

"I'm sorry I yelled at Mordachi. I'll apologize to him later. And thank you. For your help. I'm not used to help, not really. I don't know how to react, anymore. But you're doing this for us, and that was nice. Thank you."

Joe stepped forward, tipped his hat. Slapped his hand against the newly sanded wood.

She blanched at the thought of not being able to afford paint, and her eyes found her feet again.

"You're here, Cherry. Like it or not, you're home."

Joe's voice was softer than she'd ever heard. It sounded like resignation to her. Her own thoughts being spoken aloud.

# Chapter Four

LATE SUMMER WAS harsh in Darling. The kids needed new clothes and Cerise needed to get out of that horrible house of memories. It was time to go shopping.

She bundled the kids into their old junker. "This will be fun, kids. Let's go!"

If she kept her voice light enough, maybe they'd be fooled into thinking this was a fun trip instead of Cherry LaRouche's walk of shame.

"Mama! Trees!" Daisy exclaimed.

"That's right, darling."

The dogwoods would bloom come spring. Daisy will be even more entranced with them. There's a lot to be said for the anonymity of the city, but trees weren't one of them.

Cerise drove past the video rental store, which was next to the only place in town to get a haircut—also known as gossip central. Past the florist, whose husband was the butcher, and past the only diner. Darling etiquette required she pop in the diner for a little meet and greet. Cerise didn't give a plug for Darling etiquette. It had never helped her before.

The Alco store was next door to the grocery store. It had everything; batteries, hunting gear, inexpensive toys that wouldn't last a week. When Cerise was a little girl, her daddy would take her to the hardware section of the store and let her try to cut the thickest chain she could find.

"Use all of your strength, Cherry."

All her tiny strength had only dented the chain, never cut it. She wondered if she could cut it now.

Cerise stopped Old Sal seconds before she felt the engine was going to die. She helped Daisy out of her car seat, then leaned over to undo Jonah.

"Behave, okay? Good kids."

The tired bell dinged when she opened the door. Jonah clapped his hands over his ears and hummed.

"Why, Cherry LaRouche, is that you?"

The voice was uncomfortably high and reedy, but it was a warm, familiar voice.

"Hi, Monica. How—?"

Cerise didn't have time to finish the question before she was enveloped in a cloud of too much perfume. She was nearly smothered by Monica's puffy T-shirt.

"I missed you, darling," Monica whispered. She pulled away and her heavily mascaraed eyes shone with moisture. "Oh, and your little ones." She leaned down and smiled at them. "Hello, children. Aren't you beautiful? You must be Jonah. And you're Daisy."

Jonah sat on the floor and began to spin in a circle.

Cerise frowned. "How did you know their names?"

Monica laughed. "Maybe you forgot how small towns work, my dear. They know everything."

"Hello," Daisy said. She sat on the floor and began to spin beside her brother.

"Aren't they both beautiful. You two have your grandmama's gorgeous hair, don't you? Why, they look so much like Iris." She took Cerise's hand in an uncomfortable grip. "I'm so sorry about your mother, dear. She was such a wonderful woman. So important to this town."

Cerise felt her throat close. A sound came out of it that she quickly turned into a cough.

Monica released her. "Now what can I do for you? Need some things to start your new life back home?"

Darling would never be home. Never. "Some clothes for the kids, please. They're growing like weeds. I think they've both gone up a size since we left the last place."

"And where would that be?"

Cerise ignored her prying.

Monica chattered on, catching her up on the gossip going around town. The church had been renovated and repainted. They had a new pastor now since the last one had taken up with the organist. Split their families right in two, that one did. The dogwood festival was coming up. The organist's husband? He'd started the church's float on fire during the last festival. Wasn't that just wild? Little angels with wire wings and robes made of bedsheets leaping off everywhere. The choir screaming. Sounded better than they did in church. And that fire? It was so merry! It burned and burned and burned.

While she spoke, Monica expertly picked out the necessities for the children's wardrobe. She pulled out a pair of boy's shorts, took a second look at the LaRouche's ratty clothes, and decided on something cheaper. Cerise straightened her spine.

"Now that comes to a hundred-and-thirty-seven dollars, Cherry. Most of it will have to be ordered in. Was there anything you need for yourself? A nice dress, maybe? Something that covers more?"

Cerise looked down at her cutoffs. "No thanks, Monica. Mom left some clothes behind. I can make do for a while." She fished the money out of her purse and handed it over. It almost physically hurt her to see so much going at one time. "I'm looking for a job. Do you know if anything is open?"

Monica counted the money carefully and handed back the change. "I'll keep an ear out, honey. I'll call you when the rest of the clothes come in."

Cerise loaded the bags into Old Sal. The grocery store was only a few steps away. The kids balked.

"I know it's already been a long day, kiddos. Just a little longer. Here, you can sit in the cart."

Cerise's muscles strained as she hefted Jonah into the children's seat in the cart. Daisy went into the basket itself.

"Shall we see how fast we can go? Let's run!"

The kids giggled, but it wasn't a game. Cerise could feel Darling creeping into her bones, winding around her nervous system like a malignancy. She breathed in the despair-like spores. The last thing she needed was the new growth of fresh despair blooming in her lungs.

She pushed past two shoppers standing around, comparing avocados.

"Overripe," the first one declared. Her eyes glittered when she saw Cerise.

"Do you see who's here?" she whispered to her friend. They both turned to look.

Cerise hated this town. She couldn't breathe here. At least she could cry in the privacy of her own bathroom if she could just get back to it. Wanting to go to the house? The irony wasn't lost on her.

They were standing in the checkout line within minutes. Cerise was slightly out of breath.

"More," Daisy yelled. Jonah grinned and flapped his hands. Cerise laughed.

"I can't do anymore. Mama's tired." She still smiled as she loaded her items onto the check stand. A gallon of milk. A loaf of bread. The cheapest box of tampons she could find.

"Cherry."

Cerise looked up at the cashier, and the grin fell from her lips.

"Wendy. It's been a while."

Wendy twisted her lips in the smile that had made Cerise's

stomach run cold in high school. She ran the items across the scanner. "Nice way to avoid saying, 'Good to see you.'"

"Good to see you."

"Liar."

*If I can just make it to the house. If I can just make it to the house.*

"The total is twelve-thirty-three."

Cerise blinked. "It can't possibly be that much. I added it up. It should be under ten dollars."

"Do you think I'm stupid?"

It was a trick question. Wendy was going to twist this like she twisted everything else, and Cerise wouldn't be Cerise anymore, but plain old stupid Cherry.

"I just think you're mistaken. And I don't have that much on me right now."

"Don't you? Bet you could pick some change up pretty fast. You're dressed for a quick sale. There's gotta be at least one old perv or two who would pay for a piece of Cherry Pie."

Nothing had changed.

Cerise's cheeks burned.

Jonah rubbed his eyes and started to fuss in the cart.

Daisy stared between the two women with wide eyes.

"Stop being nasty, Wendy, especially in front of my kids. Scan it again, please. I'm sure the machine made a mistake."

Wendy twirled her hair around one finger. "No mistake. Pay up or put something back."

Cerise opened her mouth to say something, but Jonah grabbed onto the cart handle and shrieked. He leaned forward and bumped his head against the handle repeatedly. Cerise stuck her hand there to cushion the blow.

"I don't have time for this. Here," she said and pointed at the tampons with her other hand. "I'll put those back. Hurry, please."

Wendy didn't move. "What are you going to do without them? Sit in the dirt outside all day? That's disgusting."

Jonah was fighting harder. He got past Cerise's hands and the crack of his forehead against the metal was horrifyingly loud. His screams increased.

Cerise started to push the cart through, leaving everything behind. A hand fell on her shoulder.

"Hey, there, Cherry. Just a sec."

She recognized the voice immediately, even after all these years. It reminded Cerise of bonfires and English tests and far too many nights sitting on top of the car with her friends after the sun went down. Cerise looked up, and Runner's familiar lopsided grin still made her stomach twist in the best of ways. His blond hair was overlong, touching his collar, and she swallowed hard at the way his green eyes caught the light. He looked better than ever if that was even possible.

He turned to the pouting cashier.

"Wendy, darlin', I think we all know the machine runs up the wrong prices every now and then."

"I don't need your help. We were—"

"I know a pretty girl like you don't want these little kids to go home without milk and something for sandwiches. Try again, would ya?" He rolled right over her words.

Wendy dropped her gaze and rescanned everything. "$7.14," she said. She took the ten-dollar bill that was lying on the counter. Runner reached out his hand for the change.

"I'll drop it in your purse for ya, Cherry. Looks like your hands are full."

She nodded, then decided that might be taken as rude. "Thanks, Runner."

"Not a problem. I'll be right behind ya."

Cerise managed to get the cart to Old Sal without mishap. She pulled Jonah from the cart and buckled him into his seat. His breathing settled into a more comfortable hitch when he recognized he was back in the safety of the car.

The opposite door opened, and Runner popped Daisy into her seat.

"There ya are, Princess. Now how does this contraption work?"

Cerise nearly smiled. "Let me finish up here and I'll buckle her in."

Runner raised an eyebrow. "I'm no dummy, Cherry. I think I can figure out a simple seatbelt."

"Oh, can you? These things are demonically tricky, you know."

"Says you."

While Runner fumbled with the latches, Cerise put the grocery bag in the car. She thought of her run-in with Wendy and felt her jaw tighten.

"She's not that bad, you know. Just has to make it hard for some people."

Cerise pushed Runner aside and buckled Daisy in. "What are you, a mind reader?"

Runner shrugged, his easy grin lighting up his green eyes. "Nah. But she gets under your skin. Always has. Probably always will." He opened the driver's side door. "After you, darlin'."

"I didn't need your help in there."

"Now most people would say, 'Thanks, Runner. That was mighty gracious of ya.'"

"I ... Thanks."

Cerise slid into Old Sal.

Runner leaned down and handed her a Caramello bar. "I remembered these are your favorite. Never was a sexier sight than Cherry LaRouche enjoying herself some candy."

Cerise's lips twitched into a smile. "Still a sweet talker, I see. Thanks again."

Runner nodded and slapped his hand against the car.

Cerise started up the road to the house. "Well, kids, that wasn't so bad, was it?"

Daisy was already asleep in her car seat, her pigtails waving in the wind like banners. Jonah's eyes darted back and forth, and he gnawed on a raw knuckle.

"Out of your mouth, sweetie."

He didn't listen. Cerise didn't expect him to. She slumped back in her seat. The idea of unloading the kids and the groceries seemed more than she could bear. She'd have better luck strapping her children and belongings to her back and climbing Mount Everest. It would take the same amount of energy.

She turned a corner and passed a thin figure in a too-long skirt walking up the hill. It was her old friend, Rosemary, most likely trudging her way to the home she shared with her disabled mother. Rosemary's mom had been in a wheelchair for as long as Cerise could remember. Sweet, bland Rosemary. The only fight she remembered Rosemary getting in was one in fourth grade when some boy asked why her mom hadn't died yet.

Rosemary had been weary, even then.

"I'm sorry he said that," Cerise had said. "He's such a jerk."

"He's right, though," Rosemary answered. "She just hangs on and on. Every day I open the door and don't expect Mom to be there. But she just … is."

Now, driving, Cerise pretended not to see her, but when her eyes flicked to the rearview mirror after she passed, Rosemary met her gaze evenly. She didn't look at all surprised.

# Chapter Five

$\int$HE THOUGHT SHE heard something.

Cerise blearily opened her eyes, trying to focus in the dark room. Jonah and Daisy snuggled into her side again.

An owl hooted.

She listened, waiting for the scrabbling sound she halfway remembered. It didn't come, and Cerise fell back asleep.

Enough. Enough of this. Of the uncertainty, of tiptoeing down the hall like a ghost. Iris was dead and gone. She had secretly prayed for that. Hell had a place for Cerise.

She picked up Daisy in one arm and swung the cleaning bucket jauntily in the other.

"Ready to make this a place of joy?"

"Joy?" her daughter asked.

Cerise thought. "A house of happy."

Daisy nodded.

"Let's do it," Cerise said.

She eyed the living room gravely. Stark. Unwelcoming. Too many years spent dying inside of these walls, trying to climb out.

"A house of happy," she repeated and stepped through the entryway.

Two and a half hours of solid morning cleaning made a dent into the grime of their house of happy. It was a house of order and a house of good smells. Cerise knew if she worked hard enough, and sang loudly enough, and prayed hard enough, she could turn this house into a home. Maybe her first one ever.

Daisy had fallen asleep on the ugly orange and brown couch. Jonah was in the kitchen drinking a glass of water in loud gulps.

Cerise flopped onto the other end of the couch, kicked off her shoes, and studied her daughter. Her brown curls, her smooth skin, clutching a little bald homemade doll that she had asked Cerise for. This house, this town, it was new to her. What a good little sport, being dragged along to somewhere different and strange.

Cerise felt fierceness claw at her heart.

*I'll make it up to you, sweetness,* she thought. *It will all be worth it.*

Jonah put the glass down, too hard. It shattered, a fountain of glittering blades, and Cerise was up and running before the last shards even had time to fall.

"Don't move, don't *move*," she screamed, and the sound her bare feet made as they landed on the glass was nothing compared to the sound of her heart. "I have you."

Jonah backed up, his arms thrown over his head. Cerise could see at least one hand was bleeding.

She grabbed her son around his waist, twirling him away from the counter and setting him on the table. Her feet left a gory smear of blood where she had spun.

"Let me see your hands. Let me see."

He screamed, bucking and fighting, but Cerise held him down with the strength of a mother who was used to this.

"Mama?"

Daisy stood in the kitchen entryway, blinking.

"Daisy, go sit on the couch, okay? There's glass on the floor."

Jonah continued to shriek.

"Daisy, on the couch, now!"

Daisy turned and fled.

Cerise gritted her teeth and pried open her son's hands.

One palm had a thick sliver of glass in it. His constant clutching and fighting was driving it deeper and deeper into his thin skin. She had to get it out.

"Hold still, Jonah. Stay still, all right, baby?"

She grabbed at the sliver with her fingers, but Jonah bucked violently, kicking her in the stomach so hard she doubled over. He squirmed off the table and ran clumsily toward the entryway.

"Jonah, no!" she shouted, and reached out for him. A thick work boot landed on the glass with a crunch. Jonah was swept into the air and held firmly against a warm chest.

"Where do you want me to put him, Cherry?"

Cerise glanced up to see Mordachi standing in the entryway, holding her struggling son with ease. Daisy peeked out from behind his legs.

"Here, Mordachi. On the table. He has glass in his hand."

Mordachi crunched across the floor and held Jonah down firmly. He pried open the little boy's soft fingers.

"Bleeding pretty bad, Cherry."

"His skin is thin. He bleeds easier than most of us."

"Gonna need to see the doc?"

"I don't think so. Not if I can get the glass out."

Cerise tried to pull the sliver free with her nails, but she couldn't get a good grasp. Jonah's screams were getting wilder, even more frantic. Daisy leaned her face against the wall and sobbed.

"It's okay, sweetheart," Cerise said. A bead of sweat made its way down the side of her flushed face.

Mordachi looked at her with heavy-lidded eyes. "Can't do it with fingers. Got something else?"

"I don't know where my tweezers are. They're in boxes somewhere."

"Got a knife?"

"I don't carry a knife around with me, Mordachi."

He shook his head. "You ain't the girl I used to know."

Cerise shot him a look, but he didn't seem to notice. "I have a knife in my front left pocket," he said. "Grab it."

"I don't—"

He flicked his eyes at her son. Jonah was so frantic he was gasping for breath. His lips were turning blue, his heart overexerting itself. She had to calm him down.

Cerise stuck her hand in Mordachi's pocket, grabbed the knife, and flicked it open.

"Hold him really still, Mordachi."

"Doing my best."

Cerise tested the end of the knife, finding it extremely sharp. She held her breath and flicked at the piece of glass embedded in Jonah's tender hand.

"It's not moving."

"Press a little harder, Cherry. Hurry now. Your kid's going crazy."

He was right. She took a deep breath and pressed the flat of the knife into Jonah's palm. Mordachi's muscles tensed with strain as he held the boy down. Cerise added pressure to the base of the glass until it oozed out of Jonah's hand.

"All done. All done," she said and took the boy into her arms. He fought her until Mordachi picked him up, carried him over the shattered glass, and set him on the carpet next to his sister.

"Look, all better now," he said to the kids.

Jonah ran for the laundry room and slammed the door behind him.

Daisy stared at Mordachi with teary eyes.

"Here, kid," he said, and mopped at her face with a handkerchief pulled from his back pocket. "Go keep an eye on your brother. I need to clean your mom up."

"I don't need cleaning up."

Mordachi glanced at the bloodied floor and shook his head. "Stubborn. Hold on. I have a first aid kit in the truck."

As soon as he left, Cerise hobbled to the chair by the table. She pulled up her left foot and studied the shredded bottom of the sole. Glass sparkled in the sunlight.

Cerise swore.

"They both that bad?" Mordachi returned with a small black box. He grabbed some antiseptic and a cloth.

"Maybe a little worse than I thought."

One side of Mordachi's smile hitched. "Must kill you to admit that. Hang tight. I'm going to splash some of this on the boy's hand."

"He's going to fight you."

"You'll probably do the same while I work on your feet."

Jonah began to scream, and Cerise felt the muscles in her jaw twitch. Mordachi was back in a flash. He grabbed the broom and swept the glass into a pile.

"It looked worse than it was," he said. "And Daisy's a good little one, kept trying to calm him down."

"She does a lot of that."

He dumped the glass into the garbage can and then pulled up a chair across from Cerise.

"Feet up."

"I can do this myself."

"Feet up, Cherry."

She slowly extended her foot until it was in Mordachi's lap. She was painfully aware she hadn't shaved her legs in days. He whistled.

"Did yourself some damage. Did you even stop to think for a minute about putting on shoes before you went running through broken glass?"

Cerise scowled. "What was I supposed to do? Let him prance around in that mess while I looked for shoes?"

He extracted a sliver of glass from her foot, and she hissed.

"Gotta learn to think ahead, Cherry. What if I didn't happen by right now?"

"I would have done fine by myself."

"You always say that but look at you. Look at your life. How's it going so far?"

"What are you doing here, anyway? Just pop by to be self-righteous?"

"Why not? I was bored."

She leaned forward in her chair to tell him exactly what she thought. He also leaned forward, eyes narrowed, to make sure his piece was heard. This was when Rosemary walked in, a covered casserole in her hands.

"Knock-knock. The door was unlocked so I … oh."

Her eyes went from Cerise's face to her long legs in Mordachi's lap then to her face again. Cerise rolled her eyes and drew her legs back.

"Jonah broke a glass and I got some in my feet. What are you doing here, Rosemary?"

Rosemary held the casserole out. "I brought somethin' to eat. I saw you driving your car yesterday and I thought, well."

Cerise felt that uncomfortable pang of shame as she remembered zooming on by, leaving Rosemary to walk up the hill alone. And here she was, already being rude to her.

"Thanks, Rosemary. You can put it on the counter. Mordachi was just leaving."

Mordachi pushed back his chair. He gestured at the knife and first aid kit. "I'll swing by and grab those later."

"Bye, Mordachi," Rosemary said. There was so much feeling in the words that Cerise nearly cringed.

He nodded to her, took another peek at the kids in the laundry room, and left.

Cerise and Rosemary sat in awkward silence.

"Do you mind?" Cerise asked, picking up the knife and eyeing her shredded feet.

"Not at all. Please, go ahead."

"How's your mother?" Cerise asked. Next, they'd probably discuss the weather, and then maybe math class in high school. It was pretty much all they had in common.

"Why didn't you come back, Cherry?" Rosemary asked. She was looking at her white hands, not Cerise's face, so she didn't see her stiffen. "There wasn't anybody to talk to after you left."

"I go by Cerise, now. And we didn't talk that much before."

Rosemary looked hurt. "I always thought we were friends."

"We were friends. Are," Cerise corrected herself. "Are friends. But you don't come back to someplace you hate for just one person."

"I'd come back for one person," Rosemary said. "He wouldn't even have to ask me to."

Cerise almost smiled as she dabbed antiseptic on her foot. She listened to the sound of the dryer door opening and closing, opening and closing, and Daisy's cheery humming.

"You wouldn't happen to be talking about Mordachi, now, would you?"

Rosemary blushed. She tucked her feet under her chair like a young girl.

"So, how long have you been sweet on him?" Cerise wrapped both feet gingerly.

"A while."

"A long while or a short while?"

The ruddiness faded from Rosemary's face, leaving it pale again. "It doesn't matter. He isn't interested."

Cerise almost felt bad for her. "How do you know that? Did you ever ask him?"

Rosemary turned her cornflower blue eyes on Cerise. "I don't need to ask him. It wouldn't do any good. He's just who he is. I don't think he'll ever get married. I don't think he even wants to."

It was like poking at a bruise, but Cerise couldn't help herself. "What makes you say that?"

Rosemary's eyes drifted from Cerise's face as she took in the room. She noticed the shattered glass on the counter and stood up to get a rag.

"Come off it, Cherry. You know why."

Cerise drew in a quick breath. Rosemary collected the glass into the rag and dropped it into the trash can. She mopped the counter with almost manic precision.

"You're selfish, Cherry. You always were." She met Cerise's eyes again. "It's not your fault, really. Everybody treated you like you were somethin' special."

"Nobody treated me like I was—"

"I mean, how else were you gonna act? Everybody liked you. The boys were all over you. Even after Ephraim knocked you up—"

"Rosemary," Cerise said, her voice low.

"You were still the golden child. Tell me, how is that fair?"

"Rosemary, lower your voice. You're going to upset my kids."

Rosemary threw the rag on the counter. Her eyes were full of tears. "How does that happen? When I do everything right? And nobody even looks at me?"

Cerise was torn between hugging Rosemary and hitting her. She settled on raising her chin.

"Sit down and pull yourself together. This isn't like you."

Rosemary looked at her trembling fingers where they grabbed the counter. Her lips thinned.

"I'm sorry. I don't know why I said that."

Cerise sighed and patted the chair next to her. "Sit."

Rosemary obediently walked to the chair and perched on the edge. Cerise put an arm around her bony shoulders.

"It isn't easy. It's never going to be easy. That's what this town does to you, you know? Makes it seem like you should be one thing when you're actually another. But you know what? You're good enough for this place. You're good enough for everything. And you're good enough for Mordachi."

Rosemary didn't answer.

Cerise gritted her teeth and gingerly stood up. "Come on. I want you to meet my kids. Everybody has their reason to stick around on this planet, and these little darlings are mine."

She limped to the laundry room, Rosemary following a good distance behind.

Cerise poked her head through the door.

"It's dark," she said and flipped on the light. Both children blinked at her like they were field mice wandering into the early sun. She glanced at Jonah's hand as he flapped them in the air. The cut looked good.

"Jonah, Daisy, I'd like you to meet my friend Rosemary. We've known each other since we were little girls."

Jonah rocked from side to side, eyes stuck firmly on the buttons and dials of the washing machine.

"Hi," Daisy said sweetly. She started to rock back and forth like her brother.

"What's wrong with them?" Rosemary asked.

Cerise's hackles rose automatically, but she forced herself to breathe. She was familiar with this. She could handle this.

"Jonah has a genetic disorder. It affects, well, everything. And Daisy's completely typical. She just likes to mimic her brother. Don't you, possum?" Cerise ruffled Daisy's hair. The little girl grinned.

"The boy is E's," Rosemary said slowly.

Cerise struggled hard to keep her voice level. "The boy's name is Jonah. And yes, he's E's." *From when I was "knocked up" in high school,* Cerise almost said. The words were bitter in her mouth.

Rosemary turned to face her. "So, whose fault is it? Who's the carrier of ... whatever? You or E?"

Cerise's mouth dropped open.

Rosemary pressed on. "And you used to drink a lot. Is that it? Is he a fetal alcohol baby?"

"Get out."

The words were so soft they sounded like a hiss.

"What?" Rosemary asked.

"Get out of my house."

Rosemary's slim hand flew to her mouth. "Oh, Cherry! I'm so sorry! I didn't mean to—"

Cerise gathered both of her children close. Jonah ducked away, while Daisy snuggled up and closed her eyes.

"I knew this is what it would be like," Cerise said. Her eyes burned with fire, or maybe they were just ordinary tears. "So simple. Too simple. Nothing *happened* to my son, okay? It isn't anybody's fault. He's amazing, and he's here, and I'm not going to have him listen to some silly girl running her mouth off without using her brain."

"That isn't—"

"Go now."

"But I—"

"Now!"

Jonah covered his head, dropped to the floor, and howled.

Daisy burst into tears as well.

Cerise glared at Rosemary, who finally backed out of the hallway, fled for the heavy wooden door, and slammed it behind her.

Cerise felt the beginnings of a headache pushing behind her eyes. She slid onto the floor.

"Come on, Daisy. Climb into my lap. Let's watch Jonah play his heart out, okay? Jonah, show me everything to do with this washer."

He rocked and sniffled, gradually getting to his feet. He pointed, pushed buttons, and spun dials. The door opened and closed, opened and closed. Daisy buried her face into her mama's shoulder and put her thumb into her mouth.

Cerise leaned her head against the wall and listened to the click-thump-bangs the washer made.

"I love you two."

No answer.

Click. Thump. Bangs.

# Chapter Six

THEY FOUND THE body in a tool shed. Long abandoned, overgrown with Cyprus vines. Somebody had cut the tangles away from the door. Somebody had slipped something infinitely precious inside.

He was a little boy with dark hair. At least, after he had been identified, his mother had told the police that he had dark hair. He was found with no hair at all, his head perfectly shorn and smooth like a grotesque baby doll.

His hands were perfect, soft, and clean. Only his broken nails belied what had happened to him. He was combed and brushed and studied. His thin legs with surprisingly muscular calves, his pointy ischium bones pressing sharply against the skin in his bottom. He was a child who was meant to run and jump and pick through fields and old furrows of ground. But here he was, not a mark on him. The only thing missing was his hair. And his breathing. And his spirit.

The police asked for his name. His mother couldn't answer. She just said, "My little bird, my little sparrow," and she wept and wept and wept.

They asked about his father, but she had no answer to that. They asked if the little boy had any medical conditions, if he had imaginary friends, if he hung out with any of the older boys who liked to ride their bikes down the dusty streets and throw firecrackers at old, windowless stores. They asked if she thought he had shed his dinosaur shirt and tiny red shoes somewhere and crawled into the toolshed himself. They asked her if there was a reason his heart should stop, or when he had shaved his head. They finally, hesitantly, brought up the question they had been avoiding. Was there anybody who would want to hurt such a beautiful, perfect little boy?

Later, one of the police would think back on this day and shake his head grimly. How hopeful they were. How naïve. They found a body, and thought, "What a horrible tragedy. This poor boy. This poor mother. Really, that can't be much worse than to mysteriously lose your child."

They were touched, certainly. But they were just thinking of it as a body. They certainly didn't think of it as The First.

# Chapter Seven

WHEN CERISE PICKED up the phone, her fingers knew exactly what numbers to punch. It had been years, but old habits shot through her nerve endings and taught her fingertips what to say. She was sixteen again, and in love, and Darling was still big enough for her dreams.

She was almost surprised when Ephraim didn't answer.

"Mordachi," the voice said gruffly.

Cerise cleared her throat.

"It's Cerise."

"Cherry."

His voice didn't give anything away. Cerise felt her shoulders draw together.

"Mordachi. Well, I wanted to apologize for yesterday. You were being a friend and I was ugly to you. I'm sorry."

Silence.

"Did you hear me?"

"I heard you."

The disinterest in his voice twisted something deep inside of Cerise. She wasn't herself anymore but had reverted to the old Cherry. Scared little knocked-up high school dropout Cherry. She sniffed and was ashamed at how loud it sounded.

"Mordachi, please. I'm so sorry. I didn't mean to act that way. You've never been nothin' but nice to me." She realized her grammar was slipping. She took a deep breath and very carefully repeated herself. "Anything. Anything but nice, and I know I don't deserve it, but please don't be mad at me. I don't know what I'd do. I'm in this awful house with these horrible white walls and the kids are confused and I don't have a job and …"

"Cherry LaRouche, you always did work yourself up something awful. Fool woman."

He hung up. Cerise stared at the phone in her hand before setting it gently in the cradle. The sound was horrifyingly final. She had heard that sound many times before. After the doctor told her she was having a baby. After she called to drop out of her college classes. After she begged E to take them back, to just give them a chance as a family again. The coldness of that sound never warmed.

"I don't know if I can do this," she whispered. The words were wicked things, twisting their way inside of her larynx and shredding themselves into the softness of her throat. They were malignancies of intent, and once burrowed into the quiet places of her body, of her heart, and where her spirit grows, they would never be stemmed.

"I don't know if I can do this," she said again. It was easier this time. She swallowed the bitterness down and was vaguely surprised to find her eyes tear-free.

Her children were laughing. Something heavy rolled across the wooden floor—too weighted to be a ball or a toy. It was most likely a vase or something her mother would have swatted their hands away from. Cerise straightened her shoulders and purposefully didn't check in on the children. If they wanted to destroy something from the house, they were welcome to it. Destroy it all. Knock holes in the wall with her mama's Things of Value. Burn the place to the ground and dance in the ashes. It didn't matter. The house was a place like Darling was a place. The things were only things. People were what mattered, and Jonah and Daisy filled this place with joy. They built innocence on the bones of this house like flesh. Joy would run through its walls like finely placed veins.

*I don't know if I can do this,* she thought again. Her lips parted so she could say it, but the breath wouldn't come. *Speak,* the cancer of despair seemed to urge her. *Say it aloud. Let your ears hear. Let your misery coat the walls like fire smoke.*

Jonah laughed again, high and free, and Daisy's bubbles of glee followed. It sounded like music. It was a song of triumph.

"I can do this," Cerise whispered. The malignancy of desolation cried out as she spoke, but Cerise blinked the color back into her eyes.

There was a loud knock at the door. Mordachi stood there, a brown paper bag in his hands.

"Here," he said, and shoved the bag at Cerise. He turned to leave.

"Wait." She stepped onto the front steps. "Don't go. I wanted to—"

"Got something in the truck." He disappeared into the thick foliage outside.

Cerise peered after him.

A soft hand clutched at her arm.

Jonah was reaching for the bag.

"Should we look inside?" Cerise asked, and Jonah huh'd happily.

She set the bag on the counter.

Daisy scrambled over and tried to climb up Cerise's body.

"What's in there?" she asked.

"I don't know. Let's find out."

They opened the brown paper bag with a reverence that was saved by some for Sundays. Cerise pulled out thick sandwiches. Roast beef on homemade bread. Apples. An orange. A couple of bananas. Daisy loved bananas.

Mordachi thumped into the house and shut the door behind him.

"Thought you guys would be hungry. Haven't eaten lunch,

have you?"

Cerise shook her head, unable to answer.

Mordachi nodded to the food. "Well, then. There you go. I ate already. This is all you."

Cerise swallowed hard. "Thank you, but I don't need your charity."

Mordachi walked right to the cupboard that held the plates. Years of repetition told him where everything was. He pulled out the same stark white plates that he had eaten off when he was ten years old. The same chips, the same scratches. There should be comfort in such familiarity, but there wasn't. Familiarity breeds horror, too.

"Cherry, this has nothing to do with you. This is about a guy who had too much food and brought some over. It's called being neighborly. Has it been so long that you've forgotten what being neighborly means?"

It stung. Cerise opened her mouth to say something, but Mordachi was already setting the plates on the table.

"Come and get it, kids. There's more'an enough to go around."

"Thank you," Daisy said, and climbed into her seat.

Mordachi rested his hand on her hair.

"Ain't nothing. Jonah, want to sit down?"

"He won't sit. He won't eat anything, either, except maybe the apple. He only likes crunchy things."

Mordachi handed the apple to Jonah. He took the sandwich from the little boy's plate and dumped the meat out.

Cerise automatically reached for Mordachi but caught herself. How many times had she done the same thing to his brother? Touching him, calming him, trying to keep the temper at bay. Her hand trembled. She laced her fingers tightly together.

Mordachi stepped past her, dropped the pieces of bread in the toaster. He scooped up the extra roast beef and added it to a sandwich already piled high.

"This is yours, Cherry. Go on. You always were too skinny."

She eyed the sandwich. "I can't eat all of that."

He shrugged. "You're gonna try. You need to keep your energy up. I have plans for you this afternoon, my dear."

Her eyes widened, and she felt sick inside. "Plans?"

He reached for her, and she jerked away.

Mordachi sighed and showed her the toast he had reached past her to get.

"No matter what I do, you always think the worst of me." He dropped the toast on Jonah's plate.

"No, you're wrong." Impulsively, she leaned her head against his chest. "I'm sorry, Mordachi. Of all the people in the world, I think you'd be the last one to hurt me. But there's something ugly that's inside of me now. A place that's all rotted out. And even when people are being nice, I keep thinking that they're only looking for an angle."

He ran his hand over her hair, patted her head like he had just patted her children. "S'okay, Cherry."

Then he was quiet, thinking about calming barn cats or the weather or the way that Cerise's hair had blown in the wind when she was a child, Cerise didn't know. But she was glad he was here, that he hadn't let her stubbornness run him off.

She was good at running people off.

She saw something glinting by the front door and craned her neck to get a better view.

"What's that? What did you bring?"

Mordachi's face broke into a wide smile. "Cherry LaRouche, we're gonna have ourselves a party."

Paint. Mordachi had brought over several cans of paint. Cerise slipped to her knees and clapped her hands like a child.

"Oh, Mordachi! I'm so excited! What colors do you have? Can we see?"

He grinned and popped a screwdriver under the lid.

"Lots of colors, Cherry. A little bit of everything. See, some of this blue. Some of this red. A little bit of green, and lots of this orange. Even some pink for the little one. You like pink?"

Daisy had wandered over and stared in awe at the pink paint. "Pink," she said and ran back over to the table.

Cerise couldn't keep the smile off her face. "What are they all for?" Her eyes were far away, like the Cherry of before, when Mordachi gave her his box of crayons once, and they had drawn all over the underside of the kitchen table until his dad caught them and gave Mordachi the whipping of his life.

"I do a little woodworking every now and then, and that means painting if the customer wants it. I don't have a lot of anything, but I have lots of little different things. Do you like it?"

Her eyes glowed. "I love it, but what's it doing here?"

Mordachi looked at his big black boots on the pristine carpet, like he thought he was making the place filthy just by being in it. He breathed lightly. Cherry wondered if he was thinking delicate thoughts, as though that would lift him high enough that he couldn't leave mud on the carpet.

"White walls are like a prison for you, Cherry. This ain't your mom's house no more; it's yours. Make it yours. I have brushes and tarps in the truck. I'm busy today, but I can give you a hand later on in the week if you want it."

She couldn't stop staring at the paints and their beautiful colors. "Mordachi. It's wonderful."

He glanced at the kids, still eating at the table. "They're my family, Cherry. You're my family. I don't have anybody now, and suddenly you all showed up. These kids can't live in a museum, and this house ain't built for kids." His eyes bored into her. "You know that, and I know that. Make it a good place for them."

He nodded and disappeared out the front door. The house suddenly seemed empty and bare, like a blank canvas. She thought she caught a whimper from the walls, edging back from the color.

"Children," Cerise said, smiling at the cringing walls. "I think we're going to have a splendid evening. First, I'll find us some music. Then we're going to have ourselves some fun."

Could this place become something more than a horror? Could it really become a home?

She looked at her children, buzzing around the cans of paint. The door where Mordachi had been.

Maybe, yes, it could be something more than it was. For the first time, she believed.

# Chapter Eight

SADA'S TINY BODY was found slowly, laboriously, in pieces. She had been a little girl with dark hair and even darker eyes. Her eyes had held secrets and laughter and childhood charm for six years. Now her eyes held nothing at all.

Her hands were discovered first, hanging from the Crying Trees like a rosary. The man who discovered them stood for a long time, staring at the soft fingers and delicate ribbons of bone until he fell to his knees. He didn't see something pale and shadowy flit through the trees.

The police called her father, Azhar.

He fell to his knees, also.

# Chapter Nine

THERE WAS A wailing, a painful sound wrenched from deep inside of a person. The wailing made Cerise stop cold, and she wrapped her thin arms around herself. But they were too thin, too white, even after all this time in the Southern sun, and as she pressed her hands to the fluttering in her stomach, she felt a strange humming sensation there, a strange pressure.

Her hands were bone, pressed against the tattered remains of her womb and diaphragm. The wailing tore itself out of her mouth, rocked her head back from the force of it, and Cerise made a noise that stunned her senseless, clubbed all humanity out of her head. It was the sound of a suffering so raw that her ears began to shred. Blood ran down her face, down what was left of her body, and still the sound became louder and louder until she searched frantically for something to throw herself from to seek refuge from the sound, which threatened to consume her.

She sat up in bed, gasping. Her dark hair stuck to her wet skin, and she flailed wildly until she realized that she was in her mother's old bed, her darlings beside her. She rested her face on her knees, wrapped her arms around herself, and shook with the sobs that she wouldn't allow herself to utter out loud. Dashing her hand across her eyes, she looked at her children.

Asleep. Peaceful. Jonah's hair stuck up like a beacon, something beautiful. In his sleep, he was king of his world, just a sweet little boy. Not an afterthought. Not a mistake. There was nothing lacking, nothing that any stranger could point at, and

Cerise wished this would transfer over into his waking life.

"You are enough," she whispered and leaned over to kiss his hair. "You are exactly right."

Daisy's blue eyes darted behind closed eyelids.

Cerise hoped that she dreamed of rainbows and popsicles, and all the things a child should dream about. Not houses with frightening white walls and whispering tongues that licked you while you slept. Not a mother who had a chip on her shoulder and bandages on her feet.

A sound. Cerise was out of the bed before she realized it. She padded to the window. Listened.

Scratch. Scratch, and a thump.

The sound of something moving surreptitiously, a sound of wrongness, of something being where it shouldn't be. She knew that sound, had heard it on many of the nights when she had worked in seedy motels and parking lots. It was the sound of husbands being unfaithful, of desperation and greed undressing in the dark.

The floor undulated under her feet, and the walls whispered. She felt a pressure building behind her eyes and a tension in her shoulders that nearly crippled her.

"Quiet, quiet, quiet," she whispered the mantra. A prayer, asking the otherworldly to shush.

Cerise moved the curtain, slowly, carefully, but couldn't see anything outside. The thing eased itself around on the roof. She pressed her hand to the glass and closed her eyes. Perhaps if she willed it away, believed strongly enough in fairies and gods and whatever it was that people believed in, it would go away. Go away and leave her and her children be.

The sound again, and she smacked her hand against the window sharply. It was a small movement of triumph and fear, an insignificant rebellion against the evil monsters of the world, but it was enough. A scrabbling sliding and something skittered across the eaves far more nimbly than she would have thought possible. Then silence.

Cerise kept watch over her children for the rest of the night, but the sound didn't return. It would eventually, she was certain but for right now, they were safe. Next time might be a different story.

"I'm going to be prepared, my sweet ones," she whispered. Daisy turned comfortably under her words. "I will take care of you and do the very best I can. There might not be much value in me, but there's one thing I know, and it's love. I'll fight for you, any way that I have to."

The sun rose. The window, which had seemed so dark and dismal before, filled with colors. Shadows were banished. Monsters were vanquished. Cerise's fears shrunk and stumbled until they were a much more manageable size.

"Mama," Daisy said, her bright eyes peeping over the blanket. "Today?"

Cerise smiled. "First we're going to have baths and breakfast. Do you remember the paint Uncle Mordachi brought us? We're going to make the house into something extraordinarily beautiful."

The little girl sat up, her hair a glorious mane of tangles. "I help?"

"Of course."

Jonah stirred, rubbing the sleep from his eyes. They opened and seemed clear and bright until the reality of life dulled them. It broke Cerise's heart to watch him disappear. He was a fairytale prince under a magical spell and was only fully himself when asleep. There were glimpses of him here and there during waking hours, but that thin moment between sleep and wakefulness blunted something inside of him. No matter how strong the spirit is, the body couldn't fight against it. The battle was fought over and over but couldn't ever be won.

Cerise felt the sadness in her smile, so she let it drop.

"Jonah can help, too. Let's go. We have a big day today."

Cerise's wounded feet hurt. Too much standing. Too much dancing. Too much spinning and balancing on stools to get that one spot right there, up in the corner. So much color that she caught her breath. Teal behind the fireplace. Pink in what would be Daisy's room. Red and blue for Jonah. Lavender in Cerise's.

They were the happiest of sore feet. Bare except for her bandages, they were spattered with tiny spots of color. They were spattered with joy. The house had been a house of laughter this day.

Mordachi was right: tiny splashes of many colors. Enough for a wall of this and a mantle of that. She painted the molding in the downstairs bathroom a bright burnt orange, the color of the sun. Her mother was probably spinning like a top in her grave.

Cerise wished she could paint her mama's casket burnt orange, too. Maybe give Iris some whimsy in her life. A reason to let her hair down.

"I want a burnt orange casket," she said to Daisy. Daisy had paint in her eyebrows and wore a smile. Her paintbrush was wet with water, and she was 'painting' the bathtub neat and clean, inside and out.

Jonah was happily playing in the laundry room. She could hear the doors opening and shutting. She had hoped to paint it green before nightfall, but it would have to wait until tomorrow.

Dinner time. Bath time. Storytime. Bedtime.

A Louisiana storm was brewing. She swallowed hard, angry that the wind and thunder still made her shiver.

A truck growled up the way. Cerise turned around expecting to see Mordachi, but she sucked in her breath with surprise.

"Morning, Cherry," Runner said as he hopped out of the

truck. His pants were painted on him and his shirt was too tight. Cerise felt things stirring in places that would make a proper lady blush. "I was hoping you'd be around today."

"Why would that be?"

His smile still had the power to do things to her, even after all these years. Especially after all these years.

"Why, Cherry, can't a friend stop by every now and then just to say hi? No need to make it complicated."

Cherry's smile made it to her eyes. "You always were a complication, Runner." She leaned back on her heels. "Now, what can I do for you?"

Runner went quiet, his smile looking out of place. Finally, he shook his head.

"Look. There isn't an easy way to ask this, so I'm not even gonna try. Would you like to go out sometime? On a date." He looked like he was trying not to fidget, and the memories of Runner in his youth flooded back so hard Cerise's hair nearly blew back. But with Runner came everybody else.

"You know I can't. It isn't that I don't want to."

He squatted down, looked her in the eyes. His were so green they burned.

"But what? What's your excuse this time, baby? Things have changed since then, you see. They're different."

"You don't need to point that out."

Cerise looked toward the yard, to her children playing in the tub of clean laundry they should be folding.

Runner took her chin and turned her to face him.

"All the more reason, Cherry. You're a strong woman, but you have an awful lot on your shoulders. Let me help you out, huh? Hang around and give you a hand."

She bit her lip, and Runner laughed.

"Some things change, and some things don't. I see you still can't make a decision that will do you any good."

He stood up, blinked the sun out of his eyes.

"You're not with E anymore. He left you flat, and that's not what a real man does."

He held up his hand when she opened her mouth, his face burning with so much anger he looked like somebody else for just a minute. "Now, you know he was my best friend since we were kids, but what he did, that wasn't right. Especially to you. Especially with a baby. He didn't deserve you, Cherry LaRouche, and it's time you understand it. E always acted tough, but when push came to shove, he had a way of squirreling out of trouble. You know it and I know it."

He sighed and shook his head. He took his hat off and rubbed a hand across his hair.

"This isn't what I came here to say. I came to say, 'Have coffee with me,' and you were supposed to say, 'Why, yes, how very fine,' and it would be the end of the conversation. But things don't work like that, do they?"

He turned to leave, and Cerise finally found her voice.

"Runner."

He paused but didn't turn back around.

"Yeah?"

"Coffee—" she cleared her throat and tried again. "Coffee would be great. But dinner would be better. I'm no chef by any means, but I can cook. How about Thursday at eight?"

He turned around then, and his smile was a beautiful thing. "Been waiting over ten years to hear you say that, my girl. Don't make anything. I'll bring something over. See you then."

He drove away and Cerise found herself staring after him. Then she looked at her kids.

She hummed as she tackled the ground with her spade. The soil threw up rocks and lizards and evil things, but she didn't care. Not a whit.

# Chapter Ten

*T*HURSDAY SURGED FORWARD with an eagerness that was nearly uncomely. Cerise padded around the house, touching up paint and playing with her kids, all while watching the clock. She fed her children lunch and tried to remember if Runner liked her better in blue or yellow. She tucked her kids into bed at seven and kissed them both goodnight.

"Tomorrow you get to sleep in your own rooms. Won't that be wonderful? I love you, my darlings."

Cerise ruffled their soft hair, watching as they snuffled and cuddled together in her mother's old bed. She looked out the window, listening for the now-familiar scuttling sound, but nothing was to be heard.

"Now I guess it's time for me."

The shower was luxurious. Cerise soaped and shaved and exfoliated, rubbing a worn washcloth over the bones in her hips. Her vertebrae jutted like a broken staircase down her back. Cerise frowned, running her hands over her too pale skin. If she didn't take care of herself, she'd get sick. Being sick meant doctors she couldn't afford. Better to buy a few extra apples or another jar of peanut butter. Cerise wondered what Runner would bring over. Her stomach growled.

She sat at her mama's vanity, drying her hair. Next, she marked her mouth with red lipstick and studied her face in the mirror. It was the face of someone else, a girl long ago who went to school by day and earned money by night, while her son slept in the backseat of the car. Cerise scrubbed the lipstick off and threw the tube into the trash. She painted her lips a pale pink, pressed them together.

"This is a mistake," she told the mirror. The woman in it nodded back wisely. "The last thing you need is any type of relationship, especially with Runner."

"What relationship?" the woman in the mirror asked her. She darkened her lashes with mascara, and Cerise was almost surprised to find herself doing the same. "This is just dinner with an old friend. Nobody can fault you for that."

"Yes, but E—"

"E isn't here." The woman in the mirror worked on her other eye, became something beautiful. "This doesn't have anything to do with anybody else. This night is just about you and Runner."

She kissed her children again and made her way downstairs. This time she didn't know if the butterflies in her stomach came from hunger or excitement.

Runner was on time. He knocked lightly, and when Cerise opened the door, she found that she was barely breathing.

He was beautiful. His too-long hair was still wet from his shower, combed back from his face. Cerise kept her eyes firmly on his, refusing to let her gaze travel down the rest of him.

"You're sure looking lovely, Cherry. Gotta say it makes me happy to see that you fixed your face just for me."

He leaned over, planted a light kiss on her lips, and pressed a bouquet into her hands.

Cerise couldn't say a word.

Runner nudged her gently. "How about some water for the flowers? Poor little things might get parched."

Cerise backed up clumsily. "Oh, yes, the flowers. They're … Water. Beautiful. Thank you." She started toward the kitchen, dropped her head.

"Darlin'? You okay?" Runner put a hand on her shivering

shoulder. "Did I do something wrong? Pick the wrong flowers or something? Because I—"

Cerise turned around, her eyes alight, her smile so glorious that something tightened in Runner's gut. He swallowed hard.

"Runner, this is ridiculous. They're beautiful. You look so handsome I could eat you alive. I'm terrible at dating. Haven't done it since E, and I don't know what to do. I'm a mess. Are you sure you want to stay for dinner? I can't offer you anything after that. You might want to cut your losses now." She closed her eyes and breathed deeply, making love to the scent of the food from his takeout bags. "Oh, my lord, is that chicken fried steak you have in there? If you're going to leave, leave my half behind, will you?"

Runner set the food down. He took the flowers from Cerise's hands and set them down, as well. He pushed her against the table, pressing a firm hand to the back of her head.

"I think I'll take my chances."

His mouth on hers tasted glorious. He lifted her onto the table, and she wrapped her legs around his hips, keeping him closer. There was a hunger inside her that had nothing to do with dinner, and she teased and tasted and feasted until her lipstick was gone and her hair had fallen out of its elastic band. Her lips were swollen, and her neck raw from nips and bites. She buttoned up her top two buttons and made sure her bra strap wasn't hanging out.

"Well," she said and smoothed Runner's hair with her hand. The tenderness of the gesture almost caught her by surprise. "Well," she said again.

Runner's eyes were blazing colors they shouldn't be able to blaze, dilated and loopy looking.

"Well," he answered. He caught Cerise's gaze and laughed, his delightfully sharp teeth flashing white in the candlelight. He leaned forward and nuzzled her ear. "I don't know about you, Cherry, but we'd better stop now before I reach a no-stopping point. My boyhood fantasies are coming true."

Cerise blushed and started to dish up their dinner. It was cold, but she didn't care.

"Sweet talker," she said.

Runner caught her and spun her to him.

"I'm telling the truth. Only the truth. If you only knew how many times I imagined how it would be when you and I—"

"Runner, that was the old Cherry. I'm somebody different now. I'm Cerise. Strong, dependable, beat-down, mother-of-two Cerise. That girl you remember? She's not me."

He pressed his lips against hers. Spoke against her mouth. "It is you, Cherry. Cherry, Cherry, Cherry Pie. I know who you are."

The kisses were sweet, but the words were even sweeter. It was several minutes before Cerise realized Runner was kissing her tears, washing them from her face with his lips and tongue. Her life had been under a wicked spell, and by saying her name, her *real* name, perhaps he had broken it. Cerise struggled and was hurt and abused. Cerise never had enough or was worth enough. But Cherry? Ah. Cherry had been happy. The world is beautiful with Cherry-colored glasses.

"Cherry," Runner whispered again, and she nodded. Yes, yes, she was Cherry. In that instant, Cerise was shed like an old skin, and the bright, beautiful, new Cherry was left behind.

Runner left shortly thereafter with tight jeans and a tight Cherry-colored band around his heart. But Cherry went to bed and slept with her lips parted for the first time in years. The darkness in the walls paced and cursed and shouted, but she didn't hear. Everything was beautiful. Everything was right.

# Chapter Eleven

CHERRY STARTED HER morning on the front porch, wrapped in her mother's old robe and holding a mug of hot water in her hands. She hoped it would warm her like tea. She closed her eyes and let the cool morning breeze bring the scent of the trees to her. The nights in Darling were terrifying things, full of creatures that prowled and storms that never fully went away. But if you survived the nights, then sometimes you earned the mornings.

She had forgotten how many times she had awakened on a soft blanket in the trees, her clothes scattered around her, E's fingers tangled in her hair.

"Bound for trouble," her mama had told her before beating her with a poker where the bruises wouldn't show.

But on those mornings when the stars slipped away, and the sun blinked blearily, she didn't feel like trouble at all. She was just a girl, with a boy, and she felt more like a child than she had in any other time of her life.

A truck rumbled up the road, and Cherry squinted until she could determine it was Mordachi's. She stood and waved over her head. He pulled into her drive, and she walked up to greet him.

"Morning, Mordachi."

"Morning, Cherry. Whatcha doing up so early?"

She stretched happily. "I'm rested. It feels good. I made Daisy a doll this morning." She pointed at the scrap of cloth at her feet.

Mordachi picked it up and turned it over in his hands. It was sewn together with free, uneven stitches. White and undressed, it smiled with the simplicity of a child's toy.

"Still making these after all these years, huh?"

Cherry laughed. "They're easy. Daisy has been asking for them more and more lately. She says she dreams about them at night. She's quite specific. The last one couldn't have any hair. This one can't have any clothes. She's asked for several. One with yellow barrettes and one sock. All kinds of silly things. But I love sewing them, and it takes so little to make her happy."

Mordachi held the tiny doll in his worn hands. "Reminds me of another little girl I used to know."

Cherry grinned into her mug. "On your way up to the property?"

He nodded, thumbed at the bales of hay in the back. "Have a couple horses now. Gentle ones. Keep 'em up at the old field, with a couple of ranch hands who came through to help me take care of them. Maybe your kids would want to give 'em a ride sometime."

She opened her mouth to say no. She opened it to say horses were dangerous, that her kids were small, that their bones were so fragile she feared breaking them every time she tugged their slim little shorts on in the morning.

That's something Cerise would say.

Cherry said something different. She said, "I think they'd love that."

Mordachi eyed her, a smile brewing under his lips. "Would they? What about you?"

She shrugged. "I might love it, too. It's been years since I was on a horse. Sure you're ready to force me on one of them? Don't you want to keep them gentle?"

Mordachi laughed out loud and then peered over Cherry's shoulder.

"Morning, Jonah. Morning, Daisy. Your mom and I are talking about horses. Do you like horses?"

Jonah's hair stuck up in the back like a rooster tail. Daisy's resembled something closer to a Louisiana tornado.

"Kids? Say hi to Uncle Mordachi."

Jonah hooted and pranced to the truck. Mordachi lifted him onto his lap and let him work the hazards.

"Horses!" Daisy trilled.

"I have a gray mare that loves to have little girls ride on her back. What do ya say?"

Daisy's eyes were as big as moons. Cherry tried to smooth her daughter's hair, but it waved into the sky, as defiant as ever.

"Thank you, Mordachi. You name the time and we'll be there."

He reached into the passenger seat, grabbed a couple of bananas. He tossed one at Cherry and one at Daisy. She caught it and squealed.

"Let's whip up this boy some toast. Then let's go horse riding after breakfast. Sound good?"

Cerise tried to bubble to the surface again, but Cherry squashed her down with something that felt like delight.

"Fantastic. Let's get these little monsters and their mama into some clothes, and then what do you say, kiddos? Horses!" She started into the house, turned to look at Mordachi over her shoulder. "Coming?"

Mordachi turned off his truck and set Jonah on his feet. He reached out, squeezed Cherry's hand, and then put the boy on his shoulders.

"Ever been on a horse before?" he asked Jonah. Jonah flapped his hands eagerly. "You'll have the time of your life, son. Ain't no place as relaxing as a horse's back, that's for sure."

He set Jonah down and bustled around the kitchen.

Cherry leaned against the doorjamb, watching them.

Mordachi looked up and winked at her.

She waved shyly before heading upstairs to dress.

This is what family does. She had never realized it. Family didn't hurt and cut and shame. Family made toast and got each other drinks of water out of chipped mugs. Mordachi didn't have much luck when it came to family, and neither did she. But just maybe the two of them could figure it out, and show her kids that family is more than Mama. It's Uncle Mordachi and love, too.

The four of them were sitting shoulder to shoulder in the truck.

Daisy screamed with delight.

"Someday they'll get around to paving this part of the road," Mordachi said it automatically, the same way he always had.

Cherry laughed. "You've been telling me that since we were kids. I don't think it's ever going to happen."

He glanced at her, his smile slight through his beard. "I'm a patient man, Cherry. It'll happen one day. You'll see."

The tone of his voice seemed heavier, alluding to a meaning she didn't quite understand, but a particularly nasty bump threw her shoulder against the window.

"All right?"

"I'm fine."

"Whee!" Daisy shouted, and Jonah followed suit.

"Whee! Whee!"

Mordachi slowed, facing the boy.

"Whee!" Jonah repeated, and his grin spread wide.

"Well, I'll be," Mordachi's voice was low.

Cherry just smiled. "He does speak, sometimes. Not often. But his voice. Isn't it beautiful?"

Mordachi nodded. "It is."

"Whee!" Jonah shouted again, and then his face changed. His eyes widened, his mouth became a black hole that opened wider and wider until Cherry thought she'd be sucked in.

"Mordachi!"

He ripped his gaze from her son and stared at the road. He

cursed and slammed on his brakes.

"Hold on." He threw one arm out to protect the kids, and the truck tore through the rutted road as if it was a starving thing, and chewing through the rivets and dirt was the only thing that could satiate it.

Cherry grabbed for her children, protecting their heads with her frail hands until the pickup finally came to a stop with a horrible sound.

"Are you okay? Are you okay, my darlings? Shhh. Shhh, it's all right." She glanced at Mordachi. "What was that?"

He opened the door to the truck. "Looked like a coyote. Pretty sure we hit it. But that's unusual. They're too fast and too cautious."

The words left his mouth and then they died. They fell to the earth and rolled like marbles. His mouth still moved, but nothing was coming out. If it hadn't been for her children's whimpers, Cherry would have thought she had gone deaf.

She looked at him, then. His brown eyes were wide, not just taking something in, but really *looking* as if they had never really seen anything before in his whole life. He went pale beneath his tan, and Cherry knew what she would see before it happened. His eyes would narrow, his face would go hard, and he would look just like his brother when he said he was gone, he was done, there was no reason to stick around for rutting with a sow that only popped out retarded piglets.

She closed her eyes and turned her face away. She couldn't take it. She couldn't take it.

"Cherry." His voice was soft, but she still couldn't open her eyes.

"Cherry. Honey. I need you to do something for me."

"Wh— What?"

He spoke calmly like he was charming a scared kitten, and she realized that's what she was reverting to. She swallowed hard and opened her eyes.

"What can I do?"

He took a step away from the truck door. "I need you to slide over to the driver's side. Don't get out, just slide over the kids. That's right."

"Need your gun?"

"Not necessarily, darlin'. It's too late for that. We killed the coyote when we hit it."

"Then what—?"

"I need you to drive back and get the sheriff. Don't look," he growled when Cherry tried to see what had shaken him. "It's not something you need to see. Just go back and tell the sheriff to come up here. Then go home. I'll have somebody drop me off at your place to get the truck later."

"Mordachi, I want to—"

"Will you just listen to me, woman?" he roared, and the kids squeaked and drew into each other with fright. Cherry scrabbled for the key and struggled to turn the engine on.

"I'm sorry," he said, and rested his hand on her trembling one. "This isn't anything I want the kids to see. You shouldn't see it either."

"All right. I'll send help."

He nodded once, sharply, and Cherry slammed the truck into reverse. As she turned around on the barren road, she watched Mordachi kneel and reach out for the furry body of the coyote. No, he was reaching for something else. Something white and broken and ...

Cherry gasped. Her foot slammed on the accelerator.

"Mama?" Daisy asked.

Cherry took several deep breaths. "Uncle Mordachi wanted to stay and look at something, sweetheart. We're going to go see the sheriff for a minute. Isn't that neat? A real sheriff's station."

"Sheriff?"

She let Daisy chatter away in her baby talk, answering noncommittally as she thought about what she had seen. Perhaps, she tried to convince herself it was just a toy. Something old and unloved that had fallen by the wayside. Tears coursed down her cheeks even as she talked sunnily of parades and police cars and how sheriffs used to wear gold stars in the Wild West.

Just a toy, she told herself sharply. She pushed the truck to its limit, taking corners too fast and nearly mowing down a mailbox that seemingly popped out of nowhere. It was a doll. A life-sized, broken doll out in the middle of the road. The coyote thought it was unusual, that was all. Strange enough that the animal didn't want to leave its quarry even though a vehicle was bearing down on it. It couldn't be a child that had been torn to pieces by the wildlife. Mordachi had simply knelt to tenderly feel the naked plastic of the doll because somewhere there was a little boy or girl who missed it, that's all.

She swallowed the tears as hard as she could, but they still blurred her vision. She pulled into the sheriff's office so wildly that two cops ran out to greet her before she could even get the children out of the truck.

"Up the lane, E and Mordachi's property. On the way to the horses. We found a ... there was a coyote and we hit it and it was eating something."

Her eyes darted to her children. The policeman's gaze followed her.

"A doll," she said, and her lips twisted up. She was crying fully then. "A little doll in the middle of the lane."

"Does this ... doll ... need an ambulance?" The officer pressed.

Cherry shook her head. "It's too late," she said, and there was movement around her, sound and flurry and the children were delighted that yes, indeed, there were sirens, and they were delightfully loud and heralded commotion. Cherry couldn't stop crying even though there was so much going on around them, but she assured Daisy that mommies can be funny that way, and besides, not everybody always likes a parade.

# Chapter Twelve

THE POLICE INTERVIEWED her tenderly. Her children were in her lap because they couldn't bear to be away from her even for a minute. They knew something was wrong. Cherry could tell they didn't know what, exactly, but they were aware something made their mama cry. It wasn't her usual crying in the middle of the night, either, when nobody else was around. This time their Cherry cried in front of a *person*, a person with a shiny badge, and she could see it was a little scarier somehow.

"Somebody is missing their favorite doll, my darlings," Cherry whispered.

Daisy nodded somberly, and Cherry knew she understood all about dolls and how much it hurt to lose them. She and Jonah had once played Hidey Hole with one of her plastic ponies, burying it in the dirt of the old apartment they had lived in, and could never find it again. Losing a doll was enough to make anybody cry.

After they discussed the doll, and where the doll had been, and why the doll had been there, the policewoman got up. She and Cherry hugged—"I went to school with your mama," the officer had confided to the children—and then she climbed into her police car and drove away.

Dinner was apple slices with peanut butter for the children, but Cherry had no appetite. She cuddled with Jonah and Daisy on the couch until they fell asleep in their pile of blankets, and then she slipped away.

Mordachi didn't get there until long after nightfall.

Cherry was sitting on the front porch, a sweater wrapped around her thin frame.

He sat down heavily beside her.

"This is how I found you this morning. All happy, like today was gonna be something special."

The silence was heavy between them. Cherry sighed and leaned against him.

"For a moment, I thought today might be something special. I almost forget, sometimes."

"Forget what?"

His breathing was slow, his body warm. She liked the feel of his flannelled shoulder, of the steadiness of the flesh covering his bones. Good old dependable Mordachi.

"Forget that some people just aren't entitled to happiness. I think I'm one of them."

He looked at her then, eyes narrowing, lips opening to say something, when a truck squealed up the path, throwing dirt and rocks everywhere. Cherry buried her face in Mordachi's sleeve while he threw up his hand to protect them.

"Cherry? Darlin'? I heard. Are you all right?"

Runner. Cherry blinked at him through the glaring headlights. She heard Mordachi's voice.

"Turn those lights off. You're blinding us."

A pause, and then the lights clicked off. Runner strode over to them and started running his hands over Cherry's arms and legs like he was searching for broken bones. Maybe he was. Maybe her pain would show up physically, turning into shards and jagged edges, and his roaming fingers could catch them and put them back together.

"I'm fine, too, if you were concerned."

Runner ignored Mordachi.

"Ah, darlin', I'm so sorry. I heard what you found. Were the kids with you? Did they see anything?"

Cherry took his arm and pulled him down beside her. He sat so close that his warm thigh pressed against hers. She was almost sickened to feel the little thrill that rushed through her. Life in the sorrow. A stolen moment before grief stamped it out.

"They were there, but they didn't see anything. Mordachi made sure of that. He stayed there while I got the sheriff."

Runner slanted his eyes Mordachi's way. "Well. Thanks."

Mordachi shrugged. "You don't show that type of thing to kids. Any idiot with half a brain knows that."

Runner looked like he was going to say something, but Cherry thought of the broken little white legs and shivered. Runner slipped his arm around her.

"Cold? Maybe we should go inside."

Cherry shook her head, watched the moon. "I'd rather stay here if you don't mind." She looked too white, too thin, too embattled to be sitting there in the moonlight. As if she would break, or perhaps she already had.

Runner tightened his arm around her.

Mordachi pressed more tightly into her side.

"Did you ever think," she pondered, and her words were almost too low to hear, "we'd be here one day? Sitting on this porch together just like when we were kids?"

*It's not the same without E,* she thought, and this surprised her. For a second, she missed him. Then the moment was gone, and she remembered his angry face, his disgust when he looked at his son. Trying to waitress in her cast.

"I never thought I'd come back," she said, and she didn't know if she was talking to Runner or Mordachi or herself. Perhaps her mother. Perhaps all of Darling. "I thought when I left this town, that was it. E and I would be happy."

Mordachi leaned back, tucking his hands under his head, and staring at the sky. "E don't know how to be happy. It just isn't his way. If there isn't trouble, he'll stir some up. Happy is for people who know how to be calm."

Runner snorted. "That's for sure." He looked over at Mordachi. "So, what did you hear tonight? About the baby?" Cherry started and Runner pulled her close. "Sorry, darlin', I know it's shocking, but it's on all of our minds, isn't it?"

Mordachi sighed. "Wasn't a baby, it was a boy about four-years old. Not that there's much difference." He covered his eyes with his hands. "They're checking all the missing persons reports right now, but they can't think of anybody right off the tops of their heads."

"So, he wasn't local," Cherry murmured. She wondered how many nights she had run around the fields here in town. She thought about the rustling outside of her window at night and frowned.

"Not that they know of. A missing kid, well, you think word would travel pretty fast among these parts."

"Did the coyote kill him, then? Is that what they think?"

Cherry was glad Runner asked. She'd been thinking it, too. What happened? Did the poor darling fall off something high and break his neck? Was he lost? Was he scared? Did a toothy animal come up from behind?

Mordachi was silent.

"What? You don't know?"

He knew. Cherry could tell by the way he held his body carefully, perfectly still as he thought things over. Should he tell them, should he not? Would the information make their lives better or worse? Could it help in any way? Would it scare Cherry? She knew how his mind worked. Slow. Thorough. Taking every angle into consideration.

"Cat got your tongue?"

"Shhh." Cherry put her hand on Runner's knee. "He knows. He's deciding what to tell us. Don't press him."

"It wasn't a coyote. They're thinking the mutt just found him later. Dug him up, maybe, or maybe he wasn't buried to begin with."

Cherry felt her face go white. "So?"

"It looks like he was killed by a knife, they're saying. I'd agree. Wounds on the throat, and all. Too many to be an accident. Too clean to be an animal."

"So, somebody did it. Somebody actually killed that little boy."

Runner was thoughtful. "That's unusual. Dead kid, not local. Why would somebody bring a body all the way out here to get rid of it?"

The bile rushed from her stomach to her throat. Cherry fought to keep it down. This wasn't a body. It wasn't simply a dead thing. It was a child, just a little younger than her Jonah, and he should be tucked in at night, not moldering out in the leaves somewhere.

Mordachi's silence said too much. Cherry sighed. "There's more, isn't there."

"It's not the only body they've found lately."

Cherry's head snapped up. "What?"

Mordachi scratched the back of his neck awkwardly. "Kids have been popping up all over lately. Here. Over by Houma."

"Related somehow?"

He shrugged. "Don't know. Some are knifed. Some are hanged. Some of the … pieces … aren't all found. So, whether it's the guy that got our little one or not, there's a monster on the loose. Or several of them." Mordachi looked into Cherry's eyes. They were warm and brown and frighteningly serious. "If you ever need help, Cherry, just give me a holler. I know you don't need a man to protect you, but it's never a bad idea to have a friend on hand. Just so's you know."

Cherry opened her mouth to thank him, but Runner's laughter cut her off. "Oh, you're so good with kids, now? Something you learned from your daddy, no doubt."

Mordachi's eyes turned black, and he held his mouth strangely still. He stood.

"Been a long day. I'm gonna leave before I say something I might regret later." He nodded to Cherry. "I'll check in on you tomorrow. Hope you can get some sleep."

He walked to his truck and pulled out of the lane.

Cherry turned on Runner.

"What a horrible thing to say. You should be ashamed."

He snorted. "Ain't nothing he hasn't heard for years, Cherry. Nothing to get all bent out of shape about."

He reached for her, but she pulled back.

"You need to go home. I have a lot to think about tonight. That poor boy. Missing children. I need to figure out how to feed my own children's bellies, let alone worryin' about some crazy man carryin' them off to the hills." Her grammar was slipping again. She took a deep breath. "Thanks for coming by, Runner. It was sweet of you. But right now, I need to go to sleep more than anything. See you later?"

He stood, pulled her to her feet. He gave her a quick peck on the forehead.

"Any time you can make time for me, Miss LaRouche, I'll be here."

He opened the door for her with a gallant gesture, and she smiled as she walked inside. She locked the door and leaned against it. The sound of his truck in the lane sounded strangely reassuring.

Maybe there were people out there who would care for her, she thought. She'd been going at it alone for so long. Perhaps this would be a nice change.

But that boy. She tossed all night, seeing him naked in the road, decorating a Christmas tree, showing off a toy he had disassembled. She dreamed she invited him to their home, to be a part of their family, but he did nothing more than slowly float in the air beside them, a ghostly child without any eyes or voice, looking like nothing more than a naked, handmade doll.

# Chapter Thirteen

*T*HERE WAS UNEASE in the air that morning, settling like dust on her heart and into the crevices of her skin. It powdered everything, making the sky grainy and foreign.

"It's going to rain today, my darlings," she said. She helped Jonah step out of his pajamas, pulling on the Big Boy Diaper he still wore every day, and would possibly wear forever. "This rain is different than the rain you're used to. You're in for a surprise."

A knock sounded at the door, and Cherry sighed. "Just once," she whispered to her son, "I wish we had a little time to ourselves. I want to grieve if I want to grieve. I want to wear pajamas all day in the house and not feel bad for it. How does that sound to you?"

Jonah put his fingers in his ears and hummed a steady, tonal note.

"That's right. The knocking is too loud. I'll go answer it."

Rosemary. Her frail hands were shoved way down deep into the pockets of her jacket.

"Good morning, Rosemary."

"I hear you were out with Mordachi yesterday. That you found a dead boy."

"Don't beat around the bush, do you?"

"Can I come in?"

Cherry hesitated for just a moment, then swung the door wide. "Daisy's still asleep, so if you'll keep your voice down."

"What were you doing out with Mordachi?"

Cherry kept her voice even. "Going to see his horses. Now excuse me, I need to make the kidlets some breakfast."

Rosemary trailed behind her into the kitchen.

"Was there blood?"

"I don't want to talk about it."

"Did you hit the kid with the car, too, or just the coyote?"

"Rosemary!" Cherry slammed the jug of milk on the counter so hard that some of it spilled. "Leave it be. Especially in front of Jonah."

Jonah had wandered into the kitchen, yellow hair sticking out in every direction.

"Toe?" he asked. "Toe?"

"Yes, I'll get you some toast. Excuse me." Cherry reached past Rosemary for the bread, popped it into the machine.

Jonah covered his ears and hummed in anticipation of the metal gear work as the toaster clicked down.

"You know, I've never seen him eat a vegetable."

Cherry gritted her teeth. "I try, Rosemary. It's a textural thing. He'll only tolerate dry and crunchy right now."

"Don't they have therapies for that sort of thing?"

"They do. But I can't afford them."

"Why do you keep having kids if you can't pay for them?"

Cherry whirled around. "Why did you come here? If you want—"

"Hello, Daisy. How's my beautiful girl?" Rosemary practically sang it.

Cherry snapped her mouth shut. Daisy stood in the doorway, rubbing her eyes.

"Sleepy? Come and give me a snuggle."

Cherry watched while Daisy walked dazedly into Rosemary's arms. Something pulled in her chest, but at the same time, she was relieved Daisy had somebody else to go to. It wasn't healthy for little girls to cling to their mother and only their mother. She told herself this, but she still swallowed hard and realized her hands were clenched into fists when Daisy finally managed to pull away.

"Hungry, Mama."

Cherry forced the smile. It felt like the old days when a smile was a uniform to wear, but Daisy and Jonah deserved to have a mama who lit up when they walked in the room. She was determined to light up.

"I bet you are. I'm making some toast. Would you like some?"

"No toast."

Cherry was sure Daisy was tired of it. Toast. Water. Milk on a good day. She thought of their finances and knew there wouldn't be very many good days left, but at least there was some milk now.

"We have some apples. Would you like me to slice one up for you?"

The little girl nodded.

Rosemary watched Daisy with something like sadness in her eyes. Cherry felt her anger fall. To not marry when you wanted to marry and to be denied children when you wanted children. It had to hurt. It had to burn and twist, take root deep inside of you. The sorrow had to pulse through her veins in place of blood. She was surprised Rosemary wasn't a bitter husk by now, but no, she continued.

"How is your mother doing, Rosemary?"

"The same. She's been pretty sick this year. I can't take her outside."

"What does she do most of the day?"

Rosemary reached out and tried to detangle Daisy's hair with her fingers. "Nothing, really. Sits in her wheelchair with a blanket and a book. Sometimes some embroidery. I take her to the window so she can check the cat traps." She smiled a small smile. A lonely smile. "We have quite a few strays, so I went to the hardware store and asked for live traps. We catch the cats, she watches them for a while, and then we let them go. We catch the same cats over and over."

Cherry cored and sliced the apple, setting the plate in front of Daisy. "Does she have a favorite?"

Rosemary sighed as Daisy squirreled away from her, closer to her food.

"You know my mother. She doesn't have favorites. She doesn't like anything."

"I'm sorry."

"It's okay."

Jonah and Daisy chewed their breakfast. Rosemary watched them, then turned to the kitchen window. "I know how I am. I know I'm too blunt. Difficult. There's a way I'm supposed to say things, but I don't know how that way is. Do you understand?"

Her eyes were too blue. They were open and honest and didn't know how to protect themselves.

"I know what you're saying, Rosemary. You have a really good heart. Everyone knows it."

Rosemary studied her fingernails. Like the rest of her, they were long and slim.

"I wish I knew what they want. I wish I knew what Mordachi wants."

Cherry took a bite of Daisy's apple and handed it back to her. "Why don't you ask him? Then at least you won't have to wonder."

Rosemary's eyes were piercing. "I'm afraid I know what he's going to say, and I won't be able to stand it. It's better not to ask, sometimes." She stood. "I'd better go. I just stopped by to warn you about the storm. It's supposed to be a big one, and I remember how you're scared of thunder."

Cherry blushed. "I'm not scared of it. I just don't like it, that's all."

Rosemary shook her head. "That's right. Nothing is too much for Cherry LaRouche. I don't know why I keep forgetting that."

She turned and left.

Cherry found herself staring after her.

# Chapter Fourteen

"MORDACHI! MORDACHI, OPEN the door."

Cherry pounded on the old wooden door with the palm of her hand. Jonah covered his ears and whimpered. Daisy narrowed her eyes against the wind threatening to push the trees down around them.

"Mordachi!"

A jackrabbit ran across the lawn, sprinting out in the woods that made up the Lewis's yard. How many times had she played here as a child? As a teenager?

"Uncle Mordachi!" Daisy's tiny knuckles rapped on the door awkwardly. "Open?"

Heavy feet on the other side of the door, then the sound of the lock turning. A haggard, bearded face peered through the slightly open door.

"Yeah?"

Cherry cleared her throat, her arms wrapped around her kids. "Can we come in?" A piece of metal siding slid along the ground, and she cringed. "Please?"

He smiled, opened the door, and stepped aside.

"After all this time still, huh, Cherry? Thought you'd get used to it by now."

She hurried the kids indoors. "I didn't have to get used to it. I moved somewhere with very little wind. But now …"

"You're back."

"I'm back."

He grinned at the kids. "Hey, buddy. Hey, little lady. What do you think of all of this wind?"

Jonah wandered away and started to explore the stairs. Cherry flicked her eyes to Mordachi, who shrugged.

"Nothing here that can hurt him. A few guns, but they're locked up with their bullets in a separate case. Knives, too."

"No wind," Daisy announced. She shuddered. "Scary."

"Yeah?" Mordachi crouched down so he could see her eye to eye. "What's so scary about it? Except'n it's loud."

"It's loud," she said and nodded.

Mordachi smiled. "You've been listening to your mama too much. Nothing 'bout this wind that can hurt you. Just make sure the stuff in your yard, and your little ones, are tied down."

Cherry's head snapped up, and Mordachi laughed.

"You never let me down. You know I'm just foolin' ya. These little ones are too heavy to go off in the storm."

He grabbed Daisy, hung her upside down, and tickled her. She screamed with laughter.

"You're probably wondering why I'm here," Cherry said. She watched Jonah climb the stairs, darting in and out of rooms. "He's looking for your washing machine," she explained.

"He'll find it. Just a few doors down from where he is now. I don't care why you're here, Cherry. I'm just glad you decided to come. Guess I half-expected you when I saw the light change to storm light."

"It's been a while."

"It has."

She looked around, taking the house in. It was darker than she remembered. The paint was an ugly avocado green, and bits of wallpaper were peeling off here and there.

"It's good enough," he said like he could read her mind. "It's just me, and I'm not home much."

"But it's so dreary." She clapped her hand over her mouth.

"I'm sorry, I didn't mean to say that."

"It's all right," he said. Then his eyes sparkled. "No, you're right. It is dreary. I got no eye for this sort of thing. But you do. I bet you could do a right nice job sprucing up the place."

"But I don't—"

"I'll pay you, Cherry. Buy your supplies, whatever you want. Business is good for me. I don't spend nothing. You could go through, pick out, I don't know, draperies or coverlets or whatever it is that people put around to make things look nice."

She smiled. "The first thing we'd have to do is new paint. This is awful. This was here when I used to come over, and I thought it was awful then. I always wondered why your mother …" She stopped. "Oh, Mordachi. I'm saying everything wrong today. Please forgive me?"

He watched Daisy chase around after her brother, climbing in and out of the cabinets. "Nothing to apologize for. And I'm serious about the house. You need work and I need someone to make this place livable. It's not fit for company."

Cherry fluttered her eyelashes at him. "You have a lady friend you're building a nest for? Come on, you can tell me."

He shook his head, his smile cutting through his dark beard. "No, ma'am. No lady friends."

"What about Rosemary? She's taken a shine to you."

The look he tossed her was full of emotion. Pain and embarrassment and frustration. "Cherry. Not funny. Don't even joke about it."

"Is she really that bad?"

He sighed, rubbed a piece of soot off the wall with his finger. "There are things you want in a woman, you know. And things you don't. Psycho isn't one of them. Now, about the house."

"I'll do it. I'd love to do it. Thank you, Mordachi."

She launched herself into his arms, and they were both laughing. Then thunder rattled the old pictures and stuffed animal trophies on the walls. The wind called her name, promising the most obscene of things. Cherry pressed her face into his shoulder.

His arms tightened around her. "You really are still scared. After all this time."

She pulled away, smoothing her shirt nervously. "Wind and thunder. What kind of adult am I, huh? Are you all right, my darlings?"

Her children hooted back.

"Fun, Mama!" Daisy cried and scurried back into her cupboard. Jonah closed the door behind them with a click.

"She forgot she was scared, huh," Mordachi teased. "That's my girl. So, what can I do for you?"

Cherry studied her shoes. Her toes had worn the fabric nearly through. She should pick up another pair, but that would have to wait. Everything would have to wait.

"I'm here for two reasons. The main reason is the storm. I went through and found all the flashlights I could, but none of them are working. I can't find any batteries, and I can't run down to the store and buy some right now." Or ever, she thought. Put it on the list with the shoes. "I'd use candles, but I know the little ones would knock them right over and the house would go up like a tinderbox. Do you by any chance—"

"Have some batteries? A slew, my dear. A plethora. You like that word, plethora?"

She nodded. "Thank you. I just need enough for one flashlight if you don't mind. I don't want to take any more from you."

He waved her away. "I have a ton of batteries. What am I gonna use them for? I'm not going to send you and the kids back to the house in the dark with one lousy flashlight. What kind of man would do that? Besides, this storm … I didn't want to say something in front of the little ones, but there's something different about it. Can you feel it?"

She looked at his eyes, trying to see if he was serious or if he was teasing her. But E was the teaser, not Mordachi. She pressed her lips together.

"Honestly? I'm terrified. I feel like I want to run away screaming. Whether it's this particular storm, or because it's my first storm back in Darling, or because it's a storm at all, I feel like I'm going to jump out of my skin. I think I'm exploding, and I don't know how to keep all of the pieces in."

She felt her eyes starting to tear, and quickly blinked until they were gone. "I'm sorry. I'm just a little emotional tonight, after everything." She cleared her throat. "I keep thinking, what would happen if we hadn't found that little boy? Would the wind drag him across the ground? Was he in a hole somewhere, and the water would fill it until he floated to the top? It seems disrespectful, like the earth itself is desecrating his grave. I can't stand it. Have you been thinking about it?"

He rubbed the back of his hand across his eyes.

"I can't stop thinking about it, Cherry. I wish I could, but I can't." He opened his eyes. "You said there were two reasons. What's the other reason you're here?" He looked at her intently, so deeply that for a second, she wondered if … but no. Not Mordachi. He was like a brother to her. She shouldn't look for problems where problems didn't exist.

"The other thing is … oh, this is embarrassing."

"Come out and say it, darlin'. I can't help you if I don't know what you need."

"This is for the children," she said and bit her lip. She pulled herself together. "We don't have any food. Nothing in the house except for two apples, and the kids are … *we*. We're hungry. Could you perhaps—?"

"Kids," he shouted. Jonah and Daisy popped their heads out of the cabinet. "Come on down to the kitchen. Let's rustle you up some dinner. Then we'll make up a nice basket and you can take some stuff home before the storm really gets started. It'll be a picnic."

"Yay!" Daisy shouted and ran down the stairs. Jonah pranced behind her.

"Toast and everything," Mordachi said. He ruffled Jonah's hair.

Cherry sniffed and dashed at her eyes discreetly.

Mordachi caught her hands and kissed her fingers.

"Cherry, we're family. This is what family does. Don't ever be ashamed to ask for something, you hear? If I have it, it's yours. It's always been that way. Besides, would you turn me away if I was hungry? I'm seeing you shoving food into my hands left and right if'n that were the case. Probably some strange concoction you'd make. Wouldn't that be so?"

She nodded, unable to speak.

Mordachi put his arm around her and walked her to the kitchen.

"It's going to be a crazy storm. Let's get you some Crazy Storm Food. And maybe some things you can cook over candles or a fire in case the power goes out. You might need it."

# Chapter Fifteen

$I$T WAS STARTING to get dark when there was a pounding on the LaRouche's door. Cherry, Mordachi, and the kids were picnicking on the living room floor, with everything spread out on a cheery blanket. Tonight was going to be special; Cherry was going to make sure of it. Not frightening. Not pressing. Just special.

"Runner," she said when she opened the door. "How good to see you! Come on in."

"I'm not interrupting anything?" he asked.

Mordachi held Daisy in his lap on the floor. They gazed at each other coolly.

"Of course, not. We're having some dinner. Would you like to join us?"

Runner shook his head, leaned awkwardly against the wall.

"Nah. I was just stopping by to make sure everything's all buttoned up for the storm. Supposed to be a wild one tonight."

"That's what everybody says."

Mordachi stood. "I took care of it. Boarded up some of the loose windows, made sure they have enough stuff to get them through the night." He looked at Cherry. "I can stay if you want me to."

Runner took a step forward. "No need, brother. I can stay if Cherry needs me."

Cherry looked from one man to the other. "Are you two crazy? Nobody's staying. I'm a grown woman. The kids and I will be just fine. We were just nervous for a while, that's all. Now excuse me. I need to put them to bed."

She hustled Jonah and Daisy up the stairs and into their pajamas. She led them to Jonah's brightly painted room. It was difficult enough having them sleep without her tonight; she wasn't going to ask them to sleep without each other.

"Are you two kiddos going to be all right?"

Jonah was nearly asleep already. Daisy nodded.

"I'm glad, sweetie." She kissed Jonah on his forehead. He smiled sleepily. She leaned over and did the same to her daughter.

"I love you two. You're the best thing that ever happened to me, and don't you forget it. I'll be downstairs with Uncle Mordachi and Runner. Sleep well, my darlings."

"Night-night, Mommy."

Cherry turned around in the doorway, blowing another kiss to her children. Thank goodness they were all safe inside. Thank goodness her friends were here for a while to take her mind off the horrors of the poor dead child and the lewd whispers of the wind.

Mordachi and Runner sat silently on the couch when she made it down there.

"You don't have to stay," she said, slipping between them and linking her arms with theirs. "We'll be perfectly all right. But I am enjoying your company."

"Got nothing to rush home for," Mordachi said.

"Same here. Might as well hang around for a while. Got any coffee?"

"Hot cocoa is in the pantry."

Runner pursed his lips. "Uh. No thanks."

A shutter slammed and then laughed cruelly when Cherry jumped. Runner put his arm around her. Mordachi rubbed his palms awkwardly on the knees of his jeans.

"I'm sorry," she said, gritting her teeth. "You don't know how I wish this would all be different. That this stupid fear would just go away."

"Have you always been afraid?" Runner asked.

Mordachi answered for her. "Always. Ever since she was an itty bit. She used to come tearing over to our house in the middle of the night during storms. Her nightgown was soaked, her hair plastered to her face. Said the storm was telling her things and threatening to take her away. She'd monkey up that trellis just as fast as you please, couldn't wait to get in the room with old E and me."

Cherry blushed. "It wasn't that bad."

Mordachi laughed. "Oh, wasn't it? When it would get like this outside, we'd say, 'Better leave the window unlocked. You know Cherry's gonna show up here looking like a drowned rat.' Be darned if it didn't happen every time."

Runner snorted. "Sure wish I lived here then. Maybe you could have run to my house."

"You missed out on a lot," Mordachi said. His voice was edged. "You showed up when things were getting good. When Cherry was going out with E and things had settled down some."

"Let's not talk about that," Cherry said. Her voice was so quiet they could barely hear it under the wind and rain. "Sometimes the past just needs to stay in the past."

They chatted for a bit more before Cherry pleaded exhaustion.

"If you need me, holler," Mordachi told her. She nodded.

"Sure you don't want me to stay?" Runner asked after Mordachi stepped into the night. His eyes glowed a sultry green. "I could take your mind off the storm." He slid his arms around her and pulled her close.

"Tempting," she said, and playfully nipped the underside of his jaw. "But not tonight. I still need … I still need time for that."

Cherry thought his eyes narrowed briefly, but surely she'd imagined it.

"Of course. No rush. Call me when you need me."

His boots crunched on the gravel outside, and Cherry shut the door. Locked it. Leaned against it and wondered if she was making a terrible mistake.

# Chapter Sixteen

DAISY WENT MISSING at storm light.

The old house shifted and groaned in the wind, and lightning painted sinister patterns on the bedroom walls.

Cherry started awake. She flailed and protected her head with her arms. Realizing she was alone, Cherry took a deep breath. Mama wasn't here. Ephraim wasn't here. The house pressed close around her, malevolent and waiting. She tried to ignore it.

She needed a drink of water and slipped out of bed, her oversized T-shirt clinging to her sweaty skin. Cherry flipped the light switch. Nothing. She felt her way to the closet and grabbed a flashlight. The light danced across the floor and on the walls. To the bathroom. She checked behind the door and shower curtain before running the sink. Splashing her face with water. Scooping it into her mouth.

She padded across the wooden floor to check on the kids, avoiding the spot on the far left that squeaked horribly. Easing the door open, she peered inside. Jonah slept on his stomach, his fuzzy head covered by his Sesame Street pillow. His oxygen tank was nearby.

She didn't see Daisy. She crept closer, lifted the pillow and blankets.

She wasn't there.

"Sweetie," she called softly. "It's Mama. Do you hear the storm outside? Are you hiding?"

Nothing. Cherry shone the light around the room. Nothing.

"Sweetheart," she called a bit louder. "Where are you? Don't be afraid. I'm here."

She checked in the closet, under the bed. No Daisy. Panic climbed into Cherry's throat like a clawed animal, but she kept herself in check.

"Daisy, no hiding. Where are you?"

Cherry pulled the clothes aside violently in the closet, banging doors as she checked. Not in her room. Not in the bathroom. Not downstairs in the kitchen cupboards or the laundry room or anywhere else she could see.

The house snickered, then it howled.

A particularly bright flash of lightning made Cherry suck in her breath, and the thunder booming outside made her lose it in a rush. Jonah screamed in his bed. Cherry screamed in her head.

"Daisy, come here. You're scaring Mommy."

She wouldn't wander away, not in a storm like this. She'd come running straight to Cherry, just as she always had. Something was terribly, terribly wrong.

She leaned against the wall, letting it support the weight of her and the fears that were settling close to her heart. She couldn't do this by herself. She had thought that so many times during the years, before gritting her teeth and making the impossible happen. But this was too much even for Cherry, a woman whose years were counted by sorrows.

The rain came violently, battering at the windows with a force and a fury that reminded her of her ex-husband. She nearly retched but put her hand over her mouth and continued to search more frantically.

Jonah's screams were becoming hysterical. If he didn't calm quickly, the panic would be more than his broken body could handle and they'd be in the ER for sure. Not tonight. It couldn't happen tonight.

"I'm coming, baby," she said as normally and cheerfully as she could. Her teeth were chattering, but she had to sell the lightness to her son, had to convince him nothing was out of sorts. "What a loud storm! The rain will help the grass and flowers grow. It'll be so beautiful in the morning, just you wait and see."

He was sitting on top of his covers, his face scarily flushed and the whites showing all around his eyes. Cherry groaned as she picked him up, shifting the flashlight awkwardly as she did so. "You're getting so heavy, darling. My big boy." Jonah wrapped his arms and legs around her, and Cherry kissed the top of his head, wiped her tears against his hair.

"Come downstairs with Mama, okay, sweetheart? I'm looking for your sister."

He wept, crying open-mouthed against Cherry's neck. Her heart made the same sound deep inside, but her children were her concern, her only reason for living. Jonah's heart was beating so hard she could feel it against her own chest, and she knew it was becoming weary, the muscle stretching and swelling as it did whenever it was forced to work so hard, squeezing blood through the aortic valve that was too narrow and surgery could not fix.

"Hush, darling. I know you're frightened, but there's nothing to worry about, okay?" She walked carefully through the house, careful not to jostle Jonah. His sobs were starting to die down to whimpers. The heat in his face was beginning to cool as well. This was good.

"That's right. Breathe deep. Keep calm. Everything is going to be okay."

Cherry was still a terrible liar. Her throat closed, and she felt like she was coughing up the words. Not a movement in the house, not a single stirring in the shadows. If Daisy was in this house, her plump little legs would have been pumping their way up the stairs to calm her frenzied brother. She was born with more empathy than most of the world would ever experience. Cherry and Jonah were kites buffeted on the high winds, and

Daisy was the string that kept them both grounded.

Her little girl wasn't here. She wasn't inside. And she was terrified of the unfamiliar woods and the darkness that surrounded the house. She never would have stepped foot outside without Cherry holding her hand.

Lightning lit the room, and she pondered vaguely how white Jonah's skin looked in the light, how close to death. Then the thunder cracked, and her son threw his hands over his ears, shrieking so hard his nose began to bleed.

"Your headphones, your headphones," Cherry muttered. Still clutching her son, she shifted him to one hip and climbed down the stairs. She set the flashlight on the counter and rifled through the kitchen drawer until she found his headphones. She put them on his head, still cooing soothingly, and they hurried to the wooden front door. It stood open, too heavy to sway even in the winds of this storm. Cherry felt dizzy, leaned against the wall again to make sure she didn't drop Jonah.

"No. No!"

Her body shook, but she forced herself forward, peering out into the raging night.

No Daisy. No tracks. The rain had turned the dirt lane into a river of mud. She took hold of the doorknob, turned it firmly in her hand. Unlocked.

Jonah shifted in her arms and moaned. Cherry closed the door with a sound that made her jump. She locked it firmly. She didn't realize she was sobbing until Jonah turned his head to look at her with curiosity.

"Come with me, b-baby," Cherry said, forcing a smile that felt like a grimace. She was certain her shattered heart and terror seeped around the edges, and her son would be able to read the despair and outright horror in it. She turned her face away. "Let's go get the phone."

She held the phone to her ear. Three numbers, but they

were nearly impossible to remember and even harder to dial with hands that had lost all feeling.

"911, what is your emergency?"

She sobbed again, and the raw desperation of the sound sickened her. "H-hello? This is Cerise LaRouche. S-somebody has taken my daughter."

"Cherry? Is that you? Did you say somebody took Daisy?"

And Cherry broke down. She dropped the phone and slid down to the floor, her arms around Jonah, who—his world rocked by his mother's unheard-of display of emotion—began to scream. Twenty minutes later the police knocked and eventually broke through the door, finding Cherry and Jonah in hysterics on the kitchen floor. The officer put his arms around them while his partner picked up the phone and said, "We're here," and hung it up.

# Chapter Seventeen

*T*HE STORM BLEW out by morning just like Cherry's heart. The Darling City Police crawled over her house, her property, her fences.

She held Jonah on her lap, rocking back and forth restlessly.

"Did you see anybody?"

"Hear anybody?"

"Does anybody have reason to hate you?"

They asked about her taxes. They asked about her old johns. They asked about Daisy's father, if he had any reason to want his daughter back, and Cherry bared her teeth at this.

"He doesn't even know she exists. It isn't him. It isn't him."

But who could it be? In her mind, she saw the tiny broken body of the doll—the *child*. It could be her daughter, for all she knew.

"No," she screamed and fell to her knees on the floor. Jonah tumbled out of her arms, howling, and an officer pulled him close awkwardly, trying to hug the boy into quietness.

"No!" Cherry screamed again, and she was on the floor and weeping. Daisy was gone, she was gone, and there was a monster about.

"She'll be all right," a faceless officer told her. They were all faceless at this point, just shiny badges on stiff suits that were lovingly, pathetically pressed with a care that was nearly wretched in its earnestness. "We'll find her. We take care of our own, Cherry. We'll find your little girl." The officer reached out, touched her shoulder gently.

"No," Cherry shrieked and jerked away. She glared at the

officer with a hate that made her eyes burn even more than the tears. "You won't find her. Don't you get it? Don't you understand? This place, this town, it's nothing but death! It takes everyone, everything I love, and it twists it, reshapes it. Couldn't you feel it in the storm?" She choked, and Jonah squalled, fighting, and beating his head against the officer's chest until he was forced to let the boy go. Jonah ran to his mama, burrowing under her arms until she held him without thinking.

"Calm down, Mrs. LaRouche. We'll do everything in our power to get your little girl back."

Cherry hated him then. Hated with a hate that was more than hate. It wasn't his fault, and she knew this deep down. He knew it, too, and this was why he bore it with the weary grace of those who serve.

"You won't find her. She didn't wander away. Do you understand me? She was taken. By this town, or a monster. Something horrid."

"Perhaps the storm just scared her."

"She did not wander away!"

"You don't know that, Mrs. LaRouche. Don't jump to conclusions."

The door burst open. The sound of several men shouting, people trying to hold somebody back. Mordachi pushed through them like they were children.

"Cherry," he said, and dropped to the ground. He ran his rough hands over her, over Jonah's fuzzy hair. "I heard. Is it true? Is she—?"

"She's gone," she said, and the words broke the last bit of strength inside her. Wore it down, ground it to tiny stone bits under their weight.

He held her, rocked her and her remaining child. Footprints had been washed away by the rain. The wind had blown every bit of evidence away.

"A monster," he whispered as he rocked what was left of his family. "A monster."

# Chapter Eighteen

THE HOUSE WAS full of people. People trying to be comforting. People trying to do their jobs. People Cherry didn't know, didn't care about, didn't bother with.

"What are you doing here?" she asked, the few times she found the strength to speak instead of screaming. "Why are you here? Why aren't you out looking for my daughter?"

There were things to look at. Closets to check, stuffed animals to poke. Questions to ask, information to find, process, study.

"Too slow, too slow," Cherry muttered, and then she turned to the room. "I need to look for my daughter. Do you understand? I can't be here."

A man came forward. She thought she recognized him as one of the officers who had arrived in the middle of the night, but she didn't remember. She didn't care.

"You need to stay here," he said. She was sure there was emotion in his voice, but to her ears, it sounded robotic and rehearsed. "What if she comes home? What if there is a telephone call? You can't leave the house. We have plenty of men looking."

"But why aren't *you* looking?" She threw a vase across the room. It shattered, and Jonah screamed. The yelling and shrieking became so loud, Cherry didn't realize when she was the only one left screaming like her mother.

Mordachi forcefully hauled her out of the door after directing two other flannel-clad men to care for the boy.

"I'll come with you," he said. They were both breathing hard on the front porch as the door slammed shut behind them. "Let's go look for Daisy."

He took her hand, and she was grateful for it, for having something solid to tether her to this world.

"Otherwise, I'll float away," she said.

He simply looked at her.

They didn't speak, just called Daisy's name until their voices were hoarse. Still, she called. Still, he called. There wasn't anything else to do. Nothing else to be done.

"She's so little," Cherry said once, and the tears started rolling silently. They dripped onto her faded tank top, and she didn't bother to wipe them away. Water dripped off the too-wet trees. Louisiana and Cherry were both crying.

It became dark.

Cherry's feet hurt from her worn shoes.

Mordachi touched her shoulder gently.

"Want to go home? Want to keep looking?"

She thought, biting her lip. She didn't want to go home, not ever. She wanted to call her little girl's name until Daisy heard it, until she realized there was a brilliant light in this dark place. She wanted to scream and scream until Daisy broke free from whatever nightmare she was living in and ran joyfully through the trees and bogs until she came home, until she, the tiny moth, found her flame. Her mama.

"How am I supposed to go home?" Her voice sounded tearless, calm, and Cherry felt pride that it was under control. "How am I supposed to crawl into my bed and sleep soundly when Daisy is out here somewhere? That's not what a mother does."

"I think we should at least check on Jonah. He's probably afraid you're not coming back by now."

Jonah. Her other little one. Her other darling.

"He doesn't understand what's going on," she whispered. Mordachi leaned closer to hear her. "He must be so scared."

"We're all scared."

He took her hand again, surprisingly cool in the muggy after-storm heat. She gently pulled away.

"If I had just let you stay," she said.

"Don't say that. I've thought it a thousand times. Don't say it aloud."

Her lips closed, but her mind repeated it. *If I had let you stay. If I had let Runner spend the night in my bed. If there were more of us. If I was more careful, this wouldn't have happened.*

The house was blazing with light and activity. She stepped through the doorway and voices hushed. Jonah was sobbing on the floor, refusing to be comforted.

An old woman stepped forward—Mrs. Getchell from two miles up the lane.

"Cerise, you're gon' need somebody to set with you tonight."

"Mrs. Getchell, I don't particularly feel like …"

Mrs. Getchell glowered, and her frizzy gray hair managed to look offended. "Oh, hush. You act like you ain't got a lick of sense. Put that boy to bed and tuck him in good. He's been near hysterical without you for these past few hours."

Cherry opened her mouth, but Ardeth Getchell was not to be stopped. "Don't sass me, child. Take care of your son, and then catch some sleep yourself if you can. You need someone in the house just to be here, who won't talk you to death like these no-accounts and their incessant questions. The pain in these bones keep me up at night, and I have no interest in conversation."

Cherry nodded, just once, and took Jonah up to bed. She washed him, dressed him in shorts and a shirt that was soft, so soft, like his hair and his eyes and his calming cries. She tucked him into her bed and crawled, fully clothed, beside him.

"Let's pray, my darling," she whispered and nuzzled her

nose into his hair. He threw his skinny arms around her neck, and she prayed for them, for her little girl, for the morning to come and tell her everything was still a bad dream.

But that wasn't how it happened, and Cherry knew it. Life is a nightmare, and it just goes on and on and on.

# Chapter Nineteen

*D*AWN ARRIVED AND everybody was gathered in Cherry's front yard. Police with their dogs. Men and women from town. Cherry saw Monica from the dry goods store, her bright lipstick drawn with a shaky hand this morning. Wendy's father and mother and three older sisters. High school kids. Strangers. People she didn't know, but who seemed to know her. Milling. Standing. Staring.

A fistfight broke out in the back of the group, two men who held a grudge from long before Cherry's time. It went on for far too long until somebody wearily stepped in.

Mordachi set a pair of red rain boots on the step in front of Cherry. She looked up at him.

"We're going through some rough terrain today. There will be snakes and bugs. Your shoes won't hold up to that."

The boots were shiny and red. On a normal day, Cherry would marvel at them. On a normal day, she'd thank him.

"I bought a pair for Daisy, too. I'll give them to her when we find her."

He walked away as Cherry buried her face in her knees and cried.

"Daisy LaRouche, two-years old. Brown hair, blue eyes, last seen wearing a purple and white nightgown. Here's her picture. We're going to divide the town into sections and each team will be assigned to a specific area." The officer cleared his throat, darted his eyes at Cherry. "I don't need to tell you the seriousness of this matter. At this point, we're looking at a possible abduction. And regarding some other circumstances, which, uh, involve minor children, we—"

"You mean the murdered kids?" The voice from the back was shrill. The words were too ugly, too horrible, and Cherry opened her mouth and worked her tongue, trying to get the sour taste out of it.

"Harold." The officer's voice was calm, but the rebuke was there. "Remember where you are."

He turned to Cherry. "Cherry, if she's to be found, we'll find her. I can promise you that, darlin'."

"No, you can't." Cherry's mouth moved in ways that made her feel ugly, but it kept the crying inside. "Are we ready to go? Can we please look now?"

He turned toward the volunteers.

"Move out."

Darling had never seemed so large. A group of older women hit all the stores, asking questions. "Have you seen this child? She went missing last night. Can we put this picture up in your window?"

Every door was knocked on. People were asked to search their back rooms, in case a terrified little one went crawling back there, scared of the storm. Owners peeked inside doghouses, under beds and tables, in closets and under stairs.

"Daisy? Daisy, sweetheart?" they asked. "Are you here? Your mommy is out looking for you. If you're here, please come out. I'll call your mommy and you can go home."

While the older women knocked on doors, the rest searched outside. "The body walk" it was called, but nobody breathed the name aloud. The volunteers walked, shoulder to shoulder, making sure they didn't miss anything. A flash of fabric in the grass. A tangle of hair that could be mistaken for weeds.

"We'll find her," Mordachi whispered.

Cherry's gait was strange, a sort of sloping, awkward slog.

The shock was hitting her system in a new way, that half of her body wasn't responding to the simple WALK command from her brain.

He put a hand on her shoulder, but she pulled away.

Mordachi stared at his offending hand, at their calluses and strength. A child was so tiny. A neck was so fragile. He put his hand in his pocket and continued to clamber through the tall grasses.

The searchers stared at the area directly in front of them, eyes narrowed and darting back and forth to miss nothing.

But Mordachi knew too much. That day when he had discovered the dead child in the road, a member of the police department had whispered some of the other information they had. Missing children all over the parish, turning up in the most twisted of places, in the grisliest forms. Tiny hands missing. Hair shorn, eyes and mouths sewed closed like horrifying little dolls. They were found in baskets and hollows and trees. Mordachi's eyes roamed through the magnolias and dogwoods searching for anything delicate and white and shining in the leaves. He peered up into a weeping willow, and the man beside him stopped.

"Whatcha looking for, Mordachi?"

Cherry halted, turned around. Her dark eyes looked frosted over in the morning light, but she turned them on Mordachi with a strange intensity that seared him.

He forced a half-smile. "Just checking to see if she's up there. Kids love to climb."

Cherry's voice was cold, as frosty as her eyes. "She's too little to climb." She stumbled forward again, staring at the ground, feeling her way tenderly with her feet. Careful not to step on water snakes or little girls who could be … sleeping, yes, sleeping in the grass.

The man next to Mordachi continued staring at the weeping willow, the Crying Trees, and a line formed in the skin between his eyes. He caught Mordachi's gaze, and Mordachi gave a short, subtle nod. The man's face darkened, and he nodded back. He whispered to the grizzled fellow next to him, who did taxes and taxidermy and sewed up torn stuffed animals for the town's children, and said something in a low voice, gesturing to the trees. The taxes/taxidermist muttered something to Rosemary next to him. She made a small sound that she turned into a cough, and then whispered discreetly to the man next to her. The information was spread quickly and quietly, how it is always spread in small towns.

*Look in the trees,* they whispered. *Check the trees. Sometimes small, precious things hang from their branches.*

The silence was muggy as the hot air pushed into their pores and forced sweat from the inside out. They had started out calling the little girl's name, but soon voices were hoarse and the pain of not getting a reply, well, it damaged the heart. Better to pretend one doesn't care. Better to stare intently into the grasses and steal glimpses into the trees when the missing one's mother isn't looking. What if you call a child and she never responds, not ever? Better not to call, then.

Small, ghostly forms slipped through the trees and watched from the branches. Dead boys with missing feet. Pretty little girls with plaits and overalls and empty eye sockets. They tried to call out, but it's difficult to speak when your throat has rotted out and the Handsome Butcher made you promise to keep his secrets. They watched and listened and tried to think back to when they went missing. Did anyone search for them? Did their mamas and papas call their names? They couldn't seem to remember.

Nearly two hours passed like this. Hair stuck to sweaty faces. Clouds of mosquitoes lazed around them like misfortune. Then there was a shout. Everything changed.

"I think I found something!" A small man, wiry and strangely youthful, jumped to his feet. "It looks like an old suitcase. Do you want me ... I mean, should I ...?"

Cherry stumbled.

The wiry man's wife rushed to Cherry's side and held her arms out to catch her.

"Let me do it." John Holfield, the lawyer who originally called Cherry about the house, stepped up. His eyes met Cherry's briefly before he jerked his gaze away.

The wiry man backed away in relief. He watched his wife hover around Cherry and loved her more than he had ever loved her before. They had two sons who had been young once. They could imagine the horror of losing one.

John hesitated, but he glanced at Cherry's white face and gritted his teeth. He grabbed the corroded buckle and forced his newly awkward hands to paw at the latch, to grasp the latch, to open the latch.

The metallic click was harsh in the suffocating silence.

He opened the suitcase.

It was full of bones.

The wiry man's wife made a sick little moan in her throat, the sound of something hurting, and reached for Cherry, but Cherry stood strong and firm on her own.

Somebody turned their head to the side and retched. Somebody started praying out loud to their god.

"Let me see." It was the grizzled taxes/taxidermist, who had been discreetly eyeing the trees for strangled little girls while Cherry wasn't looking. He peered into the suitcase, picked up a couple of bones, and studied them.

"These are old bones. And this skull, it's canine. I bet we stumbled upon somebody's pet. Put 'em in this suitcase and took 'em out here to rest." He put the bones back and closed the suitcase. His intelligent eyes sought out Cherry. "Ain't your little girl, Cherry. God be praised."

The sigh of relief was like a wind, a breeze that energized the group.

Cherry turned to Mordachi, wearing a strange smile.

"Of course, it isn't Daisy. I knew that all along."

Mordachi tried to smile back, but then Cherry's eyes were rolling in the back of her head, seeking refuge someplace inside of her skull, and her body collapsed from the knees up. He reached out to grab her the same time the wiry man's wife did.

"Help me take her home," he said to the man beside him. They picked her up together, this woman who had been a child in their midst years ago, and who was once again nothing more than a child in her vulnerability.

She regained consciousness about halfway back and soon walked while leaning heavily on Mordachi. Her face had a strange gray-green coloring to it, and her eyes had turned into something Mordachi had to look away from.

"I was dreaming," she said.

"What about?"

She sighed. "There was a man with a beautiful face. He was scratching on my bedroom window, at night, just like … anyway. I didn't want to let him in, but he had something to tell me."

Mordachi kept his voice even. "Did he, now."

She turned to him, looking like the little girl she had been. She had been made of pigtails, her frog collection, terror at storms, her mother, and blood.

"He said the most horrifying thing. I don't know if I can repeat it."

"You don't have to. Look, we're almost back. You can lie down. I'll take care of Jonah, and—"

She grabbed his sleeve. The frost in her eyes had melted and they were rivers now, filling and leaking down the sides of her face, dropping into her shirt and onto her red boots.

Mordachi wrapped his hands around hers, around her grip on his sleeve.

"What did he say?"

"He said his daughter had gone missing, too. That he looked everywhere, but he finally found her."

"That's good."

The words were comforting, but Cherry's face showed it wasn't good at all, that this man with the beautiful face hadn't brought comfort, but more fear than she had been feeling previously.

"But that wasn't all he said, was it? What else did he tell you?"

She hoped he would say it was a dream. *It was a dream and a dream under duress, at that.* Soft things, soothing things. He should practice until his lips can say them slow and easy, but she knew she couldn't buy it. Daisy was stolen, stolen by storm light, and the town of Darling had tipped on its head. Men searched the grass and trees and suitcases for little girls, and dreams can be real.

"What else did he say?" he asked again.

Cherry stared at her house in the distance. Tall, imposing. Full of activity and people and her son, full of walkie-talkies and their static. Full of everything but her daughter, and hope.

"I hate that house," she said, and the anger and vehemence in her voice nearly made her sound like a monster herself. She turned back to Mordachi, her teeth bared. "He said, 'They found my little girl in pieces.'"

Mordachi staggered like Cherry had been staggering. He pulled himself upright with effort, but it seemed he still struggled to breathe.

"Just a dream," he said. His face screwed up like the words tasted foul.

Cherry looked away from him.

"Yes," she said. It was a hollow word, spoken in a hollow voice. They both knew she was lying.

# Chapter Twenty

THEY DIDN'T FIND her. Hours and hours of searching, peeking under and into and around everything in and about Darling, and there was no Daisy. Cherry wanted to yell. She wanted to throw things and scream the worst, cruelest, most hateful words she knew. She wanted to fall to her knees and pray. Not finding her missing daughter was hell. But ...

"No Daisy, no body," Mrs. Getchell said. The woman behind her tried to hush her, but Mrs. Getchell shooed her away. "Oh, stop being all delicate. Cherry knows what's up. Think she isn't grateful for it?"

Cherry was grateful but still wished she was snuggling sweet Daisy in her arms. What kind of comfort is the lack of her little girl's body?

The living room was buzzing again. Mordachi had taken Jonah for a ride in his truck to calm him down, to spend some time together, to look down the back roads and check for deer and little girls hiding behind trees.

Cherry looked at Mrs. Getchell, at her unpleasant mouth and furrowed brow. "Mrs. Getchell? I'm going to do the news conference soon. Will you stand by me?"

"If I must," the old woman said. Her eyes were flint, dark and hard, and unmoving.

"Thank you."

Darling had its own public service station, a tiny thing that talked about rodeos and school bakery sales and the importance of getting the flu shot. Now it was going to be used for something Very Important, and the somber atmosphere covered the porch like a dark umbrella made of sorrow.

They set up on the front porch. The police chief spoke first, talking into a podium borrowed from the local church, and being careful to speak into the microphone.

"Daisy LaRouche. Two years old. She went missing last night during the storm."

Cherry heard his words, but they blended together until they didn't make any sense anymore. Daisy. Missing girl. Possible abduction. These things didn't go together, didn't sound like they ought to be said out loud. Shouldn't he be saying how Daisy loved paints, just like her mama? How her pigtails waved triumphantly in the air like banners? That Daisy loved her Jonah?

The chief of police turned to Cherry, and the silence was thick and expectant. A question. An introduction. She looked at him and blinked.

"Go," Ardeth Getchell said, and the gravel of her voice propelled Cherry forward, like a toy with a key in its back.

She stood at the podium, staring at her white hands, at the lone news camera.

"M-my name is Cerise. Er, Cherry. Cherry LaRouche. I grew up here in Darling, in this very house."

*Identify yourself as a member of the town,* she had been coached. *Let them know you're one of them. Folks here take care of their own.*

The muscles in Cherry's face froze, and she brought her hands up to massage them. Saw the trembling in her fingers, the veins running underneath her skin, and dropped them again.

"My mama died not too long ago. Iris LaRouche. I came back after her death with my two children. Jonah and Daisy. Now Daisy has gone missing." Her voice cracked, and she cleared her throat, tried again. "Missing. She's only two. She's just a little girl. Please, if you have seen her, can you please bring her back to me? She must be so scared. *I'm* so scared."

She paused, wondered if there was something more she should say. If there is somehow a magic word that will make it all right, that will touch the darkest heart. Wouldn't most people bring in a lost child? Unless that person was a monster, something that screeches in the night and scratches at bedroom windows. What would persuade somebody like that?

"Please," she said again because it was the only magic word she knew. "Please" and "Abracadabra" and "I can pay you," but she didn't think any of those words would help now. It was too late. Her little girl was too far away.

The police chief nodded at her kindly. She dropped her eyes and started to step away from the podium. Then. Then, she thought, if there is a monster, it won't understand niceties like "please" and "thank you" and "I beg of you to return my daughter to me in one piece, alive and breathing." Horrors only understand horror. Monsters only speak the language of blood.

"I want to say," she said quietly, and the buzzing that swarmed around her stilled. "I want to say," she said louder. Cherry stared deeply into the camera, her eyes changing from teary pools into lakes of fire. "If somebody has my daughter, and you mean her any harm, I will kill you."

The sudden silence was heavy. Cherry's breast heaved under her worn tank top, and she licked her lips. "Daisy is mine. She's not for you. You can't have her. If you don't return her to me, I will hunt you down and I will smear your pieces across the floor. Do you understand me?"

She nodded once, resolutely, and then padded, barefoot, into the house and shut the front door.

The onlookers swept themselves into a frenzy.

Mrs. Getchell smiled.

# Chapter Twenty-One

$\mathcal{J}$ONAH OBVIOUSLY WANTED to be held. The sounds, the sirens, the lighting crews, terrified him. Strangers trekked through his bedroom, and clever fingers poked and felt around the blankets on his bed, stuck themselves into toys and worn-out shoes. Jonah hated the fingers, the noise, the people. He just wanted his mama and his baby sister, whom he couldn't find. Cherry watched as he searched everywhere. In the potty. In the faucet. She wasn't even in the washer and dryer, and that was more than he could comprehend. He looked at Cherry in confusion. *Why wouldn't she be there?* she imagined him thinking. *If Mama let her go away, anywhere she wanted, why wouldn't she be at the washer and dryer, where things were always so happy?*

Jonah threw back his head and wailed.

Cherry wanted to run to him, but the policeman shook his head.

"Not now, ma'am. We have something important to discuss. If you could just—"

"Important?" Cherry's eyes were doing that thing, that thing they had done during the news conference, and the officer reacted as if she were a dangerous animal. "Do you somehow think my son, my other child, isn't important? Why? Because he isn't missing? Because he *isn't all there?*"

This was taking an ugly, unexpected turn.

Cherry walked to Jonah and scooped him up. He was all gangly legs and brittle bones, sharp elbows and pointed knees.

He sobbed into her shoulder, his open mouth leaving wet stains on her clothes.

The officer looked to his superior for help. His superior pretended to be interested elsewhere.

"Miss LaRouche," the officer began again, "I certainly don't mean to imply what you think I'm implying. But we need to talk to you, to go over some details and make sure we're being as thorough as we can."

"So, ask me in front of my son. Can't you see I can't leave him now, that he's beside himself? You want me to go gallivanting off, making him afraid I won't come back, that I'll disappear like his sister? Who we'll find, by the way." She readjusted her grip on Jonah, trying to keep her wits about her while he screamed in her ear.

Mordachi looked over, caught her eyes. She flashed him a furious glance.

"I'm afraid you don't understand, Miss LaRouche. Perhaps you could find somebody to watch your son while we go down to the station and—"

That was it. The stress, the crying, the pounding pain in her head, the fear that Daisy was gone, that she was dead, that she wasn't simply hiding, but she'd never be found and hugged and kissed and her hair tied into pigtails again, it was enough.

"Now you listen to me," she said, and the venom she tasted made her forget all the hours she'd spent scrubbing the Louisiana drawl out of her voice. She sounded like her daddy, like her neighbors, like her *mother,* and this realization made her angry all over again. "Listen good. I need to tend to my son, you understand? He needs me. He doesn't understand what's going on, any more than I do. The stress isn't good for his heart. If we could all just calm down, if the noise could just all go away ..."

She blinked and was horrified to find tears in her eyes. Treacherous, traitorous tears. She blinked again, and they evaporated in the fire she conjured up. The heat felt good. The fear and hate and ugliness from the house, from the very land itself, powdered her skin with residue. She breathed it in, and it stuck to her lungs in lethal patches. Her eyes glowed with supernatural strength.

"But ma'am," he started again.

Over his shoulder, she saw Mordachi and the police chief in deep discussion. Mordachi looked at her with something like pity, and Cerise LaRouche wasn't going to have pity.

"My child is missing. Do you understand that? Out of my house. Out of my *house*, where she should be safe, but something came and took her." She thought of Daisy, of her soft cheeks and wide, clear blue eyes. Something went out of her, something broke. What she thought were bones were really papier-mâché. She sagged but continued to stand on her feet, holding her wailing child. The unholy light in her eyes dimmed. "I need my son," she finished lamely. She nuzzled him, and his crying softened a little. But not enough. Too much stress, too much blood sailing through his body at too fast a speed. She imagined a rocket screaming into space, a torpedo or bullet hitting its target. Only this target was delicate artery walls and fragile veiny webbing. This was his life, and she couldn't lose another, she just couldn't.

The deputy looked uncomfortable. "I'm sorry for your situation, Miss LaRouche. I really am. And we're doing our best to find your daughter."

She turned her back on him. Enough. The situation was dealt with. It didn't exist at all.

She felt a strong hand on her shoulder.

"Cherry," Mordachi said, "you're misunderstandin' the situation. They want to question you as a suspect."

He said something else, maybe. Something about how it would all be okay, how he'd pay for Johnny H's lawyer services if she wanted. Or maybe he discussed bluebells and honeysuckle because it didn't make a lick of sense to Cherry.

"They think I hurt my baby?" Her voice sounded strange. High, frantic. Or maybe that was just Jonah's cries.

"You'll be fine, Cherry. Let me take Jonah. I'll take good care of him, you know I will."

He took him from her trembling hands. Jonah squalled but Mordachi just held him close and stared at Cherry.

"Run along, girl. I'll feed him dinner. If you're not back by bedtime, I'll put him down, too."

Cherry stared past him.

"It's just protocol, ma'am. Shouldn't take too long. Now if you would just come with me, I'll give you a ride to the station and we can get started."

He took her elbow to guide her, but she jerked away.

Mordachi nodded at the door. "Go. Get through the questioning and then come on back home to your boy."

Jonah was snuffling, exhausted by his fear and screaming. Cherry raised her head and swept past the deputy toward the police car.

The Darling jail was as small as the town itself. Ian Bridger was set up in the single questioning room. There was a table, two chairs, and reams of copy paper and Styrofoam cups stacked in the corner.

Cherry stepped inside and raised her eyebrow.

"We don't have a lot of extra room here," he said.

"Are you going to be questioning me, Ian?"

"I will."

"How's your daddy doing? Have any kids?"

"This isn't easy for me, either, you know."

He pulled out a chair and Cherry sat down. He walked to

the other side of the desk.

Cherry's eyes were red and swollen. Her face was puffy from crying, her hair wild and tumbling around her face like a cloud. She was still beautiful, just as beautiful as the day she left town. Ian was two years older, had hung around Ephraim every now and then, and their departure left a little bit of a hole in him.

"I don't understand why I'm here. I would never do anything to Daisy, to either of my children. Why are you wasting time? You're one more person who could be out there hunting for her."

"This is important."

"Then get started already."

He meant to do it gently. He meant to show her how kind he could be, how sympathetic, how strong and resourceful not only the Darling PD could be, but how trustworthy he, Ian, could be. But her eyes, the fire and the—dare he say it?—hate that flared in them, well. That changed everything.

"When is the last time you saw Daisy's father?"

"Before she was born, I assume."

"You assume?"

"I'm not certain who he is."

Ian swallowed. "You were having a relationship with more than one man at a time?"

"You could say that, I suppose."

"You were a prostitute."

Cherry met his eyes, but the fire burned out and she looked away. "I was never a prostitute. I was … just a woman trying to make enough money to feed her son."

"I'm sorry, Cherry. I'm not bringing this up to hurt you. I just need to know anything that will help us find Daisy. Could her dad have come for her? Did you let him know where you were? Does anybody have a grudge against you, from back then?"

"I told you I don't know who her father is, Ian. He wouldn't have come. And I don't think anyone else hates me that much.

Nobody really thinks of me at all."

He didn't want to say it. "Could it be Ephraim? Think he'd feel any sort of paternal feelings for her?"

Her eyes flamed back to life, and in truth, Ian was glad to see it. A broken Cherry was much harder to deal with than a spirited Cherry. As long as she was fighting, there was still hope. Ian felt in his heart that when she gave up, when she let the embers of her rage die, there would be no light to lead Daisy back home.

"Ephraim has nothing to do with this. That man doesn't have a paternal bone in his body. Ephraim's *son* was starving. Ephraim's *son* was barely making it through the night. His lungs weren't getting enough air, his heart was beating too hard and enlarging. Ephraim left his *son* there to die, and me to hold his broken body, so I certainly don't think he'd suddenly take an interest in my illegitimate daughter."

"It's been difficult for you. Raising two kids alone, first in the city and then here. Your mother's death. I bet it was particularly hard to come back home where everybody is always meddling in your business."

"It was."

"I heard you still haven't found much of a job."

Cherry frowned. "Well, I'm trying. Mordachi was going to pay me to redecorate his house. I've been doing laundry for the neighbors, which is"—Ian saw the look on her face. *Embarrassing,* it said. *Humiliating. Servitude*—"convenient because Jonah loves washers and dryers. We always have them going, anyway, so might as well get some use out of it."

"You're tired."

She played with her fingers. "I'm always tired."

"It must be tough to get up during the night with a baby."

Her fingers stopped twitching.

"Babies need milk and food and love. They grow out of their

clothes awfully fast, don't they, Cherry?"

"Silence.

"Daisy's sure a cute little one. Happy. There are a lot of people who would love a little girl like her. And what a relief to you, maybe, to give her a home that would love her, would take care of her, make sure she's fed properly, and given everything she needs. Your house doesn't even have heat, does it?"

"Stop it."

"A selfless act, really. Then you could focus on Jonah, who needs you so badly. Without Daisy, you could give him the time he deserves, the medical help he needs. Maybe you could afford better doctors. Your attention wouldn't be divided. In fact, lots of folks would pay big money to adopt a child. How far would that go towards—?"

"Stop it!"

She jumped to her feet, sending the chair tumbling backward.

Ian kept his face placid, but his heart was beating fast. The fire was back. Daisy could find her way home.

*Fight, Cherry, fight,* he thought. *Burn so bright that you burst into flames. If you did something to her, we'll find out. If you didn't, she'll follow the sparks until she comes to the raging bonfire that is her mother. Don't leave that little girl out in the cold.*

"Do you know where your daughter is?"

"No."

"Did you sell or give your daughter to another individual or individuals?"

"Of course, not."

"Miss LaRouche, did you commit an act of violence against your daughter? Is she hurt or dead because of something you did?"

She was more than a bonfire. She was a nuclear holocaust. Bright enough to lead any and all of the lost souls home. Maybe the ghosts of the murdered children could find her and be comforted. Ian hoped so.

"Stop it! Just stop!"

He didn't stop. Not for several hours. Not until he'd asked her every question six different times in six different ways. Not until she lit and eventually blew out like a candle. Not until she demanded a lawyer, which she should have done at the beginning, and he drove her back to her house in charred, smoldering silence.

She hopped out of the car, slammed the door. Ian nodded at her back. Then, he turned the car back toward the station. He had a report to write.

# Chapter Twenty-Two

THE LIGHTS WERE on, but the house certainly couldn't be called welcoming.

*I hate it,* Cherry thought. The police car pulled away behind her, sounding like gravel and dirt and abject desperation and despair. *I hate this place. All I ever wanted was to get out. Why couldn't you let me do that much, Mother?*

She headed for the door, her steps slowing until she eventually stopped. Stared. Rubbed her eyes with the palms of her hands and took a deep breath. She reached for the doorknob.

"Cherry." Her name was spoken so softly that she almost missed it. "Don't go in yet. Come over here."

She hesitated, looked around. Cold, dark night. Hungry night full of bones and teeth.

"Jonah's asleep. Ardeth is sitting by him. Come on."

She looked over her shoulder once more, then turned and followed Mordachi's voice to the side yard. She could see his dark shape and the shine of his eyes up in the old magnolia tree.

"Come down from there. You look ridiculous."

His white teeth shone in the moonlight.

"When's the last time you were up here?"

She leaned back, cracking her back. "Oh, a long time ago. Probably the last time I was up there with you. When we were kids."

He reached a hand down to her.

She shook her head.

"Uh uh. No way. How can you even think of playing around at a time like this? Do you know what they asked me about down there?"

"Climb on up and tell me."

"No."

"Why not?"

"Because it isn't dignified."

He laughed. "Since when have you worried about that?" He reached for her again. "Remember how good it used to feel to hang out in this tree? Don't you want to at least try and see if it feels the same way again?"

She looked at Mordachi in the tree, back at the house, and at the tree again. Kicking her shoes off, she grabbed his hand and used it to hoist herself to the next branch.

"Atta girl."

It was more difficult than it used to be. Her body felt weighty, unsure. More fragile and full of bones than when she was younger.

"There's your branch, Cherry. Just waitin' for you. Almost there."

Her feet scrabbled against the bark, and Cherry could feel the life of the tree pulsing beneath her. Steady. Certain. She wondered how many times she had scurried up here, bringing a book or a pencil, hiding from her chores, or just enjoying the sunshine. Most of the time Mordachi was with her. E never was.

She was surprised to find she was breathing so hard.

"When did I get so old?" she said and flopped on her branch.

It curved against her back the same way. She fit, just perfectly.

"Welcome home, Cherry."

The tree's branches dipped gently in the breeze. The night smelled of grass and flowers and the too-wet scent that made moisture stick to her skin.

"I missed Southern nights," she said, running her fingers across the bark of the tree. "When I lived up north. The nights just didn't seem right."

"The nights didn't seem right here without you," he said. He sighed. "Why do you always have to make it so hard? We could have helped you. You didn't have to take care of both the kids alone."

"Guess that isn't a problem anymore, right?" She laughed, and it was a hurtful, bitter sound. It tore the inside of her throat and mouth like something jagged, something too sour. "With only half the kids, it's only half the trouble."

"Don't say that." Mordachi leaned toward her. His brown eyes reflected the moon in disquieting ways that made her stomach twist. "It isn't right. Don't say it again."

"But that's what they told me down at the police station. They think I did something to her, Mordachi. They think I did something because I was *tired* and *stressed.* Ian said—"

"I don't care what he said. He's a hanged fool and you are, too, if you're gonna give any weight to his opinions."

"But—"

"They're trying to figure it out, Cherry. They're looking at everybody. Heck, they'll probably be looking at me next. They're starting in the center of the circle and working their way out. That's what cops do, and they're gonna try for you. Even more, they're going to try for Daisy. Ain't a person on that force who doesn't have a little girl or niece or sister of their own they see when they're looking at Daisy's picture. If they have to be harsh or hurt your tender little feelings while they're doing their job, then so be it. You've dealt with worse."

The wind whistled through the branches in a soothing, familiar way. Cherry studied the sky.

"That's probably the most words I've ever heard out of you at one time."

He shrugged. "Don't say much unless there's something worth saying."

"I like that about you."

"Didn't use to."

Cherry studied her nails. She'd been biting them again.

"I was a little impatient when I was younger."

"You wanted someone fast and flirty and quick with wit and words. I could never be that."

Cherry opened her mouth to say something, but there was nothing to say. He was right. Absolutely right. He had just described his brother to a tee.

Mordachi abruptly swung out of his branch, landing easily on the ground with a quiet thud.

"Night, Cherry. Get some sleep. Something amazing is going to happen tomorrow, I can feel it. Maybe tomorrow will be the day we find Daisy, curled up asleep in somebody's backseat."

He took off without a word, and Cherry watched his back until it disappeared in the dark. The cold, snarling dark that took things like hopes and dreams and precious, precious little girls.

# Chapter Twenty-Three

DURING THE NIGHT, they found a little girl in the most northern part of the parish. Unlike some of the others, this one was completely intact. Her eyes were swollen closed, and her mouth was stitched shut. She had bright yellow barrettes in her dark hair and wore a single white sock. Or it had been white, once. It was black with dirt and leaves and the stale stench of death, now. But when her mother had put it on her only four or five days ago, it had been the purest of white. With a ruffle. For a party that would never take place because the only party that happened that evening was a search party.

Her beautiful dark skin was too clean. She had been bathed, her hair brushed out like a doll's. Her clothes were gone, and this made the tiny, ruffled sock seem even more out of place.

*I'll protect her,* the sock seemed to say. *Her modesty and dignity. I can do that much for her.*

But, of course, it couldn't. A sock can only do so much, *cover* so much. And this girl was nude and dead, and not even the delicate ruffle and cheery barrettes could bring sunshine to the situation.

When her parents rushed in to claim her, there were shouts and tears. The sock stayed on her foot, valiantly. Like everything else in the midst of this madness, it could only do what it could.

# Chapter Twenty-Four

CHERRY WOKE UP with Jonah's skinny arms twined around her neck. She didn't trust him in his own room, that the night and creatures would stay away. She kissed his hair and carefully disentangled herself from her small son.

Ardeth had made coffee, which smelled too strongly of earth. Cherry shivered.

"Don't you have a home to get to?" she asked the old woman. There was an edge to her tone, a sadness. How was it possible to be both at the same time? She hadn't meant either emotion to get the better of her.

"One home is just as good as another. At the moment, I'm needed more at yours."

Ardeth served coffee to the policeman doing paperwork on the living room couch. Then she poured herself a cup and settled in at the table. Cherry sat beside her.

"Mordachi seems to think it might be a day for miracles," she said. She picked at her fingers, drawing blood from the hangnails.

"Why not?" Ardeth sipped from her cup. "It's gonna be a day for something. Why not miracles?"

"I don't believe in miracles."

Ardeth's old eyes were sharp. "Now, that's no way to talk. Your little girl needs somebody to believe she'll come home."

Cherry wrinkled her nose. "Because miracles happen every day, isn't that right? Well, not in my life, Mrs. Getchell. If life has taught me anything, it's that you'd better bundle up and bring an umbrella, because the universe is gonna send a storm over ya. And it's fixing to stay for good."

Ardeth raised her eyebrow.

"Bitter words from the darling of Darling. Better watch yourself, Cherry LaRouche. You're slipping back into your native speak. Heaven forbid somebody would mistake you for a small-town Southern girl."

Cherry flushed. "You make it sound like I'm ashamed to be from here."

"Aren't you?"

Cherry tried to say no, but the words wouldn't come.

Ardeth nodded.

"You're a lot of things, girl. Spoiled. Entitled. But you're not a liar. And you're a good mom." She took a sip of coffee, murmuring into the cup. "Heaven knows you didn't get that from your mother."

Cherry nearly goggled. "What was that? About my mother?"

There was a squawk from upstairs and then a panicked scream.

"Better go get your little one. He doesn't know head from tail with all this craziness going on. Hug him tight and bring him down to breakfast. I'll get something for him."

Ardeth stood with a pained groan and walked to the fridge. It was stuffed full, fuller than it had ever been. Her neighbors couldn't find Daisy, but they could make casseroles. Sorrow and hope and apologies played out in the form of pies and chicken soups and carrot cakes that were brought over from nearly everyone in Darling.

Cherry trudged upstairs, pulling her robe tightly around her. Jonah was looking in the closet, squeaking unhappily.

"Jonah, I'm here, sweetheart," Cherry said, and the relief in his eyes when he ran to her, hands flipping in agitation, nearly broke her heart. She sat on the bed and pulled him into her lap.

"I'm here, I'm here, I'm here. I'll never leave you. Never."

He buzzed into her shirt, his lips not working right, not forming the words he wanted to say. "Mama," he would have said. Or "I love you." Or "Please don't ever leave me because I don't know what's going on," or "Where's Daisy hiding? If you go away I'll be totally alone, and I just can't face the world without you."

But that is all too much for a little one to say, so he buzzed, and cried, and didn't twist away at first when Cherry wiped his tears.

After he was dressed and his wispy yellow hair was combed as well as it could be, Cherry slipped on some of her mother's oversized jeans and a yellow T-shirt.

"Today is going to be a day of miracles," she told Jonah as they carefully made their way down the stairs. "We must be prepared for everything."

"Morning, son," Mrs. Getchell said and placed two pieces of toast in front of Jonah. He hooted at her and touched the toast three times with his left forefinger. When it passed inspection, he wolfed it down.

There was a loud knocking on the door.

Cherry groaned. "It's too early to deal with anybody." She eyed Ardeth. "Can't I just pretend I'm not home? At least until noon?"

"A day of miracles," the old woman reminded her. She washed Jonah's face with a washcloth while he writhed. "Can't let them in if you don't open the door."

The knock sounded again. Forceful. A little frightening. Cherry breathed out slowly and stood. She was surprised to find her hands were shaking.

"A day of miracles. A day of miracles." Her bare feet moved closer to the door, which seemed to loom ominously over her.

When the heavy knocking started up again, she cringed.

*Cherry LaRouche,* she scolded herself. *You are stronger than this. What if it's news about Daisy? What if somebody found her?*

This thought changed everything. Her head emptied of monsters, emptied of howling winds and dolls in several little pieces. She flew the last few feet to the door. The lock stuck, and she felt hair stick to her damp face as she tried to wrestle with it. The door sang on its hinges as she flung it open.

It wasn't her daughter. She wasn't in the arms of a friendly fireman, drinking from a sippy cup. She wasn't wrapped in a sheet or a tarp or covered in weeds or water. There wasn't a neighbor or an officer twisting his hat around and around in his hands, trying to keep his face from collapsing while his eyes bled compassion.

It was a man. A man with dusky skin and dark eyes framed with even darker lashes. He stood at the door, his hand raised to knock again.

He was so beautiful. Cherry recognized that face, the smooth skin, and high cheekbones. The compassion and intent that blazed behind his delicate glasses.

She dropped right where she stood, collapsing to her knees, staring up at him with an open mouth like a child. She knew what he was going to say before he said it.

He licked his lips, trying to take the bad taste from his words.

"They found my little girl," he said. "In pieces."

# Chapter Twenty-Five

CHERRY'S HEART WAS beating too fast. Faster than Jonah's. Harder than a human heart should be able to beat. If she had seen a ghost or a bull or anything else that should terrify her, she wouldn't be nearly as afraid as she was of this man at this moment.

"I'm sorry," he said. His voice was soft and gentle and riddled with horror. The lilt of his words sounded beautiful—if the words of a demon could be beautiful. "I'm sorry," he repeated. "That isn't what I meant to say. I meant to say hello. It is nice to meet you. My name is Azhar Patel."

Cherry didn't rise. She didn't speak. She stared at his face until she thought it would singe and curl like burning paper, but his kind, tortured expression didn't change.

"And you are Cherry LaRouche. Your daughter is missing. I saw you on the news."

She nodded once. Glanced over her shoulder at Jonah, now finished with the toast and tiptoeing over to the laundry room. Ardeth's keen eyes ran up and down Azhar. She lifted a brow and followed Jonah.

"Could I come in?"

"No," Cherry said, and the spell was broken. She swallowed hard, got to her feet. "No, you can't come in. But I can come outside."

He stepped back, and her delicate bare feet gripped the front porch like a bird's. This was madness. Lunacy. The wood was firm. It was real, even though it rolled and bucked and chattered beneath her. She desperately needed something real.

The man sat on the steps, far enough away that his elbows and knees didn't encroach on her space.

"I obviously frightened you. I apologize again. This wasn't how I wanted our conversation to start."

"It isn't that," Cherry said. She studied him, his profile, his painfully, painfully tender eyes. The beauty of his face struck her even more here in the sunlight than it had in her dream.

"I mean, it is that. But not just that." Cherry pressed her lips together to keep the words in. The words that tumbled out of her mouth like pearls weren't making sense.

Azhar didn't seem to mind. He ducked his head, a nod, the most beautiful nod Cherry had ever seen. It held such grace and sorrow. His neck looked ready to snap under the weight of the thoughts he carried.

"How long has your little girl been missing?" he asked politely. As if he were asking her where she had picked up her new sweater.

"Four days," she answered just as politely. *Isn't this absurd,* she thought, and panic fluttered in the corners of her vision like wings. "How long was your little girl missing? Before they … they found her."

He sighed, and she heard the emotions in that sound. *Forever,* he would say. *Eons. Eternities. Since before the world was.*

"She was gone for nearly three weeks. If you look at the calendar, that's all it was. Eighteen days. Which isn't really very long at all, if you think about it." He turned to her, the intensity in his doe-eyes clawing to release itself from his courteous professionalism. "But time is funny, isn't it, Miss LaRouche? Only eighteen days, but it felt longer than any other period in my life. Nights and days and sleeps and awakes mean nothing when you're in your own special kind of hell."

She sat down beside him on the porch steps and wrapped her arms around her legs.

"Yes. Four days. It isn't long at all. But I'm aware of every single second." She wanted to put it better than that, but she didn't know how else to say it. Cherry looked at him, and he watched her quietly.

"I understand," he said softly. She knew he did. He was probably the only one who could truly understand her torment. "I've been where you are." His voice had the hollow rush of reeds in the water. Calm and cooling and terrifying at the same time. "Sada was missing for four days. Once."

"Tell me about her."

Cherry didn't want to hear, not really. But she knew he needed to speak. He didn't come to her because he had information that would help in finding Daisy, or because he could take the fear away. He came because he needed to speak. And she was going to listen because—

*One day this could be me, talking about Daisy, about when she had been missing and there was still hope and before she, too, was found in pieces.*

—she was a good person, and that's what good people did. And she needed to hear somebody speak, something else to focus on because her own thoughts sent her screaming inside.

He sighed and leaned back on the porch. Azhar closed his eyes, and Cherry felt like the light, the sparkle had gone out of the world.

"Sada was so young. So sweet. Shy to everybody but her mother and me. To us, she smiled and was full of questions. She had pigtails."

"Daisy has pigtails," Cherry murmured.

Azhar's eyes slowly opened. "I know. I saw her picture. In fact, I ..." He pulled a crumpled piece of newspaper out of his pocket, smoothed it out. It was Daisy's smiling face. Cherry felt the muscles in her face contort with an unbearable sadness. "I'm sorry," he said. "I kept it because she ... my Sada—they are very similar. And if I see a little girl, I want to be able to hold the picture up. To the girl, you see, and know if she is your daughter or not."

His words were stilting, the rich accent thicker than ever.

"You want this to help you recognize her. I know," Cherry said. His nervousness held her together. One of them had to be strong, and if he was awkward, then it was Cherry's job to hold him together. Maybe this was what she needed.

"I'm grateful for your help, Azhar. Tell me more about Sada."

He carefully folded Daisy's picture and put it back in his pocket. Then his fingers were too bare, and he studied them as if he hadn't seen them before.

"She comes to me in dreams. My Sada."

Cherry chilled. "Of course, she does."

His eyes flicked to hers, and the intensity in them made her suck in her breath.

"No, Miss LaRouche. I don't dream about her. She comes to me in dreams. There is a difference."

"What does she say?"

A bird whistled from the tree nearby, and Azhar turned to watch it.

"I came to America when I was fifteen. It was such a change from home, but I loved it. Loved everything about it. I went to good schools. Found a good job. Met a wonderful woman, who became my wife. Sada looks like her, you know." He winced, a slight tightening around his eyes. "Looked," he corrected himself. He turned back to Cherry. "Your daughter looked like you."

"Looks. Looks like me. Yes, she does."

Azhar's eyes followed the bird again. "You have another child, yes? A boy?"

"Yes."

The bird cleaned under its feathers, then flew away. There was loss on Azhar's face as he watched it go.

"That is good. That you have another. I had Sada and that was all."

Cherry felt her chin tremble. Not with tears, but with something darker and deeper.

"My son doesn't just replace her. One child doesn't simply take the place of another." She stood on shaky legs and balled her hands into fists. "And Daisy isn't dead. She's missing. That's different. I'm sorry for what happened to your daughter. It's a terrible thing. But that's not what is going on here. This is a completely different situation." Tears were there, but they were the hateful, spiteful kind. She rubbed at her eyes with the back of her hand. "Please go."

"Miss LaRouche, I'm sorry to have upset you. I only wanted to—"

"Go. I don't know you. You're a stranger to me. I'm sorry for your loss, but it has nothing to do with me." She turned for the front door.

"He has a name," he said. Cherry stopped, her hand stretched out to the doorknob. "This killer, this monster who takes our children from us. Boys, girls, it does not matter. But he has a name."

"What is his name?"

"Sada calls him the Handsome Butcher. She says he looks like a prince. She tells me at night when she comes."

Cherry faced him. "Mr. Patel, people simply don't come in dreams. That isn't the way it works. I'm so sorry, but I can't tell the police to look for this Handsome Butcher based on a dream you had. I hope you can understand."

It was like he didn't hear her. "She tells me what he did. The things he told her. He said she was beautiful, like a doll. And then he did things, ugly things. But not until after she was dead. He doesn't want them to feel pain, I think. He's a monster, but a monster in the most unusual sense."

"Mr. Patel. Please."

"And they are like dolls, these little ones. He can pose them and place them and take them apart like toys. He isn't interested in sex. He isn't interested in hurting them. He just wants to play. But they don't always go back together, you see. They aren't like real dolls in that way. Sometimes the pieces, they don't *fit*. And he tries so hard to make them *fit*. Why won't they fit right?"

"Mr. Patel. Azhar. You're scaring me." His eyes cleared then, and he looked at Cherry's face. He instantly bowed his head. "Forgive me. That isn't what I … Forgive me." He stood and bowed his head again. "Forgiveness. Please."

Cherry's heart broke. She reached out a hand. "This is hard for both of us. I never knew anything could be so hard. But please, don't say it again."

Azhar met her eyes. His were dark, liquid, and haunted. "I need to go. I had hoped we could talk longer, but I fear I need to leave. It was a pleasure, Miss LaRouche. I truly hope you find the peace you are searching for. It is difficult when you receive the call telling you your little one is … well, you know. And it is horrible, of course. But you live. And you breathe. And your son will help you get out of bed in the morning. You will need him. Goodbye."

He left quickly, walking down the driveway into the trees.

"Daisy's alive," Cherry whispered after him. "She's just missing for a while. My Daisy will come home alive."

# Chapter Twenty-Six

CHERRY STEPPED INSIDE the house, shut the door, and leaned against it.

"Who was he?" Ardeth Getchell asked. She stood at the kitchen sink, drying dishes with a faded yellow towel. Everything was faded. Everything was rags. Cherry closed her eyes against the house and the noise and the shrieking of her heart.

"He's disturbed. Oh, I don't think he'll hurt us," she said when she saw the glint in Ardeth's eyes, "but he has things to say. About Daisy. Things I don't especially want to hear."

Ardeth nodded. "I'm afraid you'll see a lot of that, and more is only gonna come. Misery brings out the crazies, sure enough." She shrugged. "But it brings out the best in people, too. Look for it and you'll find it." She nudged Jonah, who ran into Cherry's arms. "This one has missed you. Why don't you sit back and be a mom for a while?"

Cherry knelt and hugged Jonah close to her. "She's right. Isn't she right? I'm sorry, darling. I've been so preoccupied with … but I miss you, baby boy."

There was a pounding on the door. Frantic. Uncomfortable in its insistence.

Cherry sighed. "I don't want to see him anymore. Why won't he go away?"

Ardeth looked at her, and Cherry shook her head. Jonah moved closer against her, and she cuddled him. She frowned, and put her cheek against his, her hands against his thin legs. He was warmer than usual.

"Cherry. Cherry, it's Runner. I know you're home. Please open the door."

"Runner." Cherry stood, pulled Jonah up onto her hip, and ran for the door. She swung it open.

Runner swooped her into his arms.

Jonah struggled, squawking, and slid onto the floor. He crawled away, Ardeth right behind him.

"Cherry. Oh, my girl, I just heard. I just heard. I'm so sorry, I didn't know. Are you all right? Have they found her?"

He smelled like soap and detergent and sunshine.

Cherry twisted his dark T-shirt under her fingers and was surprised to find herself crying into his chest.

He picked her up like a child, holding her close, and her feet dangled over the floor.

"Oh, darlin'. My girl. I'm sorry I wasn't here. I'm so sorry you went through this all alone."

"She wasn't alone." Mordachi wiped his feet on the mat.

Cherry felt his hand on her shoulder. Too heavy. She shrugged it off and wrapped her thin arms around Runner's neck.

"Thank you for taking care of her while I was gone," Runner said. He nodded at Mordachi, who didn't nod back.

"Just where exactly have you been all this time? Four days is a long time to go missing."

Runner didn't answer him. He kissed Cherry's hair and set her gently on the ground. He ran his hands over her face, brushing the tears away, smoothing her puff of hair away from her eyes.

"Don't cry. Don't cry. We'll figure something out. Find her somehow."

Cherry sniffled. "Where were you? I really needed you. I still need you. How could you just have heard?"

He held her close. "Shh. I'm here now. I was out of town for some work. But I'm here now."

Cherry brightened, her breath catching in her throat. She held onto Runner's shirt again.

"Gone? You weren't at home?"

"Nope."

"Do you think maybe Daisy found her way to your house somehow? Maybe wandered there during the storm? We've checked all around, but if you weren't there. Maybe nobody checked it yet."

Runner ran his green eyes over her too-big shirt and rumpled hair. "Maybe. Yeah, that's quite possible. I haven't had a chance to go home yet. I stopped by here as soon as I heard. Hey, why don't I run over there right now and look around? I'll look real good for her."

Cherry's brown eyes were huge. "Can I come?"

Runner's face changed just for a second, growing dark and stormy. Something in his eyes reared, pressing its ugly face against the glass of his pupils. "Cherry, I don't—"

Mordachi interrupted. "Jonah looks like he's ready to have a meltdown. Maybe now's not the best time to leave him. What do you think, Cherry? Besides, I brought you guys some lunch."

"Lunch?" Cherry's lips turned down. "It's hardly past morning. Besides, I want to go with Runner. You don't mind, do you?"

Runner scratched the back of his head, his blond hair flopping over one eye. "It's not that I mind, Cherry. You know I'd love to spend time with you. But if there's a problem, or if I do happen to find her and she isn't … If she's …" He put his arms around her, bent his face down until their foreheads touched. "I'm worried about you, baby. Do you understand?"

She didn't, but she was too tired to push. She was too tired for anything. First, the strange and handsome Azhar Patel, who said her daughter was dead, and now Runner was saying something similar.

She felt dizzy.

"Hold on a second, darlin'. Let's set you down."

Runner scooped her up and strode over to the couch. He put her down.

Mordachi unfolded a blanket on top of her legs.

"I feel like this will never end," she said. Her voice sounded strange like it was too far away and coming through a fog. "Will this ever be over?"

"It will end when we find her. Safe and sound," Mordachi said.

Runner bent down and kissed her on the mouth. "I'll be back soon. I'll check everything out around my property, as good as it can be checked. I'll find your little girl and bring her back to you, Cherry LaRouche. I promise you."

He left without looking back, slamming the door behind him. His boots sounded loudly on the wooden porch.

Cherry looked at Mordachi. "How come you never promise you'll find her?"

Mordachi watched Runner leave without smiling. "That's the difference between him and me," he said. "I never lie."

# Chapter Twenty-Seven

CHERRY DIDN'T WANT to go, but Mordachi dragged her outside for lunch.

"It's a beautiful day. You need some sunshine. Get," he said when she complained.

He took Jonah's thin hand in his big ones.

"Come on, son," he said. "You too."

He led them to the tree at the side of the house.

"Go," he said.

Cherry stared at him.

"Climb."

"But Mordachi, I—"

"Get up there, girl."

It was easier than last time. Her feet remembered the way and her hands automatically reached for branches just like they had several years ago. She sat on her usual branch, and she fit there more than she fit anywhere else in this world.

"Catch," he said and tossed a bag up to her. She caught it easily.

"I'm sending him up," he said.

Mordachi knelt so he was eye to eye with Jonah.

"How do you feel about climbing this tree, boy? It's your mama's tree. Favorite place in the world when we were kids. Want to sit up there with her?"

Jonah looked up the sturdy trunk, up to the thick branches and their bright flowers. He made a sound like a mewling cat.

"I'm telling you no! He has brittle bones. What if he falls?"

"I won't let him fall." He turned to Jonah again. "Hear that? I'll be right behind you, helping you up. Want to climb?"

Jonah hooted, holding his thin arms out awkwardly.

Mordachi placed them properly on the tree. "Good. Just like that. Put your feet here and here. Now push."

The climb was slow, painful. It made Cherry's heart pound in a way that didn't feel good inside, but at the same time, it was something beautiful. Mordachi supported Jonah's feet, pushing him upward, while the little boy pulled and climbed and whined softly with the effort.

"Daisy, look at this," Cherry said, then quickly covered her mouth with her hand. Her eyes blurred, and she made a sobbing, choking sound.

Mordachi kept his attention on Jonah. Cherry was grateful for this.

"That's it, son. Just like that."

Cherry swallowed, and it tore her throat. She cleared it, wiped her eyes on her thin wrist, and held her arms out for Jonah.

"Come here, sweetie. You're doing it."

She watched his eyes squint, his tender muscles shake. He lost his footing, but Mordachi steadied him with one hand.

"Doing good. No problem. Slow and steady, boy."

When he reached Cherry's branch, she pulled him quickly to her, cradling him.

"My sweet boy," she cooed. "My sweet boy."

Jonah made a happy, weak sound. His chest rose and fell rapidly.

Cherry put her hand over his heart.

"Jonah, it's beating so hard. We never should have—"

Mordachi flopped on the branch across from them.

"It takes some effort the first time. Maybe the next few times. But the boy needs to climb trees, Cherry. You can't keep him wrapped up in tissue paper forever."

She glared at him, her arms tight around her son. "Don't tell me how to raise my children. What would you know about family, anyway?" The second she said it, her heart sank. "I'm so sorry. That isn't what I meant to say. I wasn't thinking."

Mordachi looked away. "It's not like I haven't heard it before."

She bit her lip. "But never from me. I never felt that way."

The leaves rustled in the wind and flowers floated to the ground. Cherry stroked Jonah's hair. The exertion had left him happy but exhausted, and his eyelids were at half-mast.

"Do you think we'll find her?" Cherry felt her son's soft hair under her fingertips. She wished it was Daisy's at that moment. Her curly pigtails and half-moon smile. The way her pudgy, warm body rested in her arms, the way she laid her head on her mama's shoulder. Life seemed just right when there was a happy, snuggly baby in her arms.

"I do."

She looked at Mordachi, studying his face, his dark beard, and the tight muscles in his arms. He was a man who had worked every day of his life, she realized. Most of it was cleaning up the messes his brother had left behind. And that she had left behind. Her cheeks burned with something hot and uncomfortable. Could it be shame?

"But do you think we'll find her alive?" The word was ugly, but it needed to be said.

Mordachi's blazing gaze nearly made her gasp.

"Of course, we will. It's only been a few days, and Louisiana is a big place. She'll turn up. Plenty of places for a little tyke to hide."

Cherry's fingers fluttered across Jonah's eyelids. He was asleep.

"I met a man today, named Azhar. His daughter went missing a while ago. She was gone for three weeks. When they found her …"

"I know who he is. I know what they found, and I'm sorry. But that's not you, Cherry. That isn't you."

"But if Daisy—"

He turned to face her. "This isn't helping. I know you want to be reasonable and rational. More than that, I know you're preparing yourself for the worst. Life's been tough on you. But don't rob yourself of your hope, do you understand? You need it. Otherwise, you won't be left standing." He settled back. "Now, eat your lunch. You're too skinny."

She ignored this and stared at the clouds. "It's noon light," she said softly.

"Hmm?"

She kissed Jonah's head, then started gnawing nervously on her nails.

"I always hated noon light."

# Chapter Twenty-Eight

EVENING BROKE THE news that another body had been found. Small, like the others. Gray and bloated, floating face down. Pulled out of the water, fingers nibbled by animals.

Cherry hit the floor with a sound like fracturing bones. When she came to, tears leaked from her eyes before she could even remember why she was crying. The shy neighbor who brought the news had told her gently that it wasn't her child.

"You should have started with that part first," Ardeth Getchell told him.

He looked away. "Yes ma'am."

It wasn't her child, but it was somebody's. What hit even closer, what tore even more fiercely was that it was somebody's grandchild. More specifically, Monica's down at the Alco.

Her hand flew to her mouth, whether to keep the horror out or the relief that it wasn't Daisy in, she wasn't sure. "Oh, no," Cherry said.

"I have to see her." She turned to Ardeth. "Will you keep an eye on—?"

"Go," Ardeth said. Her eyes were wet. "Just go."

Cherry shoved her bare feet into the red rain boots that kept permanent residence on her porch. She yanked open Old Sal's creaky door and slammed it shut behind her. She backed out quickly, spewing mud and gravel behind her.

Her chest was too tight. Her tears had started to dry when she learned that the small, misshapen body wasn't her daughter again, but now, thinking of Monica, of her too-red lips and perfumed hugs, they started anew. She drove too far, too fast, and when she reached Monica's unusual rust-colored home, she jumped out of the car nearly before it stopped.

The police were already there, of course. Some working hard, but mostly they milled, looking at the sky and the trees and the ground. Everybody knew Monica. Everybody knew her tiny grandson. But death, and more importantly, murder, was still something of a foreigner in Darling.

The young officer saw Cherry running up the driveway and leaped to stop her.

"Cherry, you can't go in there right now. You need to—"

"Ian Bridger, you settle yourself down this instant. I need to see her and you're going to let me."

"But Cherry, I—"

Her face was ferocious. "You're a man of soul. Use it now."

She pushed past him, kicked her boots off at the door, and stepped inside.

Monica was sobbing on the couch. A female officer sat across from her, her eyes too tender, frustratingly tender, and Cherry felt her hackles rise because of it.

"Monica," she said and fell to her knees in front of her.

Monica caught Cherry around the neck. "He's so little, he's so little, and then some monster ..."

"I'm so sorry, Monica. I am."

They held each other for a long time. Monica's heart beat fast and Cherry felt hers was slowing to a crawl. Was this what evil feels like? The gratitude that it wasn't her Daisy, that perhaps the monster was satiated for a little while, even if it was from gnawing on the sharp bones of another little child. She thought of the tiny boy, of the way his skin would slide from his muscle after too long in the water, and she nearly vomited.

Cherry wouldn't wish this on anybody. Except maybe to

spare her daughter, and even then it was too much to think about.

"You know what this means, don't you?" Monica asked.

Her eyes were puffy. Her mascara and nose and soul were running. Her lipstick was smeared over her teeth and onto her face.

Cherry put her hand to her own cheek and realized she must be wearing some of it. The intimacy of this, and her feelings of relief, chilled her.

"What does it mean?"

Monica hiccupped. "It has to be somebody here, Cherry. These little babies, they were coming from different towns before. But not anymore." She stared into Cherry's eyes. "He has to be local."

Cherry felt her mouth drop open and her body went cold. "No, it can't be. Somebody from Darling? But why?"

Monica's face crumpled. "Why anything?" Then she was in tears again, wailing the sickening sound that only somebody who loses a small child can make.

Cherry tried to pull away, to put some distance between her and that sound, but Monica was too strong, her grief making her arms rigid and unbreakable. Cherry scrabbled at Monica's hands, breathing heavy and fast, but she couldn't get away. Her mouth opened, and she was afraid she would wail, too, and if she gave voice to her despair, she would bring about Daisy's destruction as well.

"Monica, your daughter is here. Cherry, come with me."

The calm voice of young Officer Bridger gave Cherry some structure to hang her emotions on. He reached out and took her hands, then gently helped her up.

Monica's daughter, a dark-haired drug addict who had more children than sense, fell to the ground in Cherry's place. All was as it should be. Almost.

Cherry grabbed Ian's fingers. Her own were slim, fragile, but the bone turned to steel under her skin.

"She says it's somebody local," she hissed.

He stepped back in surprise but soon leaned in close again.

"Why would she say that?" he asked quietly.

"There have never been two children from the same area before. I think she's right. I think it has to be somebody from Darling."

"A lot of people pass in and out, Cherry. We can't keep tabs on everyone."

"But we *do*," she insisted. "This is Darling. Everybody knows everybody's business. Why do you think E and I …? Why do you think I left? We all know who the strangers are. We all know how long they stay. All of those fights springing up at the bar? The bad blood and the feuds, strangers, and people from Darling? The entire town knows about it the next day. I think Monica is on to something." Cherry needed a drink of water or a stick of gum or a bullet to the mouth, something to take the taste away.

"The idea of a local. It …"

"It makes me sick, too," she said. "But it feels right, somehow. Who else could it be?"

"We'll look into it, Cherry. You know we will."

She took his hands in hers and nodded. Ian Bridger nodded back, and his eyes said everything. They reflected their childhood together. They said if he ever found another woman this desperate, he would help her no matter what. She saw the weight of what they were up against felt so heavy it would crush him where he stood. She turned from the porch, right into the shockingly tender eyes of Azhar.

"So, you believe me," he whispered. His voice was sweet and low as an apparitional wind.

"I didn't say that."

"You didn't have to. I know you know. That he has her. The Handsome Butcher has taken your daughter like he took mine."

Cherry opened her mouth, but nothing came out.

Azhar smiled sadly and shook his head. "Come, Miss LaRouche," he said and held his hand out. "I have something to show you."

She didn't want to take it. Something told her if she reached out, if he wrapped her small hand in his, she would be crossing a point she couldn't return from.

"I can't make this all go away, can I?" she asked.

He shook his head. There was a grimness to his face, but his eyes, as always, were full of sorrow and something akin to love. The type of love you have for a small, dying animal, perhaps. The type of love that hurts more than it heals.

"No, but it does get better. Eventually. A little bit." He swallowed hard. "It's a little easier when you know because the hope is gone. It's the hope that will get you every time."

His hand was still out toward her.

Cherry took it.

# Chapter Twenty-Nine

CHERRY AND AZHAR started up the dirt lane. The clouds were pulling low, and the wind was picking up. She shivered.

"Are you cold?"

"Oh, no. Do you see the light? How it's darkening because of the clouds? It's storm light."

"Storm light?"

"I get nervous during storm light."

He didn't say anything for a long time. Cherry regretted her words. How silly she sounded. How poorly put together.

"Sada disappeared during storm light."

She turned to look at him, but he was watching something in the distance.

"She was afraid of storms, always. The wind, especially. She would pull her blankets off her bed and sleep in the hallway because there weren't any windows. In case they broke and cut her while she was sleeping. Her mother, she was so angry."

"Where is her mother?"

Azhar shrugged. "Who knows? She left. After. Stayed in her room after the funeral, then one day she came out. She walked past me and drove away. I don't know where she is."

Cherry looked at her red rain boots as they moved over the ground. "I'm so sorry."

He didn't say anything.

She cleared her throat. "You said you had something to show me?"

"Of course." He dug into his shirt pocket, pulling out a worn picture. He ran his thumb down it and handed it to Cherry. "Sada."

She was beautiful. A small girl with beautiful golden skin. Her eyes were, if possible, even more liquid than her father's. He was right; she did have pigtails. Beautiful black pigtails which would surely wave in the wind.

"She reminds me of Daisy."

"Yes."

She swallowed hard, handed the picture back. "Do you think she reminds *him* of Daisy?"

"I don't know. Not all the children look alike. Boys, girls, it doesn't seem to matter. The monster has an appetite for … sweetness. It might not matter how the source of this sweetness appears. I do not know."

They were walking farther and farther away. Cherry realized she was peering behind the logs and trees.

*I'm still looking for my daughter as if she had wandered away. I know she didn't wander away. This man has forced me to know it.*

"He cut off her pigtails," Azhar said suddenly. "Took her legs, took her arms. Left her head. But somehow, it was the pigtails that gave me the most horror." He watched her with moist eyes. "Isn't that strange?"

She didn't want to think about it. "Do you have any idea who did this?"

"I told you. The Handsome Butcher."

"No, do you have any idea of who *did* this? A name? A description? If he took your daughter, and if he took mine, aren't there clues or something?" She spread her hands helplessly. How does one do this? How does one find a madman?

"Clues won't help you, my friend. He won't be found. He doesn't want to be found. He just wants to kill, to play, and that is what he'll do. We can't stop him."

Cherry stopped in her tracks. "I don't believe it. Not for a second. Someone will stop him because he has to be stopped. He has my little girl, and—"

His calm, lilting voice cut through her. "If he has her, then she is dead. I am sorry. It is only a matter of her being found."

Her body jerked, jolted as if it were run through with electricity, but it was something more akin to horror, and revulsion, and hate and shock and extreme, enervating pain.

"I am sorry," he said again, reaching for her shoulder.

She pulled away.

"She's not dead."

He didn't answer.

Cherry took a step away, too fast, and he had to double his speed to keep up with her.

"She's not dead, don't you understand? As her mother, don't you think I'd somehow know if she was dead?"

"No, you wouldn't." The calmness in his voice made her grit her teeth. "You wouldn't know like my wife didn't know. Like I didn't know. Like the other mothers didn't know."

"But this is different."

"It isn't."

She wanted to slap him. This want grew inside her until she rolled her sweaty palms against her shorts.

"I'm not trying to be cruel. I'm being truthful. I told you the hope will get you every time. It is a thing of beauty, at first. Like a balloon. But when that hope is taken from you, then ..." He shook his head. Azhar met her gaze. "That is when you want to die. Not when she disappears or when people leave horrible notes taped onto your door, or say they saw her when they never did, or when people tell you this is their god's punishment for some kind of sin. It is when hope is gone."

His voice had risen. He fiddled with his glasses.

Cherry nearly pushed his hair back from his eyes, to make

things clearer for him.

"This is when you want to die," he said again. "As I think my wife wanted to die."

Cherry chilled. "You think that's where she went?"

"As I said, I do not know. I have more to show you, but we are here now."

Cherry looked around. They were in a wooded area that looked just like everywhere else.

"Here? Where's here?"

He sat down on a rotting log that had fallen over and gestured for her to take a seat beside him.

"This is one of the crime scenes. Where a little girl was found. Her name was Heather Long. Look around, Cherry. This is where they found her. Most of her anyway. Here. I have pictures."

Cherry's mouth went dry. "P-pictures? Of this little girl?"

"Of all of them. Except for this newest one, of course. They haven't been released yet. But here, this is what I wanted to—"

"No." She stood, backed away. "I don't want to see them."

Azhar's head swung to her, his eyes wide.

"Why don't you want to see them? I could show you the peace. There's peace, afterward, you know. First, the hope is there, and you worry and hope and dream, but then there's such peace." He stood, took a step closer. Tried pressing a small stack of photos into her hands.

Where had they come from? How many children?

"I won't look at them. Azhar. You're sick." She spun away from him, darting up the road as quickly as her heavy red boots would let her.

He followed. "Miss LaRouche. Please. You need to see the peace of the children."

She didn't realize she was crying until she heard herself sob, when her panting and sobbing became one tangled, ugly thing.

He reached for her, and she pulled away. He reached farther and grabbed her shirt.

"Miss LaRouche, please!"

She screamed. She screamed and screamed and screamed.

He pushed her to the ground, crawling on top of her to hold her body down, his hand over her mouth.

"Please don't scream. Please. This isn't going the way it should. I don't want to hurt you."

She lay in the cold mud, kicking, clawing at the hand over her mouth.

He wrapped his legs firmly around hers. His eyes were wild. "Please. Don't make this harder. I just want to tell you about the peace your little girl has. If you would only let me show you."

Her tears ran over his hand.

His eyes tore from hers and he glanced at his hand, which covered her mouth, her face. Azhar looked down at his body, holding hers to the ground by force. His eyes shifted back to meet hers again. Stricken with guilt or fear or something Cherry couldn't quite put into words, he said, "I'm so sorry." With that, he quickly rolled away from her, drawing himself together and covering his face with his hands. "I only wanted to … I'm so ashamed."

Cherry scrambled to her feet. She cast one last look at Azhar, muddied and disheveled, sitting on the ground, his photographs scattered around him.

She turned and ran up the hill.

# Chapter Thirty

CHERRY STUMBLED INTO the chaos surrounding Monica's home. She saw Ian Bridger and grabbed his sleeve.

"That man, Azhar, he said he had pictures of the crime scenes," Cherry sobbed. She covered her face as she spoke. Somehow it made it easier. "I don't know how he got them. He said the children were at peace, now. That my daughter is dead. He said—"

Then she was crying so hard she couldn't say anything anymore, and the police took action. They were busy. They had things to *do*. Somebody to question, somebody to scream "Where are the babies?" at until they couldn't scream anymore.

"We'll figure it out, Miss LaRouche," one of them said.

She didn't know who said it, didn't care really. She just remembered being held down in the mud, the fear of it, not being able to move or scream. Did Daisy feel like that? Is that what happened? Was her little girl really not *lost*?

"I'm going to be sick," she said to nobody in particular and retched into the mud. She wiped her mouth with the back of her hand, ashamed, but nobody was looking at her. They were worker ants, swarming around Monica's house, around the wooden stairs, and the police cars. After taking Azhar away, nobody paid Cherry any mind at all.

She staggered to her car, oblivious to the mud that smeared over the upholstery. She needed to go home. To shower. To hold her son and pray for her daughter. Then, would search again.

"Cherry," Mordachi said when she walked inside her mother's house. His brown eyes took in the mud and filth and despair.

"Oh, Cherry." He took a step toward her, but she held up a thin, trembling, dirt-streaked hand.

"I have to clean up. Just a second. And then … Where is Jonah?"

Mordachi pointed to the living room where Jonah sat on the floor, stacking an old set of wooden blocks. Stacking, knocking them over. Stacking one, then two. Knocking them over.

"He's sitting so quietly," Cherry breathed. "And playing so appropriately."

"Go shower. He's fine. We'll talk later."

She nodded, and on impulse, rushed over, stood on tiptoes, and kissed Mordachi's cheek.

"Thank you," she whispered and hurried away.

The water from the shower was as warm as she could make it, which wasn't much, considering the state of the plumbing. Mud and filth ran down her body. She scrubbed her hair with cheap shampoo, rubbing the clumps of dirt out of it frantically, watching the suds run down her pale stomach and legs.

She was breathing much too fast, sputtering in the lukewarm water. Cherry stilled herself, head bowed, water washing away the terror, the ache from her bones. Was Daisy dirty? When was the last time she had a bath? The Handsome Butcher, if that's who he was, seemed to leave behind remarkably clean children. So, he washed them obviously. Was this before or after—?

She shut off the water and stepped into a thin towel, rubbing it down her body almost brutally. No time for this. No time. She threw on some clean clothes and ran downstairs.

"Cherry …"

"Mordachi, give me a second, will you? I want to hug my son."

Jonah didn't want to be hugged. He squawked and struggled away. Cherry knew she shouldn't push this, *knew* it, but she wanted him in her arms, in her care. She wanted him safe, needed that contact. She tried again. Jonah screamed and threw a block against the wall.

"Come here, darlin'."

Mordachi, sitting on the couch, held his arms out to her.

She hesitated and then walked into them.

He pulled her onto his lap. "My girl. My brave girl." He kissed the top of her head, and the arms around her, even if they were Mordachi's, were strong and warm, and what she needed. She closed her eyes.

"I don't know what to think," she told him. "What if the murderer is local? But the things Azhar said. Still, I don't think that …" She sighed and pressed her face into his shoulder like a kitten.

"So, stop thinking. You're driving yourself crazy."

She pulled back to look at him. "But—"

He kissed her, hard and sweet. Kissed her with the kind of kiss she knew he had longed to give her during their school years, the kind of kiss he wished he had given before she had driven off with his brother E. Mordachi kissed her as a man kisses a woman he's waited over twenty years to have.

"Mordachi, I—"There was another kiss, even deeper this time.

Her daughter was missing, and her hair was wet after washing mud out of it and she had been pushed to the ground by the slender hands and warm eyes of somebody who might or might not be a madman and her son was playing oh so happily and she was so tired and there was warmth and safety and oh yes this kiss.

# Chapter Thirty-One

CHERRY WAS PRIM and powdered and ready to fight. She was tired of sitting around like a good little traumatized mama. Nothing had ever come easy to her, and she wasn't holding her breath that things would change soon.

"Now, you let me talk to him," she said, leaning over the desk down at the police station. "You let me talk to him right away. None of this nonsense."

"Ma'am, I can't let you go walking in there."

Cherry leaned even closer. "Don't you 'ma'am' me. We've known each other since we were children. Don't act like we didn't. And what's the problem if I talk to him? You'll be recording it anyway, isn't that right? Watching through your little windows?" Her eyes glittered, she could feel it. "What do you think is gonna happen? Think I'll slip him a file or a handcuff key? Help him escape? Shoot, seems to me like you're not particularly interested in who took my daughter."

"Miss LaRouche, you know that isn't the case."

"Then let me talk to him. C'mon, Ian. You think he's a suspect. You even think I'm a suspect. Can't be both of us, can it?" Ian seemed unmoved and Cherry sighed. "Listen. If he knows something, I have to ask, okay? He had things he wanted to tell me. Things he wanted to show me. If he knows anything about where Daisy is … I'll do anything. Look at anything. Don't you understand?"

He understood. Cherry was ushered in and told to behave herself. They'd be watching.

Azhar sat at the same grimy little table Cherry had sat at earlier. He held his head in his handcuffed hands.

"Hello, Azhar." Cherry sat across from him, her purse tucked between her ankles. She forced a smile. "Are they treating you well?"

He didn't look at her.

Cherry felt a pang in her chest. Was it fear? Was it sorrow? She licked her lips nervously.

"Azhar, earlier you had something you wanted to show me. I wasn't ready to see it then, but I am now."

He was still silent, but she hoped he listened.

She ran her hands over her face. "Oh, Azhar, this is such a mess. They think you took her. They think I took her. Everybody is running around without any direction, and I don't know what to do. The only person who has any idea what might be going on is you, and what happens? I get you sent to jail. I'm sorry. I don't think you hurt anyone. The more I look at you, the surer of it I am. But if not you, then who? Somebody from town? I couldn't bear it if it was somebody from town."

He moved, raised his head, and his eyes were dark, beautiful, tortured, and brimming with pain.

"It is the Handsome Butcher. I wish I could tell you more, but I cannot. Sada shows me what she can, but it isn't much help." He nodded to her. "Much like your daughter will show things to you."

Cherry's mouth went dry. "But she isn't. Not yet. I think she's still alive. I know you don't believe me," she pressed when he started to shake his head, "but it's too soon. It hasn't been long enough. I need her to still be alive, you see. I need to believe I can still save her."

His look remained scornful.

"Please," she said. "At four days, you still had hope, didn't you? Don't rob me of this hope. I need it to keep on breathing."

He studied her, then dropped his eyes to stare at his bound hands.

"They think I am a monster," he said. "They think I kill children. Children." His mouth twisted. "It is the Handsome Butcher who should be here, not me." He raised his gaze to her, showing the fierceness in his eyes. "To be sitting here in his stead. It disgusts me."

Cherry licked her lips. "Do you have the pictures? What it was you wanted to show me?"

He jerked his head toward the door. "They took them, of course. Ask if you can have them. If so, I will show you."

Almost immediately, the door snicked open, and Ian set a small stack of pictures on the table.

"Thank you, sir," Azhar said.

Ian didn't answer as he stepped outside.

Azhar reached for the pictures with both hands, the handcuffs gleaming in the cheap light.

"Just a minute," Cherry said. She took a deep breath. Another. "Please." One more breath for good measure. "All right."

She braced herself for skulls and tattered clothes and bits of bone. Cherry shut her eyes, prayed feverishly, and then opened them.

The pictures. The pictures.

There weren't any children to be seen at all.

"What is this?" Cherry asked. She picked up a photograph, twisted it around in her thin fingers. "Is this some kind of joke?"

Azhar's brows drew together. "Joke? I do not understand."

Cherry grabbed another picture. And another.

"There are no children here. Weren't you going to show me the kids? How they're at peace now?"

She rifled through them, quickly, quickly. If these weren't pictures of the children, then they weren't evidence. They weren't of any use. They wouldn't lead her to the madman who took Daisy or help get her back.

With a small cry of frustration, Cherry threw the pictures to the ground. The primal nature of the sound nearly made her wince.

"Cherry." Azhar dropped to his knees, gathering the pictures with his cuffed hands. "What are you doing?"

She dropped to the ground beside him, scrabbling at the pictures, pushing them this way and that as she desperately studied each one.

"Where are they?"

"Who?"

"The children!"

He grabbed her hands then, the whiteness of her fingers swallowed in the gold of his.

"No children, Miss LaRouche. The children are gone, don't you see? All that is left behind is peace."

The door cracked open, and Ian stuck his head inside.

"Everything all right in here?"

No. Everything was a mess. Everything was out of sorts, and Cherry couldn't put it right in her head. She saw herself as Ian must see her: crouched on the floor in a sea of old photographs, clutching the fingers of a man in handcuffs.

She pulled her hands away.

Azhar graciously let her.

"We're fine. Thank you."

Ian nodded, and the door closed.

Azhar began collecting the pictures again with Cherry's help. Her hand lingered over a gentle photograph of a rolling hill, long grasses bending softly in the wind.

"Beautiful, isn't it?" he asked. Azhar stood, holding a cuffed hand genteelly out to Cherry.

She hesitated, then placed her palm against his.

He helped her onto her feet.

"It is." Cherry slid into her chair, still studying the picture. She could almost see the grass ripple. "Where is it?"

"Number Four. Zachary Sparrow."

Her eyes flicked up. "I'm sorry?"

"The fourth body. Zachary Sparrow."

"I don't understand."

Azhar sat with a grace that made him seem more foreign than ever.

"This was where they discovered his body. Well, most of it. He was missing one of his legs. But otherwise, he was intact."

Cherry's hand spasmed, and she dropped the picture.

"These are"—she searched for the words—"crime scene photos?"

Azhar shook his head, his eyes still on the picture.

"No. They are pictures of healing. Pictures of peace. Like I promised you."

"I don't understand."

He pointed at the picture. "This is where they found him. Shiny and clean. Dark and beautiful. But disposed of. Used up. Tossed away. This was a place of horrors, do you see?"

She saw.

"But then something begins to happen. Police spirited his little body away. His parents buried and mourned him. Put him back into the earth. And this area, here. It has scars."

Cherry looked closer. "Scars?"

"How can it not after such a trauma?"

"I see."

He shook his head, smiling sadly.

How beautiful would that smile be, how glorious to see it in full daylight? A smile of joy?

"The earth is a kind thing. Violence of this sort leaves scars. Dirt kicked up here. An imprint in the grass there. Yes?"

"Yes."

"It begins to heal. The grass grows and stretches and straightens out. Flowers cover the blood. The wind and rain wash away the scent of the murder."

"I see."

He smiled then, and it was as bright as she had hoped.

"Now you do."

Cherry looked at the photos again. There were easily a dozen.

"This is what you wanted to show me?"

"Yes. That there is peace afterward. Such a bad time at first. Such a bad time. But after, after accepting what has been done, it is possible to heal. Like the land. This is what I wanted you to know."

"All of these pictures represent a child who has been killed?"

"Yes."

"There are so many."

"Yes. More than the police know about, I would think. They do not know of all of the children."

She swallowed hard.

"And you do?"

He nodded. "Sada tells me. I contact the police then. Tell them where to look."

He reached for her hand, but she slid her fingers away.

"You call the police because you just happen to find all these children. You know right where they are. Mysteriously."

His eyes were intense.

"Our daughters know things, Miss LaRouche. They're all connected."

"My daughter doesn't know anything about this. Nothing."

"Are you certain?"

His voice, so silky and sincere, cut to her heart.

"Of course, I'm certain. Daisy is so little. She wouldn't—"

She thought of the dolls from Daisy's dreams. The sweet little dolls that her child had asked her to make. The oh-so-specific instructions.

This one without hair. That one without clothes. This one with yellow barrettes and a single ruffled sock.

She remembered one she'd carefully sewn with brown buttons for eyes and shiny pigtails. Daisy had shaken her head and cut the pigtails off.

"Like this," she had said and then rocked the little doll, the mini Sada, in her arms.

Cherry's stomach hurt. She tried to stand, but her muscles couldn't seem to remember how to work.

Azhar used this moment to grab her hand again. He felt warm. Far too warm. She was freezing, she realized. Freezing in the hot heat of a Louisiana afternoon. A muscle in her leg twitched, but that was all the movement she could muster.

"It will get better," he promised. His dark eyes were tender and moist with concern. "I know this feeling, this despair, but it will get better."

She managed to unlock her tongue. "Where is my daughter?" she whispered.

"She is free from pain."

"Tell me where my daughter is."

"They will find her soon. Everybody is looking so hard. Where were the search parties when Sada went missing? Who would care to look for a girl with dark skin, whose father has such a strong accent? She was gone for so long …"

Cherry stood, knocking her chair back. Her chest heaved with breaths that were much too hard to take.

"You sick monster! Where is my little girl?"

Azhar leaned back in his chair as the door flew open and uniforms streamed inside.

"I'll take pictures for you," he assured her as they grabbed him roughly and led him out. "Pictures of the grass healing. I'll name that picture Daisy LaRouche, and you will find peace."

Cherry stared after him for a long time, before finally sinking back into the folding metal chair.

# Chapter Thirty-Two

*I*AN BROUGHT HER coffee.

Cherry shook her head.

He returned with a cup of water, and she gratefully drank it.

"Tough one," he said.

Cherry slammed the Styrofoam cup on the desk. "Do you think he's doing it, Ian? Do you think he took Daisy?"

He looked uncomfortable. "You know I can't talk about that sort of thing, Cherry."

She covered her eyes with her hands, massaging them. "I want to say yes, it's Azhar because he has so much information. Because he's an outsider. And I dearly want it to be an outsider. Do you understand?"

"Of course."

"But say it *isn't* him. That it's someone else. Daisy has gone missing, and Monica's grandson is dead. Besides Azhar, I can't think of anybody passing through. That means it's somebody local."

Ian shifted in his seat. "Now, we can't be jumping to conclusions."

Cherry pushed her hair out of her eyes. "What conclusions? How are we jumping? Children are dying, and Daisy might be one of them, do you understand that?"

It was the first time. The first time she'd said it out loud. Cherry felt woozy, felt her blood roaring in her veins.

"Daisy's missing," she corrected, and the force it took, to make those words into something else, something less sinister.

The effort made her pant slightly. "Missing," she said again and glared at Ian accusingly.

Ian looked away.

Cherry stood and tucked her hair back behind her ears. "Call me when you have any information, please." She used her most professional voice. Her Cerise voice. Cerise got things done in a crisis. Cerise could handle all of this. Surely, she'd handled dark things before.

"Of course, Cherry."

"Thank you."

She was almost out the door before he called her name.

"Cherry? I'm so sorry about Daisy. We all are. I haven't really slept since you called us. We'll all keep looking, okay? No matter what you think, this is your home. You're one of us. We won't stop until we find her."

She nodded and walked her no-nonsense Cerise walk until she made it into Old Sal. Then she put her head down on the steering wheel and cried.

Ardeth Getchell stood at the door.

"Cherry, sit down. I have something to tell you."

Cherry's heart jumped. It dropped. She made her way to the couch and sank into it.

"They found Daisy?" she whispered.

Ardeth sat down beside her. "No, darling. It's Jonah."

Cherry shot to her feet. "Jonah? What happened? Where is he?" She looked around the house but didn't see him. She started for the laundry room.

"Cherry, sweetheart, he isn't here." Ardeth took her arm gently. "He isn't here. He had a bad spell. Mordachi loaded him up in the truck and took him out to the hospital in the city."

Cherry turned on her heel and headed straight for Old Sal. "When did this happen?" she asked.

"Not that long ago," Ardeth said. Her face was pale. "I called the police station, but they said you were already on your way back."

"Thank you," Cherry said. It sounded stiff, wooden, but her emotions weren't working right. She had gone from wild fear to complete numbness.

Ardeth nodded.

Cherry made the forty-five minutes to the hospital in thirty minutes, driving like a bat out of hell.

Cherry blew through the doors of the old hospital.

"May I help you?" the receptionist asked in a perky voice.

Cherry tried to keep her panic to a minimum. "My son is here. Jonah LaRouche. Emergency. Can you tell me where—?"

"Cherry."

She spun around, directly into Mordachi's arms.

"Where is he?" she asked. He held her so close and tight that her mind began to chitter. "Is he okay? Can I see him?"

"He's okay, Cherry. It's his heart. He had an—"

"Where is he?" She pulled away, grabbing Mordachi's arms. Her fingernails dug into the sleeves of his shirt, but she didn't care. "Take me to him."

He hustled her through to the room in the back of the ER.

"His mother," he said to the nurse, and she buzzed them both back through the wooden door.

"There. Third bed down," he said.

Then Cherry was running. She pulled the sheet to a small, curtained room, and her hands flew to her face.

"Oh, baby." She dropped her purse at the foot of the bed

and ran her hands over Jonah's smooth, pale skin. Cherry felt the bones of his face pressing against his flesh. So close to the surface. "Oh, my darling. Baby boy. Oh."

His eyes were closed. His skin was far, far too white, and his normally fizzy hair was pasted down with sweat over his forehead. And the tubes. Tubes in his nose, tubes in his mouth tubes coming out of his arms, pumping clear liquid into his fragile veins.

"What happened?" she asked, her voice cracking. She laid her head on Jonah's chest and felt the delicate flutter of his heart under her cheek. Too light. Too frail. His body felt too cool despite the sweat, and she tried to warm him with her hands.

"What happened?" she said again and pinned Mordachi in place with her eyes.

He sighed and pulled up a chair. Mordachi reached for her hand.

Cherry jerked away, intent on running her fingers over her still son.

"He had an episode with his heart. That's what they said. I don't know if it stopped beating, or what the thing was, but he fell and stopped breathing. He's sedated now, to rest it."

Cherry couldn't tear her eyes away from Jonah or stop running her fingers down his cheek, through his hair, over his lips.

"Just a sudden episode? What happened before? Did he have anything with nuts in it or was he outside running? You know his heart won't stand up to much running." She sucked in a breath, pulling her eyes from her son to Mordachi. "He wasn't in the tree again? Did you put him in the tree? You saw what happened last time, how tired he got. How could you?"

He reached for her hand again, and this time he held tight when she tried to take her fingers back.

"No nuts. No running. No tree. He was just screaming, Cherry. Just screaming."

"Screaming? Why?"

He shrugged, but his dark eyes didn't move from hers. "I can only guess because he's a young boy who doesn't understand everything that's going on. His sister is gone. His mom was gone. He was left with strangers."

Cherry reddened. "I had somewhere important to be, and you and Ardeth are hardly strangers." She yanked her hand back violently. "I was trying to find information on Daisy. You can't tell me that isn't important."

"Lower your voice. And yes, of course, it's important, but Jonah is important, too."

Cherry stood and pushed Mordachi as hard as she could. He hardly budged.

"How dare you? How dare you say something that horrible? My children mean everything to me. *Both* of them. Is this because he has special needs? A disability? Does that somehow make him less, in your eyes? Because let me tell you—"

"Cerise," Mordachi barked. He grabbed her shoulders.

The sternness in his voice, the use of her given name made her stop, made her cringe, made her cower in a way that had been second nature, once.

*Ephraim,* she thought. *He sounds like Ephraim. Like storm light personified.*

Her body went cold.

"Stop playing that card. You know I don't think that way, and if you don't know, then you're a foolish woman. Calm yourself down. You don't want Jonah to hear his mother like this."

He let her go.

Cherry very nearly swung at him. Instead, she closed her eyes and clenched her fists together. She took a deep breath. Held it. Let it out.

"You're right." She kept her eyes screwed shut. It was easier than looking at the compassion she knew he wore. "I know you,

Mordachi. What you think. And how you feel about us. We're family. But family doesn't mean safety. Just because we're family, that don't mean you won't leave us. Like everybody else."

She looked at him, then, and his compassion wasn't as terrible as she had feared.

He bent close and kissed her cheek.

"Family hasn't been good to either of us, Cherry, but we can be good to each other. I'm trying." He straightened. "Be with your little one. Want me to stick around for a while?"

"No, thank you. I'll be fine."

He nodded and turned to leave.

"Mordachi? Thank you. You're the best family the kids and I ever had. Why are you so nice to me?"

"I've seen who you can be. Broken pieces can be put back together."

He smiled, then he was gone.

Cherry pulled the metal chair to Jonah's bed and sat by his side. "Hi, baby. Mama misses you. How is your big, beautiful heart doing?" Jonah's breathing was slow. Regular. Cherry looked at him and wiped the first of the tears away with the back of her arm. "This is what I was always afraid of. That one day something would be too much for you. All of the times we spent in the hospital, and I told myself it would never happen again. I'd take such good care of you that you'd magically be healed somehow. If I was watchful enough, or prayed enough, or was good enough …"

She took a deep breath. Pushed the chair away. Climbed in the bed with her tiny son. She carefully wrapped the tubes and wires around both of them and curled around the too-thin arms and legs under the worn blanket.

"I love you. I love you, baby. You're so beautiful. Please don't leave me," she whispered. She kissed his forehead. "Please don't leave me."

# Chapter Thirty-Three

RUNNER SHOWED UP to Jonah's new hospital room with flowers.

Cherry was pale, drawn, sitting by Jonah's bed, and wearing a scratchy hospital blanket over her shoulders.

"The flowers are for you," Runner said. He handed them to her, kissing her on the cheek. "I have a dinosaur for Jonah."

He took a green and purple stuffed triceratops from under his arm and put it on a small tray table. Placed the toy on Jonah's bed. Looked at the tray table again.

"The bed is just fine. Thank you for coming and for the lovely gifts."

Cherry stood, but her knees wobbled.

Runner grabbed her, steadied her. "When's the last time you ate?" he asked.

"I don't remember."

"Let's get you something." He led her toward the door.

She pulled back. "I don't want to leave him. What if he wakes up and I'm not here? He hates hospitals."

Runner leaned back and looked at her. "Darlin', you're a mess. No offense. You could use a good wash and a hot meal. I happen to know this hospital provides both. Come on."

He grabbed her by the arm. She protested at first, but then her stomach growled, and Cherry grudgingly let him pull her along.

He wrapped his arm around her shoulders. "How are you doing?"

"Well, he's sleeping well. His heartbeat is holding steady right now. They don't know how long he went without oxygen, if there's permanent damage or not."

"I didn't ask about Jonah. I know he's getting great care. I'm asking about you."

She blinked. "I'm good." Her stomach growled again. "Maybe a little hungry."

"Let's fix that, then."

He walked her to the cafeteria. Cherry mentally counted the money in her wallet and picked up the biggest apple she could find. She rubbed it uncertainly between her hands.

"Why so nervous?"

Runner filled his tray high. A sandwich, some spaghetti. Fruit and rolls and some of that ever-present hospital Jell-O.

"He hasn't been this bad in a long time. Not since he was about two years old. This seemed to come out of nowhere." She frowned. "Or maybe it didn't."

He grabbed her apple and put it on his tray.

"What do you mean by that?"

Cherry followed him to the register.

Runner paid and made his way to an empty table. When Cherry sat, he slid the tray in front of her. "Eat," he said. "I've never seen a girl as bony as you. Makes me sad to look at ya."

She took a bite of roll, covered her mouth, and talked through it. "Mordachi thinks I'm not paying enough attention to Jonah."

Runner took a bite of the apple and put it back on the tray. "Mordachi's an idiot."

"Runner. That's not very nice."

He leaned back in his chair. "Doesn't keep it from being true. As if that guy knows anything about a family."

"Hey."

He looked at her, his green eyes sharp.

"Why are you always defending him, anyway?"

"The family thing … you don't need to bring it up all of the time. It's hurtful."

Runner smirked. "It doesn't bother him. He's used to it by now."

"Still."

He leaned close. "You know what, Miss Cherry. You're such a softy. You always have been. It's one of my favorite things about you."

She looked down at her tray.

"Want to know my other favorite things about you?" he asked.

She shook her head.

"Why not?"

"I can't think right now. This could be a special moment and I'd miss it because I'm not thinking right."

Runner kissed her hair. "Ah, Cherry. Sometimes I think you're a completely different woman than the girl who left Darling in her tracks. Other times I think you haven't changed at all."

She sighed, playing with her food while she looked out of the window. Dogwood trees and cane grass.

"I feel like I've changed. Like I've changed too much. I hardly remember the old me. Wasn't I happy once? Was there a time without so much responsibility?"

"High school. For a while."

"Until I got pregnant. Is that what you're saying?"

"Babies and responsibility do go hand-in-hand, sweetheart," he teased.

"Yeah, well, some people aren't built for responsibility."

"E had everything I ever wanted, and he gave it all up. The scholarship. You. Especially you. You know I'm crazy about you, right?" He slid next to her and nibbled at her ear. Wrapped his arms around her.

"Runner."

"It's never going to be the right time. I should have told you before, but I didn't. Maybe if I had said something, you wouldn't have left with E. I want you, Cherry LaRouche. I always have. And now you've come home again. We have a second chance."

He held her tighter.

"A second chance," he repeated and held her close.

She didn't answer. Couldn't answer.

He didn't seem to notice.

# Chapter Thirty-Four

"**ARE YOU MY** friend, Ardeth?" Cherry asked the old woman.

Ardeth sniffed as she reached down to smooth Jonah's already smooth sheets. The monitors beeped and buzzed and zipped.

"Don't be foolish, girl."

Cherry did feel foolish. Her cheeks burned.

"I always thought I had tons of friends," she said. Her words sounded more like a confession than she liked. "But I've come to find out, I don't."

Ardeth bustled around the room, arranging Runner's flowers, and making sure Cherry's paper cup was full of water.

"You never had friends. You had hangers-on. Boys who wanted to date you and girls who wanted to be you. Nothing more than that."

"That hurts."

"Truth hurts, child."

Cherry perked up. "Rosemary wanted to be my friend."

Ardeth's eyes were stern. "And how did you treat her, hmm? Everybody in town knows she worships you, knows how you toss her aside. Poor little slip of a thing, moonin' over Mordachi, who would marry you the second you batted your eyelashes at him. But you? You're a hard-hearted thing if you didn't know it already. Nobody means a lick to you except for your children. And look what's happened to them."

Cherry's mouth tightened and twisted and turned down at the corners.

"That's enough pouting, child. Seems to me it's time you heard these things. Seems to me it's time you change them." She patted Cherry's hand.

"Can I? Change them? Is it too late?" Cherry laid her head on the foot of Jonah's bed, watching his soft breathing. "Because you're right, Ardeth. They are all I care about. The only important things. I don't think I know how to love anybody else. If that makes any sense."

"Oh, it makes sense, Cerise. With that awful woman as your mother. It's a testament you can love at all."

Cherry chilled, looked up at Ardeth. The old woman smiled and smoothed Cherry's hair.

"Iris LaRouche had herself a right reputation. Proud. Elegant. Beautiful house, beautiful garden, beautiful daughter. Most folks bought into it. But me, I used my eyes, and I saw a woman cold as porcelain. I even saw her mean streak every now and then. How you came out of there? Well, you're a strong girl. But sometimes I see your mother in you. Don't become hard. Don't become what she was."

"Everybody seems to think Mama was such a perfect woman."

"Ain't nobody perfect. Not your mama. Not you. Not me."

Silence, interrupted only by the beeping of the monitor.

"A lot of folks were upset when you left," Ardeth said. Her voice was delicate, yet heavy with gravitas. She was leading up to something important. "A lot of folks felt you did a disservice to Darling by trapping that young football hero and then running off."

Cherry snorted, buried her face in Jonah's bed. "Trap him. He sure didn't stay trapped, did he?"

Ardeth's hand rested on her shoulder. Soft instead of bony. Tender instead of accusing.

"Like I said, ain't nobody perfect. And maybe some folks were looking for revenge. For some way to hurt you. Punish you, even, for taking the Golden Boy out of Darling. Now, how would they do that, I wonder? If they wanted to hurt you most, what would they take?"

"How could somebody be so awful?"

Ardeth stretched, popping her back. Cherry was reminded that Ardeth was a terribly old woman who shouldn't be dealing with such things like missing children and Handsome Butchers.

"Ardeth, have you always lived here in Darling?"

"Yes, child. All my years."

"So why aren't you …? How come something hasn't …?"

Ardeth laughed, and the sound reminded Cherry of stick bundles and old voodoo and peppermint candies.

"Why didn't the town change me, you're asking? I'm not a festering pool of sores and hate, how can that be so? This is what you're wondering?"

She knew she should feel silly, but she was too weary.

"Yes," she said.

"What says it hasn't?"

Cherry frowned.

"But look at you, Ardeth. You're here. You're the only one here, and I hardly know you. That's not what a soul-sick person does. It's what a good person does."

Ardeth's eyes seemed to glow then, a ring of fire shine that nearly took Cherry's breath away. Then it was gone, and they were the eyes of a crotchety old woman who made terrible coffee and saved the lives of single mothers.

"Darling will eat itself alive and everyone in it," Ardeth said. "Mark my words, it'll happen. It's happening already. You'd best be gone when that time comes, woman, or it'll take you down with it. The evil within this town is older than you. It's even older than me, and that's saying something. You think the people of Salem were always that depraved, that eager to turn on each other like dogs? Or do you think it was the same thing? Something ancient in the land that they breathed in with their air, drank with their water? Darling is just the same. It's an infection."

"I left before."

"Yes, you did. Without looking back. Without bringing anybody who cared with you. Your heartlessness saved you."

"But E came with me. I thought he cared."

Ardeth arched her brow. "Shows how much you know. You brought the wrong brother, perhaps."

"I don't want to talk about that."

"I knew your mother when she was young. Did I tell you that?"

Cherry sighed. "I bet you're going to say I'm just like her. Selfish and horrible."

Ardeth's lips turned up. "She wasn't like that at first. She reminded me more of your Daisy, except in woman form. Eyes bright. Lots of hope."

Cherry blinked. "*My* mother?"

Ardeth nodded, looking old again. Ancient. She had veins of silver running through her like old rock. She was older than the mountains themselves.

"She also used to wear her hair in pigtails when she was a bitty girl, and she climbed trees and used to sneak lollipops under her mother's nose."

"That doesn't sound like her at all."

"Time and place can change a person, can't it? She grew up. She stayed. The house sucked her breath at night. Darling wormed its way inside. It dug its tendrils into her marrow until it animated her completely. She was a marionette by the end."

Cherry opened her mouth to say something, but a child screamed from down the hall. She jerked, her head whipping to the door so quickly she was afraid it would snap.

"That sounded like Daisy."

"I bet they all sound like Daisy."

"No, it really—"

The child screamed again, and Cherry was on her feet.

"Daisy?" she shouted and ran from the room.

She heard Ardeth call after her, but she was already darting down the hall, white legs flashing, pulse beating in her throat. She peeked in each room, but Daisy wasn't there. A blonde girl. Two redheaded boys. But not her daughter. Never her daughter.

"Daisy?" she shouted, and a nurse ran out to hush her. Cherry pushed her away too hard. The nurse fell heavily against the wall. "Daisy, baby, it's Mommy! Shout again, okay? Tell Mommy where you are!"

The scream, piercing, and a garble of words sounded like hell, sounded like heaven, and Cherry pushed past a second nurse and ran, ran, ran. Her hair floated like a dirty cloud behind her.

"Daisy!" she shrieked and followed the screams of her darling daughter, of her little one.

It was a labyrinth of nightmares, of every bad dream she had ever had. Voices. Needles. White walls. Cherry had always been afraid she would end up in a place like this one day, and here she was.

Daisy's voice seemed to come from the very walls themselves. "Mama," she screamed. It was a chorus, coming from several different areas all at once. "Mama!" Two Daisy's. Three. Twelve. A hundred. Thousands of pretty little dead girls called out for Cherry. For Cherry. For …

"Cherry!"

An old woman's voice called this time, but she didn't heed it, didn't care. She was going to scoop up her girl, hold her so close, hold her to her breast and never ever let her out of her sight again.

A door. A closed door at the end of the hall. She was being chased now, the hospital staff sprinting at her in clean uniforms and cheery scrubs. Cherry ran as fast as she could toward the door, toward her little girl.

Somebody grabbed her by the arm, and she broke free. They

pulled the shirt from her shoulder, but she shook them off.

The screams, the cries of her little girl drove her forward. To find her here, maybe being hurt, maybe being taken care of, she didn't know. Was Jonah's episode meant to happen? Something divine? To bring her here so she could be reunited with—

She didn't slow down and smacked into the door. Cherry grasped the knob with both hands, but already people were dragging, pulling, yanking on her.

"No! No! Daisy!"

She scrabbled at the door and managed to pull it open, through the arms and torsos that smothered her, wrapped around her, like a nest of snakes.

"Daisy," she screamed again. Her voice frightened her—too full of rage and grief and need. So much raw need.

"Daisy!"

The door came open all of the way, and she was firmly wrestled to the floor.

Not Daisy.

Another little girl, with dark hair. A nurse with a hypodermic needle stood beside her, her eyes wide.

"I lost her again," Cherry said. She was rolled onto her belly and her arms cuffed behind her back. She blinked, her hair on the floor and in her eyes. Lost again.

Not again.

# Chapter Thirty-Five

**W**ORD SPREAD BY late afternoon. Tongues licked like wildfires. Rumors ignited, blazed, burned out as the people of Darling began to whisper.

*Cherry went crazy in the hospital today.*

*Almost lost her second kid. The retard. Wonder if it was on purpose.*

*Think she did something to him, too?*

Ardeth Getchell showed up at Cherry's house that evening. Her eyes were hard and full of so much fear and ferocity that Cherry took a step back.

"Cherry, it's time. I can't stay here anymore. Neither should you. Pack up. Stay at the hospital with your boy. As soon as he's discharged, leave and don't come back."

"Leave?"

"Look at yourself. You're falling apart, and I can't stay any longer to take care of you. It's coming."

"Mrs. Getchell, you're scaring me."

"You're right to be scared, child. You need to go. I'll be staying with my sister until things calm down."

"What do you mean, calm down?"

Ardeth eyed her sharply. "Can't you feel it? It's happened again. The very earth itself is shaking. The town woke up."

The town had teeth. Strong chops and long tongues. It yawned, gaping and wide, and then began to exorcise them.

*That Indian guy is still in custody. The one with the pictures.*

*I heard the killer is a local. One of us. The Handsome Butcher.*

# Darling

*The Handsome Butcher is among us.*

*Who could it be? Who could it be?*

*Word was that one of the cops was on the take. Pay him enough and you could get away with anything. Even murder.*

*You can't trust anybody anymore. Never could, really.*

*We need to protect our own.*

That lawyer, Johnny Holfield, had something goin' on with Iris LaRouche until she told him to hit the road. Heard he was the one that got Cherry back in town. Why would he do that, exactly? To make somebody pay?

The next time she saw Johnny H, he had his arm in a sling and both eyes blackened. When he grinned, the old bully was back in his face.

"Shoulda seen the other guy, Cherry. It felt good. Felt real good. All the way to the bone kind of good."

"I don't like this," Runner told Cherry. He leaned against the railing on her porch, shaking his blond hair out of his eyes.

Her thin cotton dress stuck to her sweaty body while she paced.

"The atmosphere in town has changed. On a dime, Cherry. People are saying you're telling everyone the killer is from Darling, that we may be looking for one of our own. I hear even the police are questioning people again, differently this time. With more force." He shook his head, then slammed his hand against the railing. "Damn it, Cherry! What do you think is happening to this town?"

"It's getting what it deserves."

"What's that?"

She turned to him, her eyes glowing in the Louisiana sunset. "This town is a place of horrors, Runner. So many secrets and lies. Everybody pretending to be something they're not. People claim they're happy here, but it's not the truth. If that was the case, then why is everybody scrambling to get out? Why are they so jealous I finally did?"

"That's not true, Cherry."

She stopped her pacing and drew herself up to her full height, which was still a slip of a thing. Runner took an involuntary step back.

"Isn't it? Tell me who's happy here. Monica? Working in that no-name store? And now her grandson is dead. Not just dead, but *murdered*, Runner. The last person he saw was not Monica, not his mommy. It was someone terrible."

"Calm down."

Her eyes flashed. "I will not calm down. Then there's Wendy. Such a spiteful thing. Always was. Think she's happy here?"

He raised an eyebrow. "You're judging someone you don't know anything about."

"What about Rosemary? Taking care of her sick mama all these years. Mordachi. You."

His eyes narrowed. "What about me?"

She should stop, she knew she should stop, but she was worked up. Too frightened and angry.

"Where should I start with you?"

His voice was dangerous. "I don't know, Cherry. You tell me."

She dropped her gaze.

Runner was there in an instant, taking her chin in his hand, forcing her to look at him.

"Don't start talking unless you can back it up, darlin'." His glowing green eyes also caught the light of the Louisiana sky.

"You were always jealous of E."

"Not a guy in town who wasn't."

"Why? Why weren't you happy enough being you? You had everything E had."

He laughed. The sound made Cherry shudder.

"E had it all. The talent. The scholarship. The brother who cleaned up after him. The girl." His eyes flashed. "Especially the girl."

"You had so many girls."

"I only ever wanted one."

Cherry couldn't look away. His eyes were glass suns, intense enough to annihilate her. Sheer immolation.

"Runner, I—"

"What? Can't do this? Why? Because of E? Because of you?"

"Because of my children. Because of my worry. Daisy's out there, somewhere. And Jonah—"

"Jonah is in the hospital, safe and sound. Somewhere you aren't allowed to be, darlin', because you fell apart. You're falling apart. You need somebody to take care of you. Can't you see I want to take care of you?"

She managed to step back and wiped her face with the back of her hand.

"I don't need you to take care of me. I can take care of myself. I always have."

He cursed. "Stubborn. You're too damn stubborn for your own good." Runner kissed her then, wrapping his arms around her and pressing her back into the railing.

"Don't," she said against his mouth, but even as she said it, she was asking herself why.

He ran his hands down her back, to her legs, onto her smooth skin. His hands were warm and lightning hot.

"Do you want me to stop?" he asked her, then kissed his way to her ear, breathed in it, nibbled on her earlobe.

"I want …" She couldn't finish her thought.

He ran his mouth down her throat. Cherry's head fell back, and his hands tangled in her hair.

"What do you want?"

"I want …"

And then she realized. She *wanted.* No thinking it through. No fastidious planning or wondering how her choices would affect her standing, her children, her plan to give them a life worth having. She was a person, too. She counted as much as everybody else.

"Cherry?"

"I want you."

He drew back, looked at her.

"Really?"

She twined her hands around his neck, ran them up into his hair.

"You. I want you. Just you."

He crushed her in his arms, kissed her with a force that nearly frightened her until she remembered this was what she wanted, and tonight she'd allow herself to take it. She kissed him back, all lips and teeth and tongue, and he pulled her to him, picked her up. She wrapped her legs around his waist, pressing herself against him.

"All right," he said. He kicked the door open, carried her inside. Kicked it shut, keeping the crickets and bullfrogs and murderers out for the night. Just for tonight.

# Chapter Thirty-Six

RUNNER OPENED HIS eyes, slowly.

He turned his head to where Cherry had curled up into a little ball, facing away from him. Her hair was a wild cloud around her face and her white skin glowed in the moonlight.

He smiled and reached out, caressing her hair. Running his fingers up her back, feeling every jutting vertebrae. She whimpered sleepily and curled up even tighter.

Perhaps one day she would move toward him in her sleep, not away. He'd have to see. He might even stick around long enough to find out. Now there was a thought that knocked a man over. It wasn't all bad.

There was a sound, disjointed and strange. A scrabbling. Something on the roof. Moving around, coming closer.

Runner slid out of bed and reached for his boxers.

He looked again at Cherry to see if she heard it, but she didn't move. She had cried last night, after Runner had feigned sleep, her shoulders shaking as she failed to muffle the sound with her pillow. Torrential tears. So many tears. He had been in awe, had seen, perhaps for the first time the depths of all she carried. Stress. Rage. Worry. Sorrow.

So much sorrow.

So many concerns in such a tiny package. He hadn't realized the extent before.

But that noise. A predatory sound, of something being where it shouldn't. It sounded heavy but surprisingly graceful like it was comfortable up there. Sure-footed.

He went to the window, peered outside, and looked up.

Nothing.

He quietly slid the window open, winced as the metal frame caught on the old wood. Finally, he had enough room where he could lean out. Look up. Nothing with wings silhouetted against the dark sky. No red eyes peered down at him.

He nearly snorted. Cherry's paranoia must be contagious. He ran his hand through his hair. Runner was just about to come back in when he heard a small, furtive scraping. He looked up again.

Something came at him, crashing into the side of his head with a force that nearly took his feet out from under him. It came a second time, harder, and wrenched him forward. He grabbed the flimsy window frame, but it wasn't enough, wasn't sturdy like he wished he had been sturdy for Cherry, and there was regret for a second, but mostly surprise.

Then, there was nothing.

Cherry heard the crash and the breaking glass and the choking sound that came from Runner's ruined face. She sat up in bed, arms wildly clawing at nothing, and turned just in time to see Runner's feet disappear from her third story window.

She scrambled from the bed.

"Runner!"

She looked down at his broken body, his leg bent awkwardly at a ninety-degree angle where a leg shouldn't bend, at his eyes that stared up at the sky, and the blood that ran down his tan body like syrup. His face … she couldn't stop staring at the carnage where his beautiful face used to be.

There were sounds on the roof, heavy, frightening sounds, but Cherry didn't register them. She just stood there in the remains of her window, hands to her cheeks, and screamed.

# Chapter Thirty-Seven

*T*HEY **THOUGHT ABOUT** bringing Cherry down to the station but decided to interview her at the house. All the trekking from the police station to Cherry LaRouche's house was getting tiring.

"He just fell out," she said. "I don't know, I was asleep. I heard something, it woke me up, and I saw him and then he was outside, and …"

Crying. Shaking. Sobbing. The deputies met each other's eyes over her head.

"Sure a lot of bad fortune coming your way, Miss LaRouche," one of them said. "Your mother. Your daughter. Your son. Your lover."

She said 'lover' in a way that made Cherry raise her tear-stained face, made fire burn in her eyes.

"I can take a lover if I want a lover. Ain't no business of yours. No business of anyone here in Darling. As for the rest, you think I don't know? At first, I thought it was random, but now I'm not so sure. Could somebody be doing this to me, do you think?"

The second officer shrugged.

They looked at each other again.

"Miss LaRouche," the first one began, "do you have any plans to leave any time soon?"

Cherry blinked. "What?"

"Any trips out of town, that sort of thing?"

With the realization came rage. With rage came hatred. Cherry stood, pulling the knitted afghan closer around her.

"You think I pushed Runner out of my window? You really think I'm capable of something like that?"

The officer raised her hands in a 'hey, don't-look-at-me' gesture. "I'd be remiss if I didn't look at the facts, and the facts say anybody around you seems to be in danger. At this time, you're not an official suspect, but considering all that's going on around here, I think it's best if you stay close to home."

Cherry gnawed at her lip. "I don't have anywhere else to go, anyway."

The detectives nodded. "All right."

"Can I see him in the hospital? Is that okay? I mean, I have permission to go back there now. As long as somebody is with me, I mean."

She stopped and looked at the floor. Squeezed her eyes shut. "Please?"

The detectives stood.

"As we said, you're not an official suspect at this time. You can do what you please. Just be cautious."

Cautious. Aware. Cherry was caught in the worst kind of nightmare. There were monsters. Terrible things were happening, and people were being stolen from her, one by one. She was alone.

She always ended up alone.

Mordachi stood in the doorway, watching her. He took a step toward her, hesitated. Dropped his hand back to his side. Turned and walked away.

She never noticed he was there.

Just like always.

# Chapter Thirty-Eight

"*I* HEAR YOU'VE BEEN looking for me." The man's voice was cool and deep, his words clipped and short.

"You're not from the South, are you?" Cherry asked.

She frowned. That wasn't what she wanted to ask him. There were other things, more pressing things, but somehow this was all she could think to say.

The man smiled, and something moved inside her. She'd do nearly anything to see that smile again.

"I'm from a lot of places. What can I do for you, Cherry-pie?"

She blinked.

"How do you know my name?"

Once again, the man smiled, and all was right with the world.

"I know all kinds of things."

She nodded slowly. "I suppose you do."

"Are you cold?" he asked her.

She realized she was shivering out under the Southern moon, sitting in the humid damp. Things crawled and slithered and chittered around her. Bugs supped on her blood. She waved one away and it flitted lazily back.

"Not much you can do about it, my dear," he said, gesturing at the mosquito. "It's the way life is. You give up blood to sate others. There are givers and takers, and you, girlie, are a giver."

"That sounds terribly one-sided."

His eyes lit up. "Then change it. Take what you want, for once."

He reached over and slapped the mosquito off her arm. It stung, and the touch of his big hands on her skin made her stomach churn.

She wiped the dead mosquito, her blood spilled around it, away.

"What are we doing here?"

He shrugged, completely at ease squatting in the foliage. His dark hair fell to his shoulders, shining in the starlight like a living thing.

"You were created to live outside, weren't you?" Cherry asked. "You don't seem to fit indoors."

"I feel at home here. I like the freedom of it. To hunt. To play. The very earth itself calls to me. We're made of the same stuff."

Suddenly he was shirtless, clad only in jeans and boots, on all fours like an animal and sniffing at something on the ground. Cherry blinked and he was upright again, looking at her with his too-sharp eyes.

Her head spun.

"What?" he asked, and the jovial tone of his voice was gone, the patience receding.

"I'm sorry. I thought I saw—"

"Thought you saw what?"

He grinned then, but it wasn't the beatific, nearly holy thing she had seen earlier. His teeth were sharp like a shark's, his face cunning, and she realized that beneath his handsome exterior ran the bones of a predator.

"You're not what we think at all, are you?" she asked. Her mouth was dry. "Perhaps we've had it wrong from the beginning."

His sharky grin widened.

"You don't think anything, do you? You know nothing about me. You, the police, the other parents, the people of these Podunk towns. You guess and guess, but you're all wrong." His grin nearly wrapped around his striking face. "Isn't that a shame?"

"Tell me your name," she said. She breathed quick and hard. "Tell me who you are, how to find you. They call you the Handsome Butcher. Who are you really?"

He stared at her, not a muscle moving. His stillness was unnatural.

She tried again.

"Where is my daughter? Do you have her?"

He was standing in front of her now, although she hadn't seen him move. He loomed over her, and she fell back. He seemed so large against the moon. She felt like a tiny thing, almost like the children he preyed on.

"It's a sickness," he said, and his eyes reflected the stars. A tear fell down his cheek, made of constellations and tiny little Saturns. "I don't want to do it, do you understand? And I'm so careful with them. I make sure they hurt for such a small time. So small. You, as a mother, would appreciate that, wouldn't you? My kindness?"

"Where is my daughter?"

Cherry scrambled to her feet. The man stood head and shoulders over her, but she pressed closer.

"Where is she? Where is my Daisy? She doesn't belong to you!"

The man winced and backed away from her fury, but Cherry didn't stop.

"She's mine. *My* little girl. She doesn't belong to you, she doesn't! You had no right to take her."

Her fists beat against his chest. She clawed at his face, leaving deep scratches on his cheek. He cuffed her hard. Cherry fell, but she was soon back on her feet again.

"My Daisy! Give me my daughter!"

A little girl with liquid eyes and a crude haircut walked up to her. She put her hand on Cherry's arm. Her touch was cold and full of sorrow. Cherry gasped and stilled, frozen to the core by the unearthliness.

"It's too late now," the girl said. Her mouth didn't move while she spoke, but her voice sounded like hollow logs and bells.

"You're Sada, aren't you? Azhar's little one."

"She's hurting me! Hurting me." The Handsome Butcher wailed and wrapped his arms around his strong body. He turned to Sada.

"She hit me. And she scratched my face. Look."

He pointed at his face and glared at Cherry. His eyes sharpened, narrowed, went from a petulant child's to the slicing predatory look and then back again.

"How can this be?" Cherry asked nobody in particular. Her head hurt. She put her hand to it.

Sada took the Handsome Butcher by the hand. He held on far too tight, and her tiny bones splintered in his grip. The sound would haunt Cherry for the rest of her life, but she didn't realize this yet.

"I'll play with you," she said to the monster. "Come on."

She limped away, hand-in-hand with him. They only got a few feet away before she turned around and looked at Cherry.

"Tell my daddy he's doing it wrong," she said. Black tears, like oil, ran down her face. "Tell him to go home. We're not us anymore. We're all dolls. Just little dolls, missing arms and legs, and eyes."

Cherry sat straight up in bed, her heart beating far too fast. She heard the familiar, upsetting sound of something scooting across the roof, but it didn't matter. None of it mattered.

*What a horrible, horrible dream.*

She tossed and she turned. She tried to get back to sleep for hours, but she kept seeing the face of the Handsome Butcher, heard the sharp snapping of Sada's deteriorated bones. Sada's oily tears and the stinging cuff against her own face.

Cherry put her hand to her cheek and was surprised to find it tender and bruised. She examined her fingernails. Two of them had broken while she slept.

*When I scratched his face,* she thought, but then quickly pushed the thought away.

Dreams aren't reality. We don't stand up to child killers in dreams. They don't give us answers. They simply torment.

She climbed out of bed, then. Put her feet on the dusty floor.

It was another day. Heaven help her get through it.

# Chapter Thirty-Nine

JONAH WAS FINALLY released from the hospital. He wrapped himself around his mother. She wrapped herself around him right back. She had sewn another doll without eyes and a tiny matching body had been found to the East. Not Daisy. Nobody from Darling, thank goodness. Nobody she knew. Just somebody young and sweet and not meant for such things. Somebody else's child.

Not hers. Not hers.

She held Jonah on her lap, sitting on Daisy's bed. The pink of the room had been so charming at first. She remembered painting it, singing, having hope for the future. Hope for some happiness inside of these walls, inside of this town.

*I hate you,* she thought to the house. *I hate you so much. How stupid of me to think I could make you a home. To think things could change.*

The wall seemed to ripple in front of her eyes. The house settled into itself darkly.

*I hate you right back, Cherry. You and your mother and your children and anybody else who dares set foot in here.*

She slid her son to the floor and stood up.

"Come on, baby. Let's get out of here for a while."

She'd been meaning to return Rosemary's casserole dish for some time. Let the house calm itself down. Cherry would try to do the same thing with her nerves.

She turned the key twice in Old Sal before she would start. When the engine turned over, Cherry released a breath she didn't realize she was holding.

"Lucky us," she told her son. He hooted in agreement.

Rosemary's home hadn't changed over the years. It was a tall building, more height than width, fit together in a way that just looked *wrong*. The wrongness of the house permeated everything else. Rosemary's invalid mother. Rosemary herself. Cherry had never stepped foot inside that home in all her life, and as she parked Old Sal, she found herself wishing fervently she'd never had to.

"Stay here, baby," she told Jonah. "I'll be right back."

Overgrown weeds grabbed at her feet as she picked her way carefully to the front door.

She knocked firmly. No answer.

"Rosemary," she called, knocking on hard wood again. "I brought your dish back. Are you home?"

She heard movement upstairs.

Jonah squawked and squirmed, seat-belted firmly into Old Sal.

"Just a second, darling," she called to him. "This won't take but a minute."

She knocked again. A small shriek from upstairs.

"Hello? Rosemary? Is everything okay?"

Cherry tried the door, but it was locked. Another small yell.

"Rosemary? Do you need help? Hold on."

She looked around frantically for another way in. She ran to the window and pounded on it with the flat of her hand.

"Rosemary? Rosemary!"

"What?"

Cherry shrieked and whirled around. Rosemary stood behind her, holding a grocery bag.

"Rosemary! I thought I heard screaming coming from inside."

Rosemary sighed. "You probably did. My mother's having a particularly bad day today. I had to run and grab some things before getting her into the bath. And I needed to get out for just a second. She doesn't remember who I am half of the time."

"Is it okay to leave her alone?"

"Who's here to help me? And it was really only for a quick grocery run. That reminds me, Wendy is saying all sorts of nasty things about you to anyone who will listen. I thought you should know."

Cherry frowned. "What kind of things?"

Rosemary looked uncomfortable. "Oh, just … things. She was real upset to hear that you slept with Runner. Calling you all sorts of names. Says she has it in her mind to ring up your husband and let him know what's going on."

"Good luck to her with that. I couldn't find E even when I wanted to. Now, you must be exhausted. Would you like me to help you with your mother today?"

Rosemary's eyes widened. "You would? Why I … Oh. What about Jonah?"

Cherry felt sick. Felt kicked in the stomach.

"What about him?"

Rosemary looked at the ground, and then back at Cherry. Her eyes were clear and blue.

"I don't want to hurt your feelings, but I don't think that would be a very good idea. She's heavy and it's hard to lift her out of her wheelchair and into the tub. I know Jonah gets excited, and I just think it's a bad idea."

Cherry looked over her shoulder at her son. He screamed and clawed at the seatbelt.

"Are you mad at me for saying that?" Rosemary asked quickly. "Because I don't want you to be mad at me. For anything, ever."

"No, I'm not mad. You're right. Here." Cherry held out the casserole dish, and Rosemary gingerly took it. "Thank you for the food. You're a good person, Rosemary. I hope good things happen to you. You really do deserve it."

She turned and climbed into Old Sal. Started the ignition.

"Cherry?"

She looked up at Rosemary.

"I'm sorry, Cherry. About Runner not talking to you. And I'm sorry about Daisy and everything. She's in a better place. She really is."

Cherry's mouth tasted like something dead. Like her heart.

"Her place is with me," she said and pulled out of the driveway.

# Chapter Forty

THEY FOUND ARDETH Getchell's body hidden in the underbrush. Her clothes were torn. Her face was purple, one eye half open, her tongue protruding. The bruising on her throat was the only vibrant thing about her, and it was very nearly a beautiful thing.

"But she left to go to her sister's," Cherry said when Officer Ian Bridger told her. "She was on her way to somewhere safe."

"She didn't make it," he said, and then he stood there awkwardly, wondering what was going on in this world. Prickly little old ladies should be sitting on their rocking chairs, staring people down from the front porch and threatening them with canes. They shouldn't be accosted while walking to and from their own homes. They shouldn't stare at their killer while their life is choked out of them. It was too ugly.

"Do you have any idea who did it?" Cherry asked. She asked out of habit, and out of politeness. She knew it was a phantom who had murdered her dear friend. Something incorporeal that slid into their dimension, killed, and then slid out again. It wasn't somebody they could find or fight. There was a reason Death was portrayed as a cipher.

"No. I wish I did," Ian said. "It looks like whoever did it broke into her house and threw around some of her things. I don't know if anything is missing. Maybe somebody thought she had money."

"Maybe somebody just wanted to make her suffer," Cherry said bitterly. "She's one of the good people left in this town.

That's reason enough, isn't it?"

"You can't think that way, Cherry. It isn't true. You can't give up hope."

"Azhar told me that hope will kill me. Maybe he was right."

"Cherry."

"I had a dream about his daughter. Do you think I should tell him?"

Officer Ian Bridger swallowed hard. "I don't know. Everything is crazy right now. I don't really know what to do anymore. And that's hard to admit for a guy like me, you know?"

Cherry forced herself to smile. "You'll muddle through. Maybe we all will. Thank you for letting me know about Ardeth. If you'll excuse me, I need to think about it for a while. Goodbye, Ian."

"See you later, Cherry." Ian stood on her front porch for a long time before getting into the squad car and driving off. He was afraid to check in the trees and bushes. He was afraid of what he would find.

Less than two hours later, Mordachi showed up at the door. His shirt was clean, and his beard was nicely trimmed.

"Marry me," he said.

Cherry looked at him, at his strong white teeth, at his fierce brown eyes.

Jonah buzzed around her, squawking with delight. He ran to Mordachi, who patted his head.

"Are you crazy?" she asked. "This isn't like you."

"This is exactly like me. This is what I should have done ten years ago. Marry me. Please."

"Why?"

"Because you can't live like this. You're not even living. You're hollowed out inside."

"You can change that?"

"I can try."

"How would you do that?" she asked but didn't want to hear the answer. She wanted to lie down on the floor and die. Step into a creek and tangle up in the weeds like any other piece of debris. Maybe she'd find Daisy there, and they could dance the dance of the dead forever.

"I know you, Cherry LaRouche. I know what makes you laugh. I know how fiercely you love. You love with your whole heart, and not everybody can do that. Why can't you love me like that?"

"I don't know if I can," Cherry whispered. Her dear Mordachi. Such earnestness and honesty and truth.

"I can protect you from the Louisiana storms. You'd never be afraid in my arms. We would always have enough to eat. You know I love Jonah. You know I love Daisy. Let us be a family. We could be such a wonderful family."

Family. The word didn't have the meaning it once did. She and E were supposed to be family. She and Jonah and Daisy were supposed to be together always. Her mother should have loved her. Her father should have, at least, existed at some point.

She looked down at her hands, which were blanched and cracked from working with the neighbor's laundry. Scrubbing out stains. Removing the signs of other people's impropriety, of their indignities.

"No, I don't think so," she said.

His jaw tightened, but that was the only reaction he made. "Why's that?" he asked.

She shrugged. Her hair was tangled, matted.

"You might make me happy," she said, and shut the door.

# Chapter Forty-One

Hope dies.
Hope died.

# Chapter Forty-Two

*D*AISY WAS THREE years old now. Would be three years old. It was her birthday. Cherry would have been throwing a party, except there was nobody to throw it for. She thought about baking a cake that wouldn't be eaten, but the idea of tossing it to the birds was too much to bear.

The doorbell rang.

It was Monica, her eyes puffy, her too-bright lips turned up slightly in the semblance of a smile. She held a beautiful cake in her hands. White with pink frosting. Colored sprinkles on top.

"Hi, Cherry. I know it's Daisy's birthday. We're going to celebrate."

Cherry's tears came, then. The tears of a woman who has lost everything and has nothing left to lose. Monica set the cake on the counter and wrapped her arms around Cherry's shaking shoulders.

"I know, sweetheart," she whispered over and over. "I know."

"I know you do," Cherry said, and sobbed harder. She threw her thin arms around the older woman. "I'm sorry. I'm so sorry."

"We both are."

Monica led Cherry to the table, sat her down in the chair. She fussed in the cupboards and found some cracked plates. Forks. Cups.

She cut a piece for Jonah, set it in front of him.

"No," Jonah said, and ran away.

"He doesn't eat cake," Cherry said. She hiccupped and wiped

her eyes with her fingers. "Nothing sweet. Never did. Sorry."

Monica smiled. "It doesn't matter if he eats it. Only that he is included in his sister's party, yes?"

Cherry was nearly embarrassed at the gratitude she was sure was shining from her eyes. It was unseemly, so much thankfulness. It was vulnerable, so much appreciation. It hurt.

"Yes."

She placed a plate in front of Cherry and put a fork neatly beside it.

"Thank you."

"Of course. Now tell me all about your little Daisy."

She sat down, red-rimmed eyes on Cherry, and began to eat.

"I can't, Monica. I don't have anything to say."

"You have plenty to say, darling, but nobody who will listen. I'm here. I'll listen."

Cherry opened her mouth and spoke about her daughter. She talked about her pigtails, about the way that holding a warm baby made everything seem okay, about when she realized she was pregnant with Daisy and how sick that made her at first, but then she guarded that little life inside of her. Cherry remembered how she had guarded her unborn Daisy with everything she had.

"She was sweetness. Something pure and joyful when everything else was so hard. And everything is hard."

Monica nodded.

"I know what hardness is, too, sweetie."

"And then she was stolen, and I have nothing left. Nothing," she cried.

Monica didn't say anything, while Jonah hissed and spit and laughed and rocked back and forth.

Cherry cried herself out. Cried like she had never cried in front of another person. She wiped her face with the palms of her hands and laughed, a shuddery sound that reminded her of a bird's wings beating as it died.

"You must think I'm insane," she said and stabbed her fork into a piece of cake.

Monica pushed the cake around on her plate. "I think you're a victim. Just like your daughter was a victim. Like my grandson. Of this Handsome Butcher you were telling me about. Of this town."

Cherry looked at her. "Of this town?"

Monica's lips thinned.

"This town has a sickness," she said. "I'm sure you know it." She looked at Cherry meaningfully.

Cherry sighed. "I hate it here. It's so petty. So full of hate. Everybody knows everything, knows all about me. Watching. Judging."

"It's more than that."

Monica's eyes burned. The flames inside them caught Cherry's attention. They made her afraid.

"This place. Darling. It's different. It does things. I know you see it. I know you feel what it does to those of us who stay here too long. You left here once. Why?"

"E and I were going to have a life together."

Monica's eyes glittered. "Yes, but why not here?"

Cherry almost couldn't answer. Why *not* here? With her mother, with the people of Darling?

She felt a chill deep in her stomach. "I couldn't raise a baby here. I just couldn't. I didn't want it to …"

Monica nodded. "So, you know."

Those words felt so heavy. Came firing out of her painted mouth like a cannon of speech. So, you know. Which meant *she* knew, too. That *she* was aware.

"People think I'm crazy," Cherry whispered. "That I'm stupid. Imagine too much, do too little. That it's my fault E left."

"It's bad here, Cherry, and it's only gettin' worse. All the things people kept inside before, it's coming up to the surface. You heard that someone broke the windows in Old Doc's house last night, didn't you? He's always been a little strange for never marrying and being too fond of menfolk. People said it for years, but talk is nothing. But action? Action is something different."

Cherry shuddered.

"And old Joe Benson shot himself in his car, right there in front of the courthouse. It was only a bad bankruptcy, no one blamed him for speculating on housing, and it's not like his uncle wasn't letting the whole family live in the second house rent free. Hey, Joe helped move you back into Darling, didn't he?"

Sweet Joe Benson, hauling in her garbage bags full of clothes from Old Sal. His wife had sent them some food to tide them over while they settled in. He was the one who put his hand on her shoulder and said that whether she liked it or not, she was home.

He knew what she was coming home to, didn't he? They all did.

"Mrs. Getchell told me to leave. You know, before she was killed. She said the town was waking up."

"Ardeth Getchell was an old bat, but she knew what she was talking about. She was here before, you know? When everything happened."

"What do you mean?"

Monica's painted brows pulled together.

"Oh, it was bad, Cherry. A bad thing. I was a little girl, but I remember some of it. The town went insane. Something went deeply wrong inside of everybody, and there was shouting and killing and the most horrendous of things. I saw … I saw …"

Cherry felt the blood leave her face as an unnatural coldness filled her veins. She wrapped her frozen fingers tightly around the fork, plunged into her possibly-murdered-daughter's pink birthday cake.

"What did you see, Monica?" She wasn't sure if she should ask, seeing as Monica looked so troubled. Her lipstick was gummed in the corners of her mouth, her eyelashes matted and clumped together. Cherry remembered a feral dog she had once seen at her old apartment, its fur twisted and dark and looking so much like Monica. It had snarled at her, snapping at Jonah. It didn't look nearly as wild as Monica did at that moment.

"I saw my father." Monica took a deep breath. Guzzled a glass of water and held it to her cheek. "My, it's hot in here, isn't it? So terribly hot."

She set the glass down, and Cherry was suddenly aware that Monica's hands were empty, that they should be holding her tiny grandson. They should be combing his hair and singing silly songs while guiding him to bed. Before his murder, before the bloat. So many precious things those hands should be holding. Stolen. Taken from her. Used and tossed in the water like trash.

She looked at her own hands, rough and dry from all the baking and scrubbing.

They were empty, too.

She tucked them around herself, watching Jonah play. Opening the fridge. Closing it. Opening. Closing. Again and again and again. The sound became a rhythm, percussion. She realized it kept her heart beating. She realized without it she would die.

Monica's voice was calm, but there was something rolling under it. Intensity. Flames. "This Handsome Butcher spawned here. I know it. Maybe he wasn't born here, but he came to Darling and was infected. Maybe he was even a good man once, I don't know."

She looked out of the window.

"He takes children. He took yours. Mine. He'll take more."

The fridge. Open. Close. Open. Stick, bang. Stick, bang. Stick, bang. Bang. Bang.

"More children, Cherry. More daughters. More sons. Unless we find him. Unless we find him and kill him."

"Kill him? What are you saying? I couldn't do that."

Monica snorted. "Somebody has to. Might as well be you."

Cherry stood. Backed away.

"I can't believe you're saying this."

Monica smiled, and it was the kind smile of a friend, not a madwoman. Or so she thought. But could she even tell anymore? Wasn't everybody mad, now?

"The sickness is growing, my dear. It's inside of you, now, as well."

"I don't know what to say."

Monica took her hand, clasped it warmly. "Say nothing. But hear. Hear and believe. There's still beauty in the world. Goodness. But here? You won't find it. You have your other little one. He gives you meaning. I'd kill the Handsome Butcher myself, but I have nothing left to fight for. I'm all hollowed out. Just as dead as our children are."

Monica pulled her hand away and stood.

"Goodbye, Cherry."

She closed the heavy wooden door behind her. It was an ominous sound.

# Chapter Forty-Three

CHERRY DROPPED BY Runner's house that morning. She couldn't help it.

She wore a yellow sundress, faded, but not overly. Courageously pretty. A nice dress. A good-girl dress. The kind of dress a woman wears when she decides to beg.

She strapped Jonah into Old Sal with a piece of toast. Normally she didn't let him eat in the car, but she needed him to be happy, to be quiet. To sit still, quite unlike a little boy at all.

Runner answered the door without any expression. Grisly stitches Frankensteined his face. His leg was in a heavy cast.

"What?"

Cherry licked her lips nervously, caught herself. She laced her fingers together firmly in front of her. Opened her mouth to speak. Closed it again.

Jonah squawked from the backseat of the car.

"Cherry, if ya got something to say, spit it out. My leg's giving me trouble. I'd just rather sit down if it's okay with you."

"Runner, I'm sorry. About everything. That you came over and this happened to you. I'm so sorry about your leg. And that everything is so awful." The words fell from her lips like water. She paused. He stared at her. She nibbled her bottom lip.

"Is that all you came here to say?"

She nodded.

He nodded back and shut the door.

Cherry's soul shattered. She felt it bursting into pieces and diamonding the air. Felt it fall to the ground around her.

She turned toward her car. Jonah's pensive face. The prospect of driving back to her house, where she'd stare at the walls and hate everything and everyone.

Cherry spun around and knocked on the door again. Harder, this time. She heard Runner curse before he opened it.

"Dammit, Cherry, what do you want?"

"Open the screen door. I want to talk to you."

He didn't move. She pulled it open and fixed her hands on her hips.

"Runner, I said I was sorry. I've been feeling terrible, but it wasn't my fault. Everybody's been treating me like a pariah, especially you." She stepped closer, stood on her tiptoes until they were nose to nose. "This has been a nightmare. All of this. I look for Daisy every day. Every second. Do you know that? I think I hear her all the time. I wake up, reaching for where I hope she's sleeping. She's never there. It kills me, over and over."

"Cherry—"

She held up a hand. "Let me finish. This town is my personal hell. I was never going to come back here, but I did, and … well, it's everything I was afraid it would be. Worse. There was nothing good in this place, except you."

His lips tightened a bit.

She continued, feeling the futility. Feeling the sorrow. But still, she had to say it, if only to convince herself she had tried. When her heart breaks the next day, or possibly the day after that, she'll have at least tried.

"You're the only bright thing in this town. I wanted … I *want* you. I do. To be with you. To spend time with you. That night was something special for me. You have to know it. Then something horrible happened, and everything was ruined again."

No response.

"I've always lived for everybody else. Obey Mama. Don't

anger E. Take care of the kids. You're the only thing I ever wanted for myself. We might be no good for each other, but I don't care. I still want you."

She looked down at her shabby shoes. Wiggled her toes in them. Swallowed hard. Sighed.

"Anyway, that's what I came to say. Goodbye, Runner."

She was halfway down the porch steps when he grabbed her, spun her around.

"Damned woman," he said, and yanked her to him. Drew her body into his. Crushed her lips with his own.

She nearly pulled away. Instead, she ran her arms around him, stood on tiptoes to kiss him better. Little purring sounds reached her ears, and she was surprised to realize they were coming from her throat.

Jonah squawked again, more insistently this time, and Cherry stepped out of Runner's arms.

"Guess we're giving the neighbors something to gossip about," she said. Her lips felt swollen and aching, and very, very alone. She flicked her tongue across them, tasting him.

His green eyes were hot on her face. "Guess so."

Jonah screamed, alone and afraid, and Cherry flushed.

"I need to go. Maybe sometime we could—?"

"I'm coming over tonight, Cherry."

"I ... yes. Please."

"There's something here. Always was. It would be a shame if we didn't explore it."

Jonah shrieked, fighting the seatbelt, throwing his body against the door.

Runner dropped another kiss on her lips. "See you later, Cherry Pie."

She couldn't speak, only nodded. Then, she ran to her car.

"Baby. Baby, it's okay," she soothed, but Jonah had disappeared, was lost within himself, and there was a changeling in his place now. She couldn't calm him down. Her son. The long ride, the terror of being left alone for so long, the confusion of seeing a man with his arms around his mother … Doing what? Hurting her? Holding her down? Constraining her like the seatbelt had been wrapped around his thin body, yanking him into place when all he wanted was to be free? It was too much. She hopped behind the wheel and gunned it for home, listening to her son shriek and scream like the possessed.

*Daisy,* she thought, and her dark eyes blurred with tears. She blinked them away. Think of Runner. Think of what tonight could bring. Her stomach twisted in a fine way, but she caught herself slowing down as she passed shadows, turns in the road, buildings that might be a good place for a little girl to hide.

Or perhaps for the Handsome Butcher to stash a tiny body.

Ditches that were always full of water. Suspicious furrows in the ground. All of these places.

She drove, and searched, and prayed. Cherry cried while Jonah screamed bloody murder in the backseat.

Her heart did the same.

# Chapter Forty-Four

JONAH HAD A potty accident in the car that soaked through his diaper. She'd scrub out Old Sal later, but right now she needed to clean up her son.

She wrestled him into the tub. He shrieked and screamed and bucked. Flipped onto his stomach, his face in the water. Flailed. Tried to struggle to his feet while Cherry used all her weight to hold him down.

"Just a second, darling. Let's wash your hair. Fast, fast, we'll do it quickly. Jonah, stop."

She sang Baa Baa Black Sheep while pouring the water over his head, getting the suds out. He struck out, catching the soft skin of her neck with his too-long nails. She bodily pulled him from the bathtub, and he rocketed his head back, catching her full in the mouth. She saw stars. Tasted blood. His shrieks were amplified in the perfect acoustics of the cold bathroom, filling her ears and head and brain and soul. Pain and sound. Noise and hurt.

"Stop it, Jonah. Stop it," she screamed.

He screamed back, covering his ears to block out his own voice.

Cherry covered her own ears, closed her eyes, and shrieked. Felt her throat tear with the ugliness of it. As loud as she could, unfettered. Just like her mama used to do during the storms when nobody else in the town could hear her. Voice and franticness covered by the sound of the rain. Throwing dishes and pushing over furniture, hidden by the growling thunder. Growling herself.

Cherry hiding under her bed, but always being found. Always being punished for being a witness.

There were far too many storms in Darling. They went on far too long.

She caught herself. Snapped her mouth shut mid-scream, forcing herself to swallow the sound. Blinked and reached for her son, who was staring at her with too-wide eyes, his mouth twisted, tears streaming down his red face.

His pulse beat in his throat. Too fast. Too hard.

No no no no.

"Oh, sweetie, I'm sorry. I'm sorry." She reached for him, but he squirmed away, his wet, naked body easily slipping between her fingers.

He cried out, wild with panic, and scrambled from the room. Bumping into walls, tripping over his own awkward feet. Running from his mother, just as Cherry had run from hers.

She went for the phone. Dialed shakily. Didn't bother to wipe the sweat from her upper lip, her hair sticking to her face.

"Hello? It's me. I need help."

The doorbell rang less than ten minutes later. She opened the door.

"What's the trouble?" Mordachi said. He looked tall and strong and exhausted. She felt a pang in her chest but ignored it.

"I can't get Jonah to calm down. I'm all worn out. I wonder if you could—?"

He nodded and stepped past her. "Where is he?"

"My bedroom."

He walked down the hall. She listened to his boots, heavy on the stairs and heavy on her heart. She closed her eyes.

"I'm sorry," she whispered, but of course he couldn't hear her.

She slid down the wall to the floor and put her head on

her knees. Listened to Jonah's shrieking, the low rumble of Mordachi's voice from up the stairs. Jonah started to calm. She heard Mordachi praise him.

Cherry took a deep breath and raised her head. "Everything all right?" she called.

"Fine. Pajamas in his drawer?"

"Yes."

This must be what it was like to have a partner. To have somebody help. To have a man in the house to take care of things when she had reached her wit's end. It felt foreign. It felt good.

This is how it should have been with E.

She slowed, practiced her breathing. Cherry leaned her head back against the wall and sighed. Stood up. Sighed again. She crept up the stairs in bare feet. Mordachi held Jonah on his shoulder like a baby, pacing the room. Jonah was sucking his fingers. His eyes were shiny and bright and sleepy.

Cherry leaned in the doorway, crossed her arms. "I can barely pick him up anymore."

"He's getting big."

"He is." She watched the two of them, and her heart did funny things. Painful things. She turned away from it.

"I'll get his medicine. He won't go to sleep without it."

The hallway groaned under her bare feet. The walls shuddered and moaned. *This town will take your son,* they wheezed. *Take everything you love, one by one by one by one.* She slapped the wall with one hand as if that would silence it. Maybe this time it would.

In the kitchen, she ground up his medicine and put it in an oral syringe. Mixed it with water. Shook it. Mordachi appeared in the hallway with Jonah in his arms. She slid the syringe into her son's mouth, pushed the plunger. Jonah took it and gagged.

"He's okay," she said. "It's like this every night."

"What is it?" Suspicion in his voice. Considering his history, it wasn't surprising.

"Just melatonin. Over the counter. His brain doesn't produce enough of it, if any. If I don't supplement it, he sleeps about three hours a night." She pressed her lips together, wondering if she should bring it up. Decided to do so, but delicately. "It isn't anything bad. His pediatrician recommended it. I know you're worried."

His dark eyes met hers, held for a beat, and then he looked away.

"Sorry." His voice was gruff.

"Don't be."

She wanted to take his hand, then. To reassure him, as she had reassured E. To tell him he wasn't alone, he was an adult now, he'd never again have to go through what his father put them through. She started to reach for him, but he had already turned away, taking Jonah back to his room. Cherry pushed her bangs out of her face, instead.

"It will take twenty minutes to kick in. You don't have to stay." She swallowed hard. "But thank you. For coming. Especially after—"

He interrupted her. "I'll stay until he goes to sleep if that's okay with you." His eyes were dark and sad and maybe almost a little bit dangerous. E's eyes.

She shouldn't have brought his father up. She shied away.

"Do you mind if I take a shower? I haven't had a chance."

Her mind shut down. Seeing her husband's eyes in his brother's face. Good, ole, dependable Mordachi was somebody else inside. Somebody with fire. Somebody with rage. Why hadn't she seen it before?

He shrugged. "Go. I have him." He held the boy closer, almost protectively. Jonah didn't struggle in his arms but seemed to go boneless. Content.

*This is what family is like,* she thought.

"I have him," Mordachi repeated.

Cherry nodded. "You do."

Her shower was running hot today. She washed her hair, conditioned it. Took special care to shave her legs. Ran the soap over her body in anticipation of Runner's hands and tongue. Wrapped a towel around her head and stared at herself in the mirror.

Her eyes were too wide, like a child's. Her mouth used to be too wide, too. It had smiled. Laughed. Sucked root beer through straws and told clever stories and rounded in excitement when she was struck by something beautiful. Birds in spring. Louisiana sunsets. E's face when he dropped to one knee and asked her to marry him. Sliding the cheap gold ring on her finger. Kissing the tears from her face and promising they would get out of town that very week. Be together forever.

Forever doesn't last very long in Darling. Nothing does.

Her mouth seemed smaller now. Shrunken with worry, with pursing, with kissing her little ones' eyes and cheeks and toes.

She missed her daughter. She missed her son.

Cherry hurriedly threw on some clothes. A soft T-shirt that read "The Best Revenge is Peace" and a ratty old denim skirt she'd worn for the last fifteen years. If only she had something sultrier, something seductive. But she'd thrown all of that away before heading back to Darling. And it had been a relief.

Jonah was asleep. Mordachi was sitting in a chair in the corner of his room, watching her boy like a falcon. A gargoyle. Something protective and a little bit frightening. Her heart skipped a beat.

"Thank you," she said. Her eyes found the floor, which infuriated her. She forced herself to look at him. "Thank you," she said again.

"You sound angry."

This took her back. "I don't mean to."

"You can be angry if you want to be."

She thought about it. "I don't want to be."

"Okay."

She sat on Jonah's bed and combed out her wet hair. "I do appreciate you, Mordachi."

"Don't."

"Don't what?"

He stretched his long legs out, his heavy boots scraping across the floor. "Don't do the gratitude thing. I hate it. Always have."

"What gratitude thing?"

"The 'Oh, Mordachi, you're ever so helpful' thing. I'm not hanging out to be *helpful*. I have no interest in being *helpful*. Men don't typically aid beautiful women in order to be *helpful* to them."

Cherry's eyes darted to Jonah, and Mordachi cursed.

"I won't wake him. But heaven forbid I should have any feelings, Cherry."

He stood, brushed past her, and the echo of his booted feet made her stomach drop.

She heard the staircase laugh as he descended it, and squeezed her eyes shut. "Wait." It was a whisper. She shot to her feet, padded after him. Stood at the top of the stairs. "Wait!"

He stopped, didn't turn around.

Cherry took a deep breath and ran down the staircase. It snarled under her feet. Roiled beneath her. Her legs buckled, but she regained her footing and headed for Mordachi. Stopped right behind him.

He didn't turn to face her.

"If you have something to say, woman, you'd better say it. I can't just stay here. I barely have any dignity left."

Her heart broke. She slid her hand onto his arm. Slid both arms around him. Rested her head against his back.

"I do love you, Mordachi. You have to know that. But not in the way you want me to. I'm sorry."

"You could learn to love me."

"I don't think so. You've always been like a brother to me. So good. So caring. Somebody I could trust."

"But that's not who you fall for. You fall for fast, good lookin' men who are selfish. Like E. Like Runner."

She didn't say anything.

He sighed and stepped away from her. Kept his back to her. "I'm leaving Darling."

She gasped. "Why? Why would you do that?"

"I can't stay here anymore. This town is eating me alive."

She wrapped her arms around him again. "Mordachi. You can't go."

He turned to face her, and the rawness in his eyes made Cherry's stomach twist.

"Tell me why I should stay. Tell me there's a reason. Tell me, and I'll stay."

She took a step back. "I can't do that."

"Please. I'll beg. I'm begging."

"I can't talk about this."

He grabbed her hands. "Just love me."

She felt the blood drain out of her face. Out of her body. Out of her heart.

"Cherry, we need to talk about this. I could be so good for you. I've always loved you. You know I'd take care of the kids. Love them. Take care of *you*. Love *you*."

She inhaled. "You need to leave. Runner … Runner will be here in a few minutes."

He stood still. Looked at his fingers clutching hers. Let her hands go. "That's your decision, then."

"I don't see why there has to be a decision. Can't we all be happy together? Like when we were kids?"

"You misremember. The only ones happy then were you and E."

He left then, and it was like watching part of her soul go. The good part. The part with all the integrity.

She wondered if she would miss it.

# Chapter Forty-Five

CHERRY OPENED THE door before Runner even knocked. His hands were deep in his jean pockets.

"Listen," he said. "I really think we should—"

"Shut up," she cut him off. Cherry stood on the tips of her toes, and kissed him.

He immediately responded, shifting his weight to his good leg. He picked her up.

She wrapped her legs around his waist as he leaned her against the railing. Cherry kissed him until she couldn't stand it anymore, then she slipped to her feet. Took his hand. Led him through the door.

He slammed it shut behind them.

Neither of them saw Mordachi perched high in the tree on the side of the house. He looked at his empty hands for a long, long time.

# Chapter Forty-Six

CHERRY WOKE UP with the sun in her eyes. She rolled onto her belly and moaned. Pulled the pillow over her head.

"Good morning, darlin'."

She blinked at the voice, remembered, smiled, stretched like a cat.

"It is, isn't it?"

Runner draped his arm around her. Pulled her close. Kissed her deliciously raw and bruised lips. He tasted like the sunrise—like hope. Maybe he brought enough hope that Daisy would be found today.

"I love you," she whispered.

He didn't answer. Maybe he didn't hear. Either way, it didn't matter. It was too soon to say she loved him, but she wanted to say it. Maybe there wouldn't be another chance.

She snuggled up against him, running her fingers down his chest.

"I'm glad you're here. Hungry?"

"Could eat a horse."

"We're fresh out of horse, but I have some homemade bread. I make a mean French toast."

"Baby, you're on."

She slid out of bed, clutching the bedsheets close to her. She picked up his undershirt from the floor.

"Mind if I wear this?"

He kissed her, bit her lip. "I like you better in nothing."

"Mmm. Maybe later. Jonah's up."

Chirps. Hoots. Bare feet scrambling down the hall.

Cherry slid the white undershirt over her head, the hem ending mid-thigh. She slipped into panties and tossed Runner his boxers.

"See you downstairs, handsome."

She met her son at the door, bent to accept his kisses on her cheeks, on her eyes, every spot he could reach on her face.

"Hi, baby. Toast? Let's go downstairs."

Jonah had forgiven her for last night. Perhaps he had even forgotten all the terror and strangeness that drove him out of his mind. She could never forgive so quickly. She was sure of it.

Toast. Jonah didn't sit at the table but took his piece and wandered. He played with the toaster, peered out of the window. He laid on his back and kicked his feet joyfully in the air.

Runner came downstairs, freshly showered, his feet bare.

"Hey, bud," he greeted Jonah. He came up behind Cherry, wrapped his arms around her, and rested his chin on her head.

"Do you like cinnamon on your French toast?" she asked.

He spun her around, pulled her close to him. Running his hands across her butt, sliding them up the hem of the undershirt.

"Darling, not in front of Jonah."

She kissed him back once and squirmed away. Pulled the hem demurely down over her thighs.

He sighed and sat down at the table.

"Your mom can be such a prude," he confided to the little boy.

Jonah ran off to the laundry room. Bang. Bang. Bang.

Cherry slid a plate of French toast in front of Runner. "Sorry, we're out of syrup. So, what are your plans for today?"

"You, I'd hoped. Just you."

She laughed. "Sounds great, but Jonah won't go back to sleep until tonight. He doesn't nap anymore."

Runner pushed his plate aside and pulled Cherry onto his lap.

"The kid's busy," he said, sliding his mouth down her neck. His breath was so hot that the rest of her body suddenly felt cold. Goosebumps. Arctic winters. Cherry closed her eyes and let her head fall back. "We should be busy, too."

Her toes curled. She ran her bare feet down his calves. He nipped at her earlobes.

Bang. Bang. Bang bang.

Cherry took a deep breath. Tried to control her breathing. Slipped out of Runner's lap with regret.

"Later. I promise."

"Sure."

She kissed him hard on the mouth. Pretended not to notice when he adjusted his jeans and drank his coffee noisily. She listened to the banging of the dryer door and thought about her daughter.

Runner started staying over more nights than not. Left a few shirts in Cherry's mother's wardrobe. Didn't mention the house whispered to him at night. That the thing on the roof still prowled. Didn't say he hoped maybe it would take the kid one evening while they were sleeping, so he could have Cherry all to himself just like he always wanted.

Monsters aren't imaginary. Runner knew that. He also knew he shouldn't say anything about it, and he wouldn't. But that didn't stop him from wishing.

During this time, Mordachi sold what he could of his possessions. He sold his horses to another family in town, and most of the ranch hands moved along with them. He practically gave the pasture away. He couldn't stand seeing Cherry with Runner. The way she hung on him. The way she looked at him. The way he acted like he was tall and strong and heroic. Like he cared about her. Like he cared about the kids.

Mordachi was leaving in the morning. Tossing what he had left in the back of his truck and driving away. Leave the house. Leave all of it. Just go.

He headed down to the Rocking JY Bar, the only one in town. He was going to sit with the guys one last time and drink a toast to misery before cutting Cherry and everything else in this dingy hellhole out like a tumor. He tipped his hat at the ranch hands who had cared for his horses. They nodded back. He sat at the bar and signaled the bartender.

He saw a nightmare out of the corner of his eye. His eyes widened and then narrowed.

The wolves were closing in on Darling.

He showed up at Cherry's front door an hour later. Runner opened it, shirtless, his hair mussed and his green eyes blazing.

Cherry pushed past him, and her hands flew to her mouth when she saw Mordachi.

"Oh, no! What happened to you? Come in and get cleaned up."

He ignored her. Just stared at her out of his good eye, the other one swollen and dark. His split lips cracked when he moved them.

"Cherry. Runner." He hated the way Runner's name tasted in his mouth, more coppery and bitter than the blood, but this concerned him, too. "I got news for you. E's back in town."

# Chapter Forty-Seven

CHERRY STARED AT Mordachi, at his swollen face and the blood that soaked into his shirt.

"Did you hurt Ephraim?" The words were out of her mouth before she could bite them back.

Mordachi's jaw tightened. "Not enough. He'll be laid out for a few days, though. I know E, and he won't come back until he's thought everything through. Till he's at a hundred percent. He's dangerous that way." He turned to Runner. "He doesn't seem to know about you two yet, but you can be sure folk'll be itching to tell him. And he's mad. Real mad. Don't think life's been too kind to him lately."

Cherry watched this with big eyes, her hands still to her mouth. Her skin felt drained of all color. Somebody had stolen her spirit when they took her daughter, and this shell that was left wasn't strong enough to function on its own.

Mordachi reached out, winced. He guided Cherry to the couch. Sat her down.

She grabbed his bloody hand. "What is he going to do? Why did he come back?"

"I don't know, darlin'." His voice was calm, but his eyes met Runner's over her head.

"Do you think he knows I'm here?"

"Can't imagine any other reason he'd set foot in Darling."

"Maybe he just wants a divorce?"

The hope in her voice hurt all of them.

Runner hissed his breath in through his teeth. "You're not even divorced yet?"

She shook her head. "He just left. I didn't know where to find him. I sent some papers to the house here in Darling, but he never sent them back." She looked at Runner. "I'm still married."

Runner ran his hands through his hair. "Oh, man. He's gonna kill me. Like, really physically *kill* me."

"Runner."

"Your brother is psycho. Messing with his wife? She's his *wife*." He turned on Cherry. "Why didn't you tell me you were still married?"

Her eyes were dead. The eyes of ghosts.

"Would it have made that much of a difference?" she asked. Her voice was ghostly, too.

Runner's lip curled in disgust. "Yeah, it would have made a difference. I wouldn't be a dead man walking right now."

Cherry was looking at Runner, then, really looking, and he wasn't the strong tree and the safe nest for her that he had been claiming to be. She shouldn't be surprised, she thought vaguely. She shouldn't be surprised, but somehow, she still was. Disappointment and regret taste sweet, like strawberry ice.

"You're this scared of E?" she asked him. Her pale fingers knotted at each other.

"Hell, yes. Are you looking at Mordachi, here? Never saw anyone who could flatten a man out like Mordachi if he had to, and just look at him. If E will do this to his own brother, what chance would I stand?" He cursed and peered out of the front window.

"Think he's hiding in the swamp, Runner? Gonna leap out like the boogie man and get you? Listen, Ephraim is still my husband, but that's been on paper only. He left us. Ran out like the rat he is. He has no claim over us. He doesn't even want it."

She looked at Mordachi and thought of his truck, of everything thrown in the back. Of his plans to leave Darling in his rearview mirror. Find a life for himself, somewhere he could fit and possibly do more than be the dutiful brother, the eyesore son, the caretaker of a dying town.

Cherry bit her lips. A new awareness dawned as she watched Runner pace.

Mordachi sighed. "You're not alone in this, Cherry. You have me. You always have me."

"But aren't you leaving?"

"No. Not anymore."

# Chapter Forty-Eight

CHERRY LET JONAH sleep in her bed that night. She wanted him close by, wanted to hear his breath and his whispering and feel his legs kick like a buzzsaw in his sleep.

"You're not staying?" she had asked Runner as soon as Mordachi left. He was already looking for his shirt. She tossed it to him.

"Nah, not tonight. Gotta get home and, you know, do stuff."

"You don't have to lie to me."

He had stopped searching around then. Looked at her. Saw she was gazing back with eyes full and clear and unclouded by her love. He sighed and sat down on the couch.

"I don't want to cut and run on you, Cherry. But if E's back in town, well, I gotta think this through, you know?"

"I understand."

And she did. She knew. Even drunk and angry, E had something about him. Charisma. A strange charm. A way of looking at you like you were either the best thing that ever crawled on the earth or something so undeserving you should be grateful to die. His own type of voodoo.

He knew how to hurt.

"I'm sorry, darlin'," Runner said and kissed her.

She didn't kiss him back.

"I know you are. Just go."

Now she was in her bed, listening to Jonah's breathing. Thinking about Daisy. Wondering why E was back. Wondering if, maybe, he had heard about her daughter. If he had come back to help.

Jonah murmured in his sleep, and Cherry stroked his hair. He chirped and settled.

At least one thing stayed the same. At least one person would always love her.

"I love you, baby," she whispered and kissed Jonah's face. "I'll never leave you."

The house whispered something ugly to her, something about miscarriages and babies that should never be. She turned on her side, wrapped her arms around her son. Refused to listen. Refused to do anything other than love.

The house didn't understand this. It had never been this way before.

# Chapter Forty-Nine

$\int$HE TOOK ALL of Runner's shirts and folded them neatly into a pile, and laid them on the couch for when he returned. If he returned. She didn't expect it.

The phone rang.

Her breath caught like it always did since her daughter disappeared. Did somebody find Daisy? Bits of her spirit? Bits of her body?

Her mouth went dry as she answered the call with a breathy, tentative voice that scared her. The hope and desperation and fear rang through like a dissonant bell. The sheer need in her voice was uncomely.

No, she didn't have time to answer a survey. No, she wasn't interested.

She hung up the phone. Took it off the hook. Looked at the receiver, put it back. The phone clicking into the cradle was such a solemn sound. A final sound. It always was. Every. Single. Time.

She knew then she would be answering the phone with her heart in her mouth for the rest of her life, but it would never be Daisy on the other end. She would never be found, not alive. Her heart told her this was the truth. Her logic agreed.

She sat on the ground next to the couch with scraps of cloth in her hands. They were old pieces of shirts and dresses she had taken from her mother's closet. They had filled her with horror while on her mother's frame, but now they were just soft pieces of fabric in surprisingly beautiful colors. She had wanted the most glorious of colors for this particular doll.

She threaded the needle, bit her lip, and sewed on a bright blue button eye. Tears ran down her face as she stitched on the second.

So blue, and so dear, and wide open and full of joy. These button eyes would never close. They'd be curious about the world forever and ever.

Her hands shook.

*Sew the doll,* the house encouraged her. She felt the glee bubble up like old water. *Sew the dolls and then the children are found.*

Dolls and children, children and dolls. Sweet innocents that the Handsome Butcher played with, bending and posing and dressing.

*You're the same,* the house purred. *You're the same, this butcher and you. Both of you create meaningless dolls out of scraps.*

Cherry's stomach lurched, but she sewed on. Simple legs. A tiny dress. She would give it pigtails like banners.

*Yes,* the house urged, *soon your child will float to the surface of the muck or fall from the trees or wild animals will drag her from the underbrush. Birds will have pecked out her eyes. Her body will be rotted from the inside out, bloated with gasses. But you will have something to bury, a corpse to toss back into a hole. Then you can make a doll for your other child. Make sure that one is nice and broken.*

The partially finished doll fell from Cherry's hands. She put her head on her knees and wept.

The house sighed. Yes. This was more to its liking. This was how it was supposed to be in the LaRouche home. The tears of broken women are the most beautiful things on earth. They shine like dewdrops, like blood drops. Oh, how they shine.

They shine.

# Chapter Fifty

*T*HEY LET AZHAR out of jail. Cops and lawyers had hemmed and hawed, dragging their feet and finding any reason to keep him inside. Basically, it came down to "He's a stranger, he's different, he's foreign, he's not one of us."

"It isn't a crime to be born outside of Darling," the sheriff finally said. "In fact, it's probably a blessing. We don't have any reason to keep him. Let him go."

Azhar stopped at Cherry's house on his way out of town. He stood on the front porch and knocked on the door just as he had the first time he'd met her. This time she invited him inside and sat him down at her kitchen table while her son spun in circles around him. She gave him a piece of pink cake that made her mouth twist in a funny way when she set the plate down.

"It's Daisy's birthday cake," she explained, and Azhar nodded.

"Happy birthday to your little one," he said, and ate the cake with such dignity that it brought tears to Cherry's eyes.

"What are you going to do now?" she asked.

"There were more children found," he answered. "I'm going to go to them, to their parents. Try to help if I can, until the Handsome Butcher is caught."

"I had a dream about him. A terrible, terrible dream."

Azhar stopped abruptly, pink crumbs on his beautiful face. Cherry wanted to wipe them away as if he were a small child.

"What did he look like?" he asked.

Jonah buzzed beside him, interested in his shiny watch. Azhar slipped it off his wrist and handed it to him.

"He looked like an angel at first. Then like a monster. It doesn't matter; it was a silly dream. But Sada was there. She said you should go home."

Azhar's face broke.

Cherry looked at her hands, at the napkin she shredded between her fingers. She forced herself to stop.

"Go home. That's what she said?"

"She said that you were doing it wrong. But it was a dream. It didn't mean anything."

Azhar looked somewhere far away, his dark eyes seeing pigtails and tiny pearly smiles.

"If I had been home, maybe none of this would have happened, yes?"

Cherry touched his fingers. "You can't say that. I was home and it happened. It doesn't change anything. It's only one more form of torture and you don't deserve that, so stop it."

Azhar laughed harshly. "Don't I?"

"If you deserve it, then I do, too. And I've been trying awful hard to convince myself that we're only human. Please don't make me think otherwise. I'm falling apart as it is."

Azhar sighed. "My daughter is dead. My wife, I think she is also dead. There is just me left, and I am only one against so many odds. But I will try, Cherry LaRouche. And I hope you try, too. For yourself. For your son." He nodded at Jonah. "It will be hard enough growing up as it is. Growing up with a murdered sister and a guilt-stricken mother will be too much for him. It is too much for anyone."

He patted Jonah's head, then took both of Cherry's hands in his and kissed them. He turned and walked out into the garish sunshine.

He disappeared and Cherry let herself muse about what life

had been like before he had ever shown up. Before his daughter had come apart like a puzzle. Back when Cherry's ideas of monsters had to do with overbearing mothers and deadbeat husbands. Back when the world was simple and not nearly so cruel.

# Chapter Fifty-One

RUNNER SHOWED UP at her door that night, his hair still wet.

Cherry's stomach twisted. Dropped. Twisted again.

She licked her lips. Tried words. Soft ones so she didn't wake Jonah or the house. So she wouldn't lose her mind and scream her loneliness and hate and fear into the wind, thereby hating herself in the morning.

"I packed up your shirts. Let me get them."

"Cherry." He was through the door, kicking it shut behind him. He dropped his cane, wrapped his arms around her, and buried his face in her neck. Breathed deep, the scent of her soap and skin. "I can't leave you. I can't. I'm sorry."

Her eyes filled with tears. She wanted to wrap her arms around him, but they were pinned to her sides.

"Runner, what—?"

He pulled away and looked at her. "I can't, okay? I tried. Out of respect to E. Out of respect to you. But dammit, Cherry, I love you, okay? I do. I always have. I need you. And you need me, more than ever. If E is back, he's only gonna cause trouble. We both know it. You don't need to handle it alone. I'm here. I'm here, Cherry Pie, if you'll still have me."

She lost her voice as she studied his green eyes—so fierce, so intense they almost scared her.

"Ephraim is going to be so angry," she said and frowned. That wasn't what she meant to say at all.

"I know. I'm worried about you, Cherry. You don't need to

deal with him right now. Not when all of this is going on. Be with me."

She closed her eyes. "Say it again."

He ran his hand down her face, cupped her cheek. Kissed her once. Murmured against her mouth.

"Be with me."

Cherry kissed him back, tasting his toothpaste and her tears. Her fingers gently touched each and every stitch on his face. She couldn't wrap her arms around him far enough, couldn't hold him close enough. He picked her up, her feet dangling off the floor, and she started to laugh through her sobs.

"Oh, darling, I'm such a mess! Are you sure you even want me?"

He kissed her. Loved her. Ran his hands over her arms and across her back. Told her without words that, yes, he wanted her, and yes, he was there, and yes, he was somewhere she could rest her back against. He was her tree. He was her nest. He meant it this time, he did.

Several hours later, in the dark of her room, their bodies wrapped around each other, he nuzzled the sweet spot under her ear.

"Did you miss me?" he asked.

"No," she answered. She turned to face him and kissed him on the mouth. "I just slept in your shirt because I'm too lazy to do laundry."

He laughed, and it was a beautiful sound. She could hear that sound every day for the rest of her life, could build her life around it. It wasn't realistic, but maybe she could allow herself the pleasure of dreaming just this once.

"I love you, Cherry Pie." He was starting to slur his words.

She kissed his forehead, smoothed his hair back.

"I love you, too. So much."

They fell asleep wrapped together, the way lovers should be.

This was contentment. This was happiness. Cherry dreamed her first sweet dreams in months. Her mouth opened and she "oh'd" in happiness.

The scrabbling on the roof worked its way into her pretty, pretty dreams. Insidious, as always.

# Chapter Fifty-Two

THIS COULD BE a new kind of happy for Cherry. Perhaps she'd find herself crying while doing dishes, and Runner would come from behind, wrap his arms around her, and hold her. Bring her little treats and wildflowers every day. Watch Jonah so she could run down to the grocery store without feeling like a bomb was ticking in her grocery cart.

"So, this is what it feels like to be in love," she whispered to him that morning. She hoped they would always be whispering. Against mouths. Against cheeks.

"You were in love with E."

"But we were children then. This is different."

Jonah hadn't warmed to him but didn't seem to mind him, either. Until about noon when the dryer broke, and there were torrents of tears. Hand-flipping. Uncontrollable sobbing and screaming.

"Why is he so upset?" Runner asked through gritted teeth. He ran his hands through his hair.

Cherry held her son as best she could. "It's his security, baby. His constant. It's always there and works in the same way, and if you push a certain button, it starts, and if you push another, it stops, and ... Oh!"

Jonah threw himself forward, hitting her nose with his forehead. Blood gushed. Cherry tried blearily to catch it in her hands.

"Cherry!"

Runner pulled Jonah from her and pushed him aside. Jonah screamed and collapsed on the floor.

"I don't think it's broken, love. But let's take care of this."

He grabbed a rag and handed it to her. Took the icepack from the freezer, wrapped it in a washcloth, and touched it to her nose. She hissed.

"Sorry, darlin'. It's gonna hurt, but you want to keep the swelling down. Otherwise … Won't that kid shut up?"

Jonah looked at the gushing blood coming from his mama's face and screamed. Banged his head against the hard floor. Banged harder.

"Jonah." Cherry stood but Runner pushed her back down on the chair.

"Sit down. Keep this on." He gave her the icepack.

"What are you going to do?"

She was on her feet again. Runner advanced toward Jonah, whose own nose was now bloodied by the constant banging.

"Knock it off, boy, do you understand me?"

Runner grabbed Jonah by his twiggy arms and yanked him up high. Jonah's feet peddled uselessly in the air.

"Runner, please. You're hurting him."

Cherry ran to her son, tried to take him from Runner's arms. Jonah's flailing arm hit her square in her tender nose, and she shrieked.

"That's it." Runner pushed her away with one hand. Hauled Jonah into the bathroom, put him in, and held the door shut.

"Mo-om! Mo-om!" Jonah screamed. The words were full of terror. Broken things, torn from a throat and a mind that didn't understand.

"Oh, baby! Runner, stop this. Let him out!"

"He's got to learn, Cherry. You can't keep coddling him like this. Don't you see what he's done to you?"

More screams. Banging. Jonah's soft fingers against the door. His head. His face.

"He'll hurt himself. He doesn't know any better."

Runner scoffed. "Check yourself out lately, babe? Your face

is hamburger. Better put your rag back on that nose."

"Open the door."

"Not until the brat shuts up. Dammit, my head hurts *so much*."

Jonah's screams raised in intensity.

Then there was the horrible sound of breaking glass.

Cherry screamed and pulled on Runner with all her strength.

"Give me my baby! My baby!"

Runner's face pulsed with the evil of Darling. He pushed her to the ground, hard. Her head cracked against the wooden floor, and she saw stars. Heard her son screaming. Heard Runner yelling. There was a chittering sound as the walls responded to the negativity. They keened. They quivered and whispered for Runner to do more, more, *more*.

He opened the bathroom door. The house reverberated with the sound of a man's fist hitting something soft. It was a sound Cherry knew far too well. Jonah's terrified wailing pitched higher. Runner slammed the door closed again.

"Don't touch my son," Cherry slurred. She wasn't certain if she had spoken the words out loud, but she must have because Runner laughed.

"I do what I want, Cherry," he said, and the voice wasn't Runner's. It belonged to something else, something old and wicked that had been sucked up from deep inside the ground. It wore Runner's ruined face and a strange, dark light glowed from underneath his stitches. "I touch who I want."

Enough. Never. No. Cherry shook her head, trying to clear it. She scrabbled to her knees but couldn't seem to do more than that.

Jonah shrieked again, and Cherry shrieked with him.

*Help me*, she thought. *Help*.

*I can help*, the entity in the walls answered back. The room rippled lazily. *Want to be strong, Cherry Pie? Want to feel the rage burn away the fear? Fire is so much easier to bear than terror.*

She wanted to say that she didn't want anything from this

desecrated mess, but it wasn't true.

*Give me the strength to stand.* She wasn't sure if she was commanding or begging, but it didn't matter. She needed to help her son.

*All you have to do is remember.* The voice was uncomfortably close now, far too loud inside her mind. *Remember.*

She did. She remembered her mother beating her with anything she could find, her eyes reflecting the lightning from the storms. She remembered walking into E's bedroom, pregnancy test in hand, to find Wendy there, her top off and E's tongue in her mouth. She remembered lying outside in the dirt, listening to the worms and ugly things slither and crawl beneath her, promising that they'd all be together soon. Everything ends up in the ground eventually.

Despair gave way to anger. Cherry hissed as she let it course through, felt her veins flood with darkness. It felt good.

She pulled herself shakily to her feet. Staggered to the kitchen drawer. Grabbed the longest cutting knife she could.

She spoke, and her cold, clear voice cut through the noise like an icicle sliding perfectly into an open eye. "Get out of my way, Runner, or I will kill you."

He stilled. Turned to look at his bloodied Cherry and the knife. "Baby. You wouldn't."

"Open the door."

He reached for her, but she slashed at him with the knife. He jerked his hand back. "You're crazy!"

"I want my son."

Jonah was in hysterics. His sobs came through the door. The screaming. The wailing. She knew she'd see blood, and his pulse in his neck, and his heart would stop. It would be too much for his tiny body this time. She knew this.

"Go. Don't come back."

Runner's eyes glowed green. "You know what, bitch? The

Handsome Butcher took the wrong kid. He should have done us all a favor and taken this one."

He spat on the floor. Took his hand off the doorknob and left.

Cherry dropped the knife. Flung the bathroom door open. Jonah was covered in snot and blood. The bathroom mirror had shattered. He had glass in his tiny fists. His face was red, but his lips were blue.

"Baby." Cherry gathered him close to her. He trembled, his screams quieting, while she rocked him in the pieces of broken glass. "Oh, my sweet boy." She ran her hands over his thin arms, his bony legs, over his ribs and face and through his hair.

"Upstairs," she told him and hauled him up each step. He was so heavy. She was so tired. She dragged him to his room and set him gently on the bed. Grabbed the oxygen tank from the corner and fumbled with the mask. Turned it on. "Breathe, baby," she whispered and held it over his mouth and nose.

Jonah struggled, but Cherry cooed and soothed and sang.

"In and out, my darling. Shall I tell you about the night you were born? It was a glorious, glorious night."

She talked. Told him stories. Reminded them about their old apartment with the strange water stains and cobwebs everywhere. Told him how strong he was, how brave. How he was the man of the house. How he always would be.

He calmed, gradually. Breathed in. Breathed out. Funny that something so simple could become so difficult. But he was a hero. A champ. A fighter.

She turned off the oxygen.

"I love you," she said and remembered the last time she had said those words, who she had whispered them to. "I love you."

She buried her aching face into his sweaty hair and sobbed her broken heart into her broken son.

Happiness doesn't belong to everyone. The darkness in her bloodstream pooled and swirled and feasted.

# Chapter Fifty-Three

MORDACHI DIDN'T EVEN ask why Cherry needed him. He just came. He always came.

He knocked on the door. Looked around at the porch. It really needed a fresh coat of stain.

Let Runner do that for her. If he was going to hang around, he might as well step up.

Only he wouldn't. Mordachi knew that. Knew deep in his heart that Runner didn't have it in him to be a real man, a real partner. That he'd always be the boy who was trying to live up to E's standards, to be his right-hand man only because he'd never be strong enough to be the one in charge.

He sighed. Stretched. Heard movement behind the door and arranged his face into a neutral expression.

The door opened slightly. He saw Cherry's eye through the crack.

"Mordachi?"

Something in his mind went primal, then. The fear he tasted from her. The uncertainty in her voice.

"Tell me what's wrong, Cherry." Something was wrong. Like the evil of the house, the disease of the town. Something had happened here.

"Mordachi, I don't want you to be mad."

Her voice was too soft, like that of a small girl. Like Daisy's sweet voice had been. For a second, he had the crazy thought that Cherry was gone, and Daisy was talking through her mother.

That they were both dead. That he was dealing with the ghosts of two little girls.

"Open the door for me, sweetheart."

The door shivered, started to open. Stopped.

It was too much. His body felt like every nerve ending was being zapped with electricity. But he couldn't move too fast, couldn't frighten her. It was just like dealing with wounded animals. Starving cats with broken legs. Beaten dogs that shied from loud noises.

"Sweetheart. Cherry. I won't be mad. I've been standing on your porch for an awfully long time. Will you please let me come in?"

Her eye disappeared. The door slowly creaked open. He opened it the rest of the way himself. She had already retreated to the kitchen.

The house had an unholy silence. A heaviness. A weight of bad feeling.

His hackles rose. "Where's Jonah?"

She had her back to him. He was almost afraid to look at her. Irrational, this fear.

"He's sleeping. He had a tough time this morning. It wore him out."

"He doesn't sleep during the day."

"Not usually."

It was a song and dance. A charade. He played his part well, stepping closer to her, his eyes roving over the room for signs of what had gone on.

He saw the cutting knife on the floor. The bathroom door open, pieces of mirror scattered around.

He swallowed hard. Reached for her.

"Is that blood on the floor?"

She turned around then, her nose swollen, the skin around her eyes purple and bruised. Blood crusted under her nose, on her chin. He saw where it had soaked into her shirt.

"Can you tell me what happened?"

Keeping his voice cool. Keeping it calm. Luring a barn cat out of hiding.

"Jonah was upset and headbutted my nose. Pretty hard. It bled. But I'm okay."

She looked at the ground. He nodded anyway.

"Okay. And Jonah. Is he okay?"

Her eyes became wet, and his fear tripled.

"I'm just going to go peek in on him, all right? See for myself?"

She nodded, and he went quietly up the stairs. As soon as he reached the second floor, he ran for Jonah's room.

He was there. Alive. Mordachi felt his blond head, checked for bruising. Cuts on his face and hands, but they had been tended to. His face was covered in dry tears. Mordachi closed his eyes, said a prayer of gratitude. Kissed Jonah's forehead. Went back down to see Cherry.

"He's sleeping well. I see he was cut. Was it the glass from the bathroom?"

She nodded again. Then her gaze fluttered up, met his.

The emotion in them made his gut hurt.

"Runner hit Jonah. He said the killer took the wrong child. That he should have taken Jonah. Like he means nothing. Like he's worthless. I had a knife, and I told him to go and never come back."

She moved into Mordachi's arms, sobbing, the way she always had when E had been particularly cruel to her. He rocked her back and forth. Careful of her tender face, careful of her tender soul. She was raw and the house was sucking the pain from her marrow, he could feel it.

"I'm sorry, darling. I'm sorry."

"You were right, you were right," she cried. He hushed her and soothed her. Told her not to talk about it. Thought to himself he had been right. Of course, he had been right, and she should have listened. But since when did she think with anything other than her heart? It had always been this way. How could he expect her to change now?

"I can't take any more, Mordachi. I just can't."

"It's okay, Cherry. We'll get through this. We will."

One person wasn't meant to handle so much pain, he thought. She needed to get out of here. Needed to take her son and flee while she still could. Before E showed up and made everything even worse. Or perhaps E would simply kill them all and end it entirely.

# Chapter Fifty-Four

**M**ORDACHI PUT A bag of groceries on Cherry's counter.

"It's getting bad out there. Darling is rumbling."

Cherry took the milk and put it in the fridge.

"About what?"

"About everything. Ephraim being back. Nobody can find him after I ran into him at the bar."

"Do you think he left?" The hope in Cherry's voice was so eager, so pure, she almost felt embarrassed. But what if God sent him away. Maybe He found a reason to answer Cherry-colored prayers.

Mordachi's face was grim as he said, "I don't think so. I think he's lying low for a few days. I messed him up pretty good."

"Perhaps you scared him, and he won't come back."

He shook his head. "You know E as well as I do. He's gonna come for you, Cherry. I'm thinking it wouldn't be a bad idea to get your mother's rifle out." He looked out the window, narrowed his dark eyes. "Actually, a gun is a mighty fine idea. People are whipped up. About the Handsome Butcher. Folks accusing folks. I hear Azhar was hassled just trying to get out of town."

"He didn't do it. Why not just let him go? You'd think they'd want him to leave after everything that's gone on."

Mordachi put the bread away, turned to face Cherry. "Part of the reason the police had him locked up so long was for his own protection. People are funny critters. They want something to hate. If the police keep Azhar, then he's nice and safe in his secure little cell. You know they're treating him right. He's not getting folks coming after him in the dead of night, and the people have someone to hate."

"A scapegoat, you mean."

"Someone who isn't them. An outsider."

"I don't like this, Mordachi."

"Neither do I."

"Anyway, thanks for telling me what's going on and for picking up the groceries."

"Not a problem. Your face will heal soon enough. It's no problem until then." He shuffled his feet, cleared his throat. "Listen, I'm sorry about Runner and Wendy. It would have been decent for her to keep her mouth shut about it for at least a week or two."

She tried to laugh but didn't quite make it. "I should have known better. I was a conquest, E's wife. The second he bagged me, of course, he'd run off to some other girl."

"They're not new," Mordachi said. He ruffled Jonah's fizzy hair as he satellited around, looking for toast. "It's been going on for a while. Not while he was with you, I don't think, but before."

Cherry carefully unloaded the grocery bags. Too carefully.

"When, before?"

Mordachi tried to catch her eye, but she wouldn't look at him. "Remember when we were out looking for Daisy? The whole town? Except for Runner and Wendy?"

Cherry's eyes flew to his, her mouth open.

He shook his head. "He wasn't choosing being with her over looking for Daisy, Cherry. I don't think he heard about it. He was busy."

Cherry's lips twisted and she swallowed hard.

"That's why he wouldn't let me go with him to check his house. Why do I care, Mordachi? I shouldn't, but I … Oh."

She sat and stared at her hands.

Jonah hooted happily, taking his bread, and heading for the toaster.

Mordachi rested his large hand on her head. It felt warm

and steady and reminded Cherry of wearing a particularly favorite hat on a cold day.

"Can't help who you love. You just do."

She heard what he was saying, what was threading under his words. He knew she knew, too. Neither of them said anything.

The phone rang. Cherry looked at it and her spirit crumbled.

"Want me to answer it?" he asked.

She closed her eyes. "Please."

He grabbed the phone off the receiver. "Hello. LaRouche residence. Yeah, this is Mordachi. She's here, but unavailable. What can I do for you?"

He went silent. His eyes darted to hers, connected. She felt the pull. The electricity. The words filling his ear filled her brain at the same time.

"They found her." She whispered the words so softly that they were little more than air, but her voice rebounded around the room like she had screamed.

"Is that right?" Mordachi said. "Where was this? When? And now? Thanks, Sheriff."

The phone slipped into the cradle. Cherry licked her lips. A fly buzzed.

"They found her," Cherry said again, slightly louder. The world around her softened, darkened around the edges.

"They're not sure. It's a possibility. They want you to come down and see if it's Daisy. She's difficult to identify."

"It's her. I know it is. I can feel it."

"Cherry."

"My baby."

Her eyes rolled up and Mordachi caught her before she slipped from the chair.

Jonah, uninterested, headed to the washer and dryer. Bang. Bang bang.

Bang.

# Chapter Fifty-Five

BLEACHED BONES. RIBBONS of calcium. Tiny fingers that should be holding dolls, holding crayons, holding Mommy and Daddy's hands.

The tests came back. This was somebody else's baby. Somebody else's Daisy.

Cherry didn't get out of bed for two days.

Nobody blamed her. For once, Darling had nothing to say.

# Chapter Fifty-Six

CHERRY HAD HELPED Jonah onto his perch in the tree. She handed him a book. He imitated looking at the pages, then put it on his head like a hat, looking at his mom.

"Fun-ny?" he asked.

She smiled. "Funny."

This is how it's going to be, she thought. Him and me. When she was a little girl and dreamed of her future family, this wasn't how she saw it. An absent husband, special needs son, and murdered little girl. She wiped at her eyes with the back of her hand. She shook her head and mussed Jonah's hair.

"We have a future ahead of us, darling. Let's talk about it."

She whispered to him of the dreams she used to have. Of getting out of town. Of owning a cheerful house somewhere as far away from Darling as she could get. Somewhere far west. Oregon, maybe. She'd have E, who adored her, and dogs and cats and raccoons. Everything.

"And money," she told him, swinging her legs from the branch. "Money for everything you could ever want. Therapies. Doctors."

"No?" he asked, and his blue eyes turned black with worry. "No?"

"No, sweetheart. No doctors."

"Is there room for one more up there?"

Jonah saw Mordachi and squawked with joy.

Mordachi tipped his hat at him. "Hiya, son. Cherry."

"Hi, Mordachi. There's always room in here for you. It's your tree."

He tossed his hat on the ground and squirreled up, settling himself on his branch.

"E hasn't come by to see ya?"

"Not yet. You?"

"Nah. I'm expecting him any day now. To come by swinging."

Jonah, encouraged by Cherry's praise, tried his book-on-the-head trick for Mordachi.

"Good one, buddy," he said and turned back to Cherry. "I'm worried about you. I don't think you and Jonah should be staying alone."

"We're perfectly fine on our own. Always have been."

"Now, darlin'. Don't get your hackles up. I'm not saying anything against you as a woman, as a mother. But you didn't see E at the bar that night. I did. He's gone wild. I wouldn't hazard a guess as to what he's capable of."

"He's capable of running out, that's for sure."

"He's capable of doing anything in order to get what he wants. And maybe he doesn't want you two. Maybe he doesn't. But chances are, he still thinks you're his property. If he hears about Runner—"

"I'm not seeing Runner anymore."

"—he'll come after both of you. Ephraim doesn't like to share his toys."

Cherry looked at the darkening sky. Soon there would be stars. They'd reflect light nobody else could see.

"I'm not his toy," she said softly. "We're so much more than that." She gritted her teeth. "Mordachi, there's something I want to ask you, and it's gonna hurt, and I'm sorry, but I need to know."

"What is it?"

She looked at Jonah, who was studying the bark of the branch. Even if he could process all the words, he wouldn't be able to process the content behind them.

"Your dad. And what he used to do. To you and the others."

"Yes."

His voice was dark. Flat. She didn't like it. She hurried on.

"Do you know why? Did he ever say why? If maybe there was something that would have stopped him?"

He was silent. The sound of the wind moving the branches, the leaves of the Dogwood shaking back and forth. Jonah's contented mews.

"I'm so sorry, I shouldn't have asked."

"No, it's okay. You're thinking about Daisy, aren't you? What the monster was thinking? How could he do it?"

"Yes, but I don't think I want to know anymore. I'm sorry for bringing it up, Mordachi."

"It's getting dark. Time to get Jonah inside?"

"Sure."

He climbed down. Held his arms out while she lowered Jonah. Set him on his little boy feet and caught Cherry when she jumped.

He held his arms around her for a long time, his face thoughtful, his mouth turned down.

Finally, he said, "I can't talk about that, Cherry. I just can't. But it might be something you need to know. In the morning, I'll drive you two out. I'll walk around with Jonah outside, and you can go. See my father. Get your answers. Ask a monster how a monster thinks."

He turned away before she could even answer. She just stared after him as he disappeared into the night.

# Chapter Fifty-Seven

*T*HE RIDE TO the prison was silent except for Jonah's cheery cooings. He loved the car. He loved Uncle Mordachi. He loved his mama. To have all three? How delightful! He missed his sister, but he had a hard time putting her face together in his mind after all this time. Like a mama, only smaller. Like a Jonah, but with ribbons.

Jonah with ribbons. Ha.

"Fun-ny?" he asked, trying out his shiny new word. "Funny?"

"Funny," both Cherry and Mordachi confirmed.

About ten minutes from their destination, Cherry reached across the seat and put her hand on Mordachi's shoulder.

"Are you sure you're okay with this? I mean, I want to know so maybe it can help me with Daisy, but I don't want to hurt you."

"It won't hurt me."

"Mordachi, I'm serious. You're so dear to me. If this is going to bother you, I won't do it."

His voice was almost a roar. "I said it's not gonna hurt me. Listen to me, woman. If it will help you, fine. If it doesn't, fine. What happened, happened. Nothing's gonna change it. But stop bringing it up all the time. I let it go years ago. I don't need you muddying up the water."

They hit a bump too fast.

"Sorry," he said.

"No, I'm sorry."

"What are you sorry for? I'm the one driving like a—"

"I'm just sorry."

They drove the last few minutes in silence. Cherry worried at her fingers, squinting at the derelict building that came into focus.

Mordachi parked the truck.

"This is it?"

"This is it."

The prison was old, squat. Unlovely. It seemed like a place of despair. A place where you handed over all your hope willingly.

She swallowed hard, opened the truck door.

"Hey."

Mordachi reached over, took her hand. She looked at his hand and then at him.

"You don't have to go. You don't have to do this."

"Are you saying this for me or you?"

A smile ghosted around his lips. "For you. Everything I do is for you."

She leaned over Jonah, threw her arms around Mordachi, and hugged him fiercely. Cherry kissed him on the cheek.

"Nothing that man says will change the wonderful things I think about you, okay? Nothing."

She was out of the car. Walking up the steps to the prison. Ready to face the original Monster of Darling.

She showed her ID. They checked the list, wanded her body, and led her to a room with a small table.

"Donald Lewis."

The guard announced the name before helping the small man shuffle inside. His hands and legs were cuffed.

He saw Cherry and grinned. "Hello, darlin'. How is my daughter-in-law?"

"Please don't call me that, Mr. Lewis."

"You look more like your mother every day."

He sat at the table across from Cherry. His blue eyes were quick, alert, and ran over her features in a way that made her slightly ill.

"Th-thank you for speaking with me."

"Not a lot of visitors, if you know what I mean. The fact that you're a beautiful woman is a bonus."

She bit her lip but decided to plunge along. "Mr. Lewis, I need to ask you about the things you did. To your boys. To some of the other kids."

He leaned back in his chair. "Already been charged for all of it. You're not gonna learn anything new. Tell that to your lawyers."

He whistled and the guard started to walk for him.

Cherry's hand flew out, rested on his arm. She bit back her revulsion. "No, it isn't for lawyers or anything to do with that. It's for me. Something I need to understand. Can you help me?"

He looked at her tiny hand on his skin. Her eyes followed his gaze, and she wrenched her hand away. Scratched at her palm. Looked at the table.

He held his hand up, stopping the guard. "What do you mean, girl? Help you, how?"

She was disgusted. This man, the things he had done. The way Ephraim had cried in his sleep as a teenager, as a man. Her throat burned. She tried to keep the bite from her teeth.

But Daisy. The Handsome Butcher. She had to know.

"Mr. Lewis, somebody stole my daughter. My little girl. Took her right out of my house. Did you hear about it?"

"Would this be my granddaughter?"

Her stomach did things. Lurched. Twisted. Nearly rebelled.

She gasped. Couldn't hide it. Donald's face didn't change expression, but his eyes came even more alive.

"No. She isn't Ephraim's."

"Whoring around on your husband, then? Does my son know?"

Cherry felt her eyes narrow. Felt the hate bubbling up from somewhere dark and deep and fanged.

"I have no idea if he knows. I haven't heard from him since he left me alone with a new baby and a pile of debt."

He grinned. His teeth were yellow and sharp. "No need to get riled, darlin'. Just asking."

"And I was just telling you."

Donald studied the room. "Had all my hopes pinned on that one. He's a good boy. Good at sports. He had lots of potential."

"Mordachi has potential, too."

His gaze sharpened on her.

"Screwing that boy, as well?"

Her face grew hot. "No. I'm not. But even if I was, it's none of your business."

"Tell me what happened. With your daughter."

Cherry's head spun. "I …"

"You said somebody stole her. Who?"

She swallowed. "I don't know. There's been talk of a madman going around."

"Somebody from Darling?"

"Maybe. Yes. I think so."

"How did you feel when he took her?"

"Excuse me?"

His eyes shone. "What was it like? When you realized she was missing? That something had been done? Were you alone when you discovered it? Did you have a friend nearby? A man, perhaps? Maybe one of my boys? I'll bet Mordachi was there, wasn't he? He was always hanging around you like a lovesick fool. When you were kids. Always. Even when I was doing things to him. Him and his brother. He didn't tell you that, though, did he? How he hurt? How he could barely walk in the morning, but still he came over to your house, to help you, to play. To climb that damned tree."

"Stop it!"

He blinked, his face beaming with innocence. "But isn't this what you wanted? To know what it felt like? To see into the mind of the man who raped your baby?"

She gagged, and Donald smiled.

"Oh, you have a tender heart. Hearts like yours are so easy to break."

"You're evil."

"I've been called worse."

Cherry took a deep breath. Closed her eyes and tried to pull herself together. She was here for a purpose. Was she strong enough to do it? Did she really want to know?

No. Yes. She needed it. Needed the knowledge and vile details to course through her, singe away everything good and naïve and weak. It was necessary to become hard if she was going to survive this. She had to become strong.

Cherry stiffened her spine. This is Cherry becoming brave. This is Cherry fighting back, the only way she knew how.

"I need to know."

He smiled again, and she shuddered.

"I'm not talking need, dear heart. I'm talking want. Delicious, delicious want. Do you *want* to know?"

She thought of Mordachi, walking around outside with her son. Thought of the things she would hear—the secrets that would no longer be secret. His pain, and E's pain, flayed open and laid out for her to dig her hands into and pull out like entrails.

She had said nothing would change between her and Mordachi, but would it? Could she keep that promise if she knew everything?

Donald sighed. "You don't want to know. Too bad. I was so looking forward to telling you. To reliving."

Cherry leaned forward, her face uncomfortably close to his. "I want to know. Now, will you help me or not?"

"Why should I?"

She didn't know what to say. Because he was a decent person underneath. Because he had a chance to help family. Because he could show some goodness, show some compassion and be more than a loser sex offender locked in a stone box.

She knew none of these things would work.

"Do what you just said. Relive, but with an audience. I will be your audience."

His pink tongue touched his top lip, and it was obscene. Cherry swallowed her disgust, forced it down into her stomach. She knew she would empty it out, later, even if she had to stick a finger down her throat. Get rid of the vileness, the disease.

He was thinking about it, obviously. Tantalized. Torn between telling her what she wanted to know and keeping it from her to maximize her pain.

She was going to have to up the ante. "Tell me, and I'll give something to you. Do something for you. Can you have gifts? I bake. Do you like pies? Cakes? I can bring you books. Visit you if you want more visits. Please, just tell me what you want. What will make you talk to me?"

"Bring me a picture of the girl."

She froze, her tongue stuck to the roof of her mouth. Her words had been pouring like rain. They dried up.

His voice was so calm. Honeyed. Glossy. She could hear E in it. Could hear Mordachi when he talked to one of his horses.

"That's not so much, is it? A picture? A picture of my daughter's baby girl?"

"I'm not your daughter."

"You married my son. That makes you family, doesn't it?"

"We're separated."

"Don't you want to *know*, Cherry? It seemed so important

to you to understand. The things I could tell you about how I think. About how the Handsome Butcher thinks."

"How did you know it was the Handsome Butcher?"

He grinned. There was so much to be said in that grin.

"You knew all along, didn't you? What happened?" Her voice was coming from somewhere deep inside, shaking. "You heard about this already. You just wanted to ask me about Daisy to hurt me."

"Daisy, is it?"

She stood. "I'm not playing your games. You had a chance to do something good. To make amends somehow. To be less than the disgusting, abhorrent monster that you are. I'm through with you."

She turned to leave.

"You are my daughter, you know. In every way that counts."

"Making a mistake as a teenager does *not* make us family."

"That's not what I'm talking about, darlin'."

Cherry stopped, clutched her purse to her chest. "What do you mean?"

"Turn around and face me."

She did, slowly. Her body moved without her permission. Like her life. Always, everything, without her permission.

"As I said, you look so much like your mother."

"Don't bring her into this. She has nothing to do with it."

He looked wistful, but then the calculating look returned. "She has everything to do with it, Cherry. You know what draws me to do what I did? Fear. The smell of it. The taste of it."

"You preyed on your own children."

"Because they were there. They were easy. But there were others, of course."

He looked at her meaningfully. She swallowed hard. "What others?"

He was delighting in this. Relishing it. He'd lie on his cot tonight and think about it, moaning at the look on her face. The look of horror and outrage and infection she couldn't hide.

"So much like your mother. Your soft, trembling, fearful mother."

The bile rose, and Cherry covered her mouth with her arm. Trying to hold it back. Trying to stop her mind from seeing.

"During storms, usually. Your father was gone so often. They slept in separate rooms anyway, did you know that? So even if he was home—"

"Stop it."

"—the wind and rain were so *loud*, you see? And she was so small. Fragile, like you. But I bet she never seemed that way to you, did she? She was good at hiding things. Bruises. Her love. Shame."

"I said, stop it."

"And the look on her face? I think of it all the time."

Cherry headed for the door again, wiped her eyes, and realized she was crying.

"And then she got pregnant."

She gasped, doubled-over, and the guard peered at her to see what was wrong.

"Miss?" he asked.

She waved him away, wrapped her arms around herself.

"She never liked you dating E, did she? Was pretty vocal about it from the start. I wonder why that would be? You were the darling of Darling. He was the hero. Seemed like it would be natural for you to get together unless there was something that made it unnatural."

Her sobs surprised her, great, heaving sounds that shook her shoulders. The guard hurried to her.

"Miss? Hey, I need a second guy out here."

Another guard appeared, took a hold of Donald. Pulled him up from the table.

"And your boy. Yours and Ephraim's. There's something *wrong* with him, isn't there? How about the girl, from a different father? Is she okay? Is she *unwrong*?"

Cherry collapsed against the guard, who pulled her through the door.

"Quiet, Lewis!" the second guard spit out.

Donald grinned. "Oh, that's right. It doesn't matter. She was murdered by the baby raper."

He laughed. He laughed and it was the most awful sound she had ever heard. Worse than E's laughter while he hit her. Worse than the house when it giggled at night.

"I always heard you were afraid of storms, Cherry. Is that true? Do they frighten you? Make you ill? Your mother hated storms, too. Bad things always happened during storms in Darling, didn't they? Something always went wrong."

He paused, and the words seared into her soul.

"These days you don't have to wait for storms."

The door shut behind him with a clang.

They signed her out. Handed her a paper cup of water. She drank it and wiped her eyes with the palms of her hands.

Mordachi and Jonah were outside, looking for frogs in the undergrowth. When he saw her, Mordachi straightened and shaded his eyes.

"Are you okay, darlin'?"

The same name his father—her father?—had called her, but there was a world of difference.

She stood on the tips of her toes and threw her arms around his neck. She buried her face against his shirt.

"Cherry?"

"He's a monster. Such a monster. I'm so sorry, Mordachi. I never understood."

He wrapped his arms around her, pulling her close. Closed his eyes and did what he had done for his whole life: he hated his father.

# Chapter Fifty-Eight

*T*HE RIDE HOME was silent except for Jonah's happy chatter. Cherry leaned her head against the window, staring at the great big Louisiana sky held up by magnolias and cypress pine.

When they were nearly home, Mordachi cleared this throat.

"I could go for a beer when I get home, Cherry. Gonna need to stop and pick some up. Do you mind?"

"Not at all."

He pulled into the grocery store, turned off the truck, and sat in his seat longer than necessary.

Cherry looked at him. "You okay, Mordachi?"

"Want anything? Like a Coke or something?"

"That would be great."

"Be right back."

Cherry chewed her fingernail and watched him walk to the store. Pause and hold the door open for two teenagers. Nodded at their thanks and stepped inside.

"Hiya, baby girl."

She froze, her finger still in her mouth.

"Now, darlin', that ain't no way to greet your husband."

Her eyes moved first. He was leaning against Mordachi's door, talking through the open window. She turned to fully face him. His face was bloated and bruised, his hair unkempt. But under the extra fat and grime, there was the youth she had fallen in love with.

"E," she said.

He smiled, and she was startled to realize his smile—his teeth—hadn't changed, even when the rest of him had. They were still sharp and beautiful and strangely mean.

"Good to know you still remember me. I got a phone call, darlin'. People have been right worried about you. Sounds like you're sleeping your way across Southern Louisiana."

"People don't know what they're talking about."

Jonah squawked, and E flicked his blue eyes to the boy. "This him?"

"This is your son, yes. Jonah, in case you had forgotten."

"Too good of a name to waste on a retard."

She laughed bitterly. "You sound like your father. Now I know where you got that particular mean streak."

"Like my … What would you remember about my father?"

"Don't have to remember. I saw him just today. In prison."

"Why'd you go talking to him?"

"I needed to know some things."

He leaned closer, his face dangerous. Dangerous and scared and uncertain. A little boy wearing the face of a man. It didn't fit. She congratulated herself on not flinching.

"What kinds of things?"

"None of your business. Now back off. You're scaring Jonah."

"I said, what kinds of things?"

She opened her mouth to say it. To say she understood why he was so shriveled and mean inside, that she finally caught a glimpse of the horrors his father wrought. That he just might be her father, too, which meant that she and her husband—

"Hey."

Both Cherry and E turned at Mordachi's voice.

Cherry closed her eyes in gratitude. Breathed deep.

E straightened up.

"Just having a conversation with my wife. Ain't no law against that."

"Move, Ephraim. You're in my way."

E stepped back, but his expression made Cherry's throat go dry.

"That's not how you show respect, little brother."

"I have no respect for you."

He pushed his way into the truck. Set the beer on the floor and tossed Cherry her Coke.

"All right?" he asked, not looking at her.

She nodded, then realized his eyes were firmly on his brother. "We're good."

"All right, then. Let's go."

He started the truck. E grabbed onto the door.

"Don't let her fool you. She don't need saving. She's a predator, that one."

"Let go or I'll take your hand off when I leave."

"If she wanted you, she would have had you. She's had everybody else this side of the Mississippi."

"Your hand."

He leaned close to Mordachi's face. "She's been talking to Dad."

"I know. I took her."

Mordachi pulled out, forcing E to step back clumsily or get run over.

"I know about you and Runner," Ephraim shrieked, his face red. "I know what Mordachi did to him, too! Nearly killed a man. Is that who you want to hitch your wagon to?"

Cherry turned to Mordachi. "What's he talking about?"

"Nothing."

"Hear anything on your roof at night?" E shouted as Mordachi drove away. "Ask what my pervert brother has to say about that."

Cherry's mouth dropped open.

"That's been you? On the roof? The thing?"

"It's not like he's saying."

Jonah started to squirm. Cherry wrapped her arms around him.

"Then what exactly is he saying?"

Mordachi cursed. "He's just trying to rile you up, Cherry. Get back at you. He knows I'm the only friend you have in town and he's trying—"

"Is he lying? About the roof? Were you up there?"

"It isn't like—"

"Were you up there?" she was screaming now.

Jonah wailed and threw his arms over his head.

"Yes. Yes, I was up there. To keep an eye on you. To keep you safe. You're so stubborn. I just felt like I needed to keep an eye on you."

Cherry felt numb, felt the horror settle on her heart.

"While I slept? While Runner and I made love?"

"No, of course, not."

Her eyes went wide. "Then what he said about nearly killing Runner. He said something hit him from the roof. That he fell out and … Oh, no."

She felt sick. She pulled Jonah closer to her, pressed against the door.

"Don't be ridiculous. You know me. You know I wouldn't do anything like that."

"I know you love me. That you've always loved me. That nobody has loved you like they love E, and you've always been jealous."

"Cherry."

"And Runner and I, it killed you, didn't it?"

"He showed what kind of man he is."

"But I still prefer him to you."

"And why is that, Cherry?" he growled. Cherry cringed away, pulling a flustered Jonah even closer. "Don't you dare pull that. The 'Oh, you're so scary, Mordachi' routine. I have never once hurt you. Never once left you, even when I should for my sake. I'm always here for you. Whatever you need, I give to you. You have two kids to take care of? Okay, I'll help you. Who was there when Daisy went missing? Who helps with Jonah? Who comes to the door to find you bleeding with two black eyes—"

"Stop the truck."

"—and broken glass and a cut-up son—"

"Pull over."

"—and a *knife* on the ground of all things? Who else would waste their time taking care of somebody like you?"

"Let me out, now!"

He slammed on his brakes. Cherry braced herself and Jonah against the dashboard, then unbuckled the seatbelt and leaped out.

"You're saying terrible things," she hissed.

"No, you're *being* terrible. Ungrateful. You're the most ungrateful person I've ever met."

She grabbed Jonah's hand. "Don't come by anymore. I don't want to see you again."

"Not a problem."

He sped away, and she kicked rocks after him. Huffed a little bit. Took Jonah's hand and started walking the last mile back to the house.

Jonah peeped.

"Not a word," she warned.

Their footsteps on the road were the only sound.

# Chapter Fifty-Nine

*I*T HAD BEEN a long, terrible day. Mordachi stomped around until he couldn't stand it any longer. He'd forgotten he had some groceries for Rosemary. Might as well drop them by. At least there was one person in Darling who would be happy to see him.

He knocked on her door. She took forever getting down to it, like usual. Most likely had to secure her poor mother somewhere safe while she was away.

"Mordachi," she breathed when she opened the door. She was wearing a too-big, shapeless dress, but her cornflower blue eyes lit up when she smiled.

"Hi, Rosemary. Sorry to stop by so late. Look, I had a few things in this here bag, and I thought you and your mom could put it to good use."

"You're so sweet, Mordachi. So thoughtful. Wait here, let me get my purse."

He pushed the paper bag into her arms.

"Oh, no. Not necessary. This is just … you know. Some things around the house. Stuff I wouldn't use."

She studied him, his hands in his pockets, the way his shoulders slumped.

"What happened today?" she asked softly. "Are you all right?"

He laughed. "No. Not so much, actually. But it's okay. Just a long day, is all."

She put the bag on the table behind her. Reached out with both of her hands. Took his rough brown hands in her soft, white ones.

"Mordachi? I know you're in love with Cherry. And she's a fine girl in a lot of ways, but she's never going to love you. And I do. Since we were kids. I wish that meant something to you."

He looked at her hands. Let his gaze travel to her wide, sincere, nearly fearless eyes.

"Rosemary, I …"

She squeezed his hands, then let go. "You don't have to say anything, but I thought you should know you're loved, even if it's only by me."

She smiled and started to shut the door.

He put his hand on the jamb.

"No, wait. It does mean something, Rosemary. Thank you. It's good to hear a man isn't alone all of the time."

She laughed. "Oh, I know how that feels. This house. Nobody ever really stops by, except for you, and then everyone's in such a hurry to go. I know what lonely is." She blinked, looked him in the eyes. "Would you like to come in for some sweet tea? I mean, if you have the time, of course."

He opened his mouth to say no, he had to be getting home, but he heard himself saying, "I'd like that."

Her smile was like sunflowers. Her thin face looked almost pretty when she smiled so brightly. Rosemary swung open the door, and he realized this was the first time he'd ever gone into her home.

"Have a seat, Mordachi. My mother is already in bed. Let me run and make sure everything's okay. Then we can just enjoy some conversation."

He watched her leave the room, then stared around him. Sunny. Yellow. Not what he expected, really, but then, what *did* he expect? Something sterile, maybe. Dreary. Grays and faded old-lady purples.

He wasn't much for being waited on. He went through the cupboards until he found glasses. Poured tumblers of sweet tea.

When Rosemary came back, he handed one to her. The surprise and joy on her face made his heart hurt. Was she so unused to basic human kindness that something this little would make her so happy?

"So, ah, how are you doing, Rosemary? We don't get a chance to talk a lot."

She sat at the table, scrubbed at a spot in her flowered dress with worn fingers. "I don't want to talk about me. I want to know why you're so upset today."

He blinked. "You never take the long road to get where you're going, do you?"

She looked at him, her face open. "Why? What's the use of that? I never understood the purpose of it."

He sat down heavily, swigged his tea. "I'm not sure I understand the purpose, either."

"You're upset about Cherry?"

"Some."

"Want to tell me about it?"

"No."

"Then let's talk about something else."

And they did. Stilted conversations about their childhoods, about the way the town's changed.

"It's unholy, Rosemary. I don't know if you can feel that. It changes people."

"Changes people into what?"

"Monsters."

She laughed. "Oh, you're so funny. It doesn't do that. It just strips the veneer away. This town lets us be who we really are."

The conversation reached a natural standstill.

Mordachi stood to leave. "It's been a pleasure. I'd like to stop by and do it again, sometime, if you don't mind."

"I'd love that."

He heard a sound from outside in the woods. Some yelling.

He walked to the window and peered out.

Men, running through the brush, armed with rifles and farming tools. Things that would hurt. Things that would bludgeon, cut, tear. Rape. Rip.

"Just a second," he told Rosemary and rushed outside. He could see a fire burning in the brush, way back.

"What's going on?" He hollered to one of the men running by. It was his old friend Trip, Monica's kin. Uncle to the murdered boy.

"They found him!" Trip shouted. He jumped from foot to foot, he was so excited to keep moving.

"Found who?"

The smoke from the fire was starting to drift this way. Trip coughed.

"The Handsome Butcher! The baby killer. Out in the woods." He jerked his head toward the flames.

"Anybody call the police?"

Trip shook his head.

"Nah. Hoping to get to him first. C'mon, Mordachi! Grab your gun! There's gonna be justice in Darling tonight!" He hooted and crashed through the brush.

Mordachi clenched his fists.

"What's going on?" Rosemary put a trembling hand on Mordachi's arm. He looked at it, and then at her.

"I need to go. I want you to go upstairs and lock yourself in the room with your mother, do you understand me? Take your gun. You have a gun?"

"Yes, but I don't know how to shoot."

"Take a knife, then. A baseball bat. Something to protect yourself, just in case."

She nodded. "What is this about?"

Mordachi started walking around the house, locking windows, testing doors.

"They say they found the Handsome Butcher. Gonna kill

him before the law stops them."

"Why would they—I can do that. I can lock up. Why don't you just go?"

"What are you gonna use as a weapon?"

"I'll find something. Just go!"

He pushed past her, headed up the uneven spiral stairs. Ducked into the first room and tested the lock on the bathroom window. It didn't catch.

"Got something I can use to board this shut?"

"I don't like having you up here. Leave, Mordachi."

"I'm not going to leave two defenseless women alone while everybody is running around like the devil is on their tails. This town is off its rocker. Won't take me two minutes with a hammer to keep you safe. I'll take it down later and fix it proper. Now, move, Rosemary. We don't have much time."

He pushed past her and opened the next room. Secure window lock, no tools. The next door. Same thing. He opened the last door and paused, blinking, at the darkness in the room. The window was nailed closed, and dusty light filtered through the slatted boards hammered to the wall. He saw something move in the darkness, heard a sound, and then something crashed against the back of his head, and he went down.

# Chapter Sixty

$\mathcal{J}$ONAH HAD BEEN drugged with his night-night medicine and was asleep in bed. Cherry wore her mother's long white nightgown, curled up on the couch with a book. Staring at it, not reading, but trying to keep herself from pacing.

Would Mordachi really do that? Try to kill Runner? This afternoon she was so sure his jealousy was coming through, that he had a horrid core like everybody else, but could it be the town itself? The disease that Monica had tried to warn her about? Was it turning Mordachi?

Or maybe it was turning her. Maybe he hadn't done anything at all, except spend a few watchful nights trying to be close to her. Trying to make sure she didn't go to pieces in a house that tried to eat her alive. He knew it would have killed her to ask for any more help than she already had.

She needed to talk to him. Needed to make things right. There was so much ugliness swirling around, and Mordachi was the bright spot. As rooted as the tree they played in as children.

She'd call him. Apologize. Ask him to stop by if he could forgive her. Tell her it wasn't romantic love, but it was love, and she loved him as strongly as she loved anybody, including her children. In more ways than maybe they knew, they were family. Perhaps he had always been her brother.

She was heading for the telephone when she heard a banging at the door.

She froze, some primal instinct kicking in, the vulnerability of an undressed woman alone with her child in the middle of the forest.

The knocking, again. Fast. Urgent. Done with the side of a fist.

She hurried over, opened the door. A young man stood outside, his upper lip fuzzy, his eyes wild.

"Yes?"

"Miss Cherry, my mom sent me. They found the Handsome Butcher. They're gonna kill him out back if you wanna go watch."

She hardly realized she was gripping her throat. "They found him? Going to … kill him?"

An unnatural light glinted and danced in the boy's eyes. "Went right into the jail looking for him, but he'd already left. Caught him leaving town. Cops weren't doing nothin'. Everybody knows it's him. Killed his own little girl and then he killed yours. And they have some other guy, too."

"Other guy?"

"The old school photographer. Found some sleazy stuff on his computer. Pictures of the kids in town doing things. Gonna kill him, too, I think."

"They can't do that!"

The boy shrugged. "Who's gonna stop them?"

"I am."

Cherry's hands shook as she unlocked the gun cabinet. She grabbed her father's old rifle and loaded it with a determination that made her numb.

"Stay with Jonah. I'll be back."

"But I wanted to go see—"

She whirled on him, a tiny force of nature in her mama's old nightgown.

"Your mother wouldn't want you anywhere near such a thing! Stay here. Keep my son safe. I'll be back as soon as I can."

"What if he wants a drink of water or something?"

"Give it to him."

She opened the door, stuffed her feet into her red rain boots. The screaming and yelling came from the distance and the sky was on fire.

"God help me," she prayed, and then she ran.

# Chapter Sixty-One

*T*HE GROUND WAS muddy underfoot. She pushed through the undergrowth, her nightdress caught and torn at every turn. But she followed the cries. The whoops and screams and hollers. The sound of men going mad.

The fires ate the sky, casting demonic shadows where they danced. Darling truly had become Hell.

She came upon a crowd of people. Faces she knew from church, from the diner, only they were hot and twisted in the firelight. They curled and sneered and shrieked.

"What's going on, here?" she asked one of the faces. Earlier that day he had been the town's butcher. Now he was something else entirely.

"Caught the killer," he said and pointed. "He was booking it out of town, and they grabbed him before he could skedaddle away, the coward."

"*Who* caught the killer?" she asked, but he had already disappeared into the crowd.

A woman turned around, and Cherry realized it was Monica. Her too-bright lipstick was smeared up the side of her face. Her mascara had run under her eyes, which were bright from smoke and tears.

"They have him, Cherry," she said. Her sharp-toothed grin was far too wide, nearly wrapping around her face. Cherry blinked and it was simply Monica again. "They have him. The monster who killed our babies."

Cherry felt sick. "They have who? Where are the police? People are going to be killed out here."

Monica took Cherry's hand. It was surprisingly cold despite the heat.

"Don't you get it, Cherry? Nobody's what we think they are. They're all monsters at heart."

"They're monsters?" Cherry asked. Her grip tightened on the rifle. "What about us? I heard there was another one, another Butcher. How can there be two?"

Monica's expression didn't change at all. "Who knows how many there are? If they're really killers or not? This other one had dirty pictures. Of *children*. Take away a baby's innocence and it's just as bad as killin'. Maybe even worse." The blankness in her eyes frosted Cherry's bones. "Think of it as cleaning house."

"How can you be okay with this?"

Monica looked at her. "How can you not be? What do you have to hide, hmm?"

"Monica?"

"You spend an awful lot of time in your nice house feeling sorry for yourself, Cherry LaRouche. Just a pretty girl waving her pretty hands and waiting for someone to take care of her. Just watch yourself. That's all I have to say. Everybody is stirred up tonight. I don't think even you would get a pass."

Cherry was about to respond, but a far-away shriek cut through the night, sharp as a cleaver, and the single solitary sound of a bullet echoed. Cherry's heart stopped, stuttered, and started again when she saw Adam Getchell, Ardeth's grandson, on his knees with his hands over his head. He was sobbing uncontrollably, tears running down his face and reflecting the firelight.

A man holding a gun pulled the trigger and shot into the mud next to Adam again, and the man howled in terror.

"I didn't do anything, I swear," he cried. His eyes were bright and wild. "I didn't do anything but look. I never touched a child, never ever, and I would never do so. Never."

The man with the gun spit into Adam's face. It mixed with the tears and the snot already there.

"You're a school photographer, you kiddie diddler. Practically a teacher. We trusted you. These kids trusted you. Your kind ain't fit to live." He put the gun to Adam's head.

The photographer closed his eyes. "No, please, they were only pictures. I never—"

The sound of the gun interrupted his words. Pieces of bone and bits of tissue spattered everywhere while a fine red spray diamonded the air.

*It's so beautiful,* Cherry thought dreamily. *Like cheerful paint on dreary white walls. Now the house will be full of* life.

Then her brain caught up with the horror of her eyes and she screamed. She gripped the rifle as if it was a magical thing that could somehow save her. Her screams were swallowed in the cheer that erupted around her as Adam's body fell heavily into the crimsoned mud.

"They got one," somebody shouted, and the cheering intensified, becoming so loud that Cherry had to squeeze her eyes shut and cover her ears like a little child hiding from danger.

Hiding from her mama. Hiding from the storms.

The ground began to tremble, feasting on the blood, and the crowd surged with new energy.

"More," they called.

Human voices sound devilish in firelight. Cherry had never realized this. She never wanted to hear the crackling of wood or the sound of humanity ever again. She wanted to be in a dark house with her children, never speaking a word again, but simply living and breathing and loving. In silence. Forever in blessed silence, so the evil things that lived in the ground could never crawl inside of her throat and turn her voice to what she heard in the trees this night.

"More."

More bloodshed, more violence, more hatred.

"Where's the other one? It's his turn."

The other one. The one escaping town. A man of quiet and good intent and unfathomable sorrow. A man who had been warned to return home by his murdered little girl.

Cherry whirled around, climbing through frenzied, clambering bodies. She waded into the thickest clump of bodies, using her rifle to push and club people out of the way until she saw him. Her beautiful, gentle Azhar. His arm was clearly broken, hanging uselessly. One liquid eye was swollen shut and his face was covered in slick blood. He was being hauled to his feet by two men. No, not men. They were demons, imps, cavorting inside this new Hell.

"Let him go!" She pushed her way through the crowd to him.

One of the men hit Azhar in the mouth. He went down hard, grunting, then tried to clamber slowly back to his feet. He spat out blood and what looked like a tooth. His broken arm showed slivers of bone in a way that made Cherry retch, a steaming mass of bile that mixed into the mud and blood. Azhar winced as they shoved him to his knees and roughly tied his hands behind him.

A man with a red shirt kicked Azhar forward. No, not just any man. It was E. Azhar's glasses flew off and landed in the mud. A woman stepped on them, grinding the wire and glass purposely under her heel.

E's shirt was open and covered in glistening stains. Sweat ran down his face, but it was his eyes that chilled Cherry. They were lit with a dark fire within that filled her with more fear than the fire without ever could. She'd seen those eyes before, and they always came with walloping fists and broken bones.

E slammed his foot down on Azhar's back, making him cry out. It was the sound of beauty dying, of something precious being ripped apart and made into something rotten.

It was very much the sound of an innocent man being murdered.

Cherry had enough.

She stepped forward, her nightdress filthy, her red boots stained, briars and thorns caught in her hair. She trained her gun on her husband.

"Ephraim Lewis. Get off him. *Get off.*"

"Cherry?" Monica was at her shoulder, her eyes pinwheeling madly. "What are you doing?"

Cherry took a step closer, her eyes blazing. Her finger was calm and sure on the trigger.

"Back away, E. Azhar, get to your feet and come over here by me."

Azhar stood gingerly and stepped behind Cherry. The crackling of the fires was the only sound.

"Now, Cherry," E said in his most placating voice, his hands raised. Cherry could smell the stink of him over the smoke. It made her stomach turn. "No need to get over-emotional."

"Over-emotional? A man was just murdered over there. You're about to do the same to Azhar here, and I'm over-emotional?"

"Cherry."

"Step the hell back."

She circled carefully around, her back to Azhar, the barrel of her unshaking gun to the crowd.

"But he killed your daughter!" somebody shouted.

She winced, but only for a second. "You have proof of that?" she asked.

"He's an outsider!"

"That's worth killing him for? We have laws for a reason. To protect people from mobs like you. Look at yourselves. Look at what you've become."

"Why, it's Cherry LaRouche. So self-righteous," Wendy said, surprisingly close to her. Cherry hadn't even noticed her creeping forward.

"Back away, Wendy. Now ain't the time."

"Are you happy to have your husband back in town? I called him, you know? Let him know you were catting around. A man's got a right to know these things, doesn't he?" She took another step forward, threateningly close.

Cherry glanced at her, and E took that second to rush forward. He wrestled the gun away and pushed her to the ground. She breathed in mud and coughed. Tried to blink it out of her eyes. Turned her head and coughed again.

She felt E's foot on her back, firmly pressing her down. Her mind scrambled, screaming inside of her head, replaying abuse after abuse after abuse in a horrid picture show as she remembered being in this position before.

Pinned. Trapped. At E's fickle mercy.

A small whine of terror escaped her throat.

"Now, this is more like it," he said.

# Chapter Sixty-Two

*M*ORDACHI FELL FORWARD. He quickly caught himself and ducked out of the way as Rosemary shrieked and tried to hit him with the board again.

"Enough. Stop that," he bellowed.

She screamed as she swung the heavy board, and Mordachi grabbed her thin wrists. He shook her like a rag doll until she dropped her weapon.

"What's gotten into you?"

She kicked at him, squirming and biting, and Mordachi held her at arm's length, backing up until he ran into something that clattered and swayed under his weight.

A wheelchair. Bones. A skeleton housed in an old, black dress.

Mordachi stared in horror and Rosemary used this opportunity to break free, dropping to the floor and scuttling to the opposite corner.

"This is your mama?"

"Don't take her! Don't take her away from me!"

Mordachi could see Rosemary's thin shape in the shadows, her wild eyes shining in the darkness.

"How long has she been dead? You've been up here all alone with her for how long, sweetheart?"

"She's mine. She's mine. Nobody else needs her like I need her."

Mordachi took a step toward her, holding out his hand. All his work with the horses, the scared barn cats, and the beaten dogs came into play now.

"It's all right, Rosemary. I didn't understand how alone you were. I wish I knew."

He heard her crying in the dim light. "Now you think I'm horrible, don't you? To keep her. You'll take her away from me, and I'll go to jail, and I'll be all alone again."

"No, darlin'. You won't be alone. You need a friend. I'll be your friend."

She sniffled.

"Really?"

"Really. Now come on out."

"I wanted to tell you."

"You did?"

"I was afraid you'd hate me, Mordachi. That you'd never speak to me again. I know what I did was wrong, but I was so lonely. And I wanted a family."

"I know. Family's awful important, isn't it?"

"Maybe we could be a family. The three of us."

He tried to smile so she could hear it in his voice, but his mouth wouldn't cooperate. He bared his teeth faintly.

"Maybe. Are you ready to come out, Rosemary? Will you take my hand?"

He held his hand out in the darkness. She hesitantly put her white hand in his.

"It's so good to finally tell somebody. I took really good care of her."

"I bet you did."

He pulled her to her feet. Hugged her to him. Her body felt as bony as her mother's remains. He closed his eyes and ran his hand over her hair.

"It's okay now, darlin'. You're okay."

She hugged him back.

"I was so alone, Mordachi. But she made me happy. Don't I have a right to be happy?" She pulled away, her eyes searching his. "Don't I?"

"Of course, you do."

"Good." She slipped out of his arms and retreated to the corner. Bent down and reached for something hidden under a blanket.

"Come say hello to Mordachi."

Mordachi took a step forward. Two. Then his legs failed to work, and he stood there, rooted, staring, and gaping and acting like a fool man with no thought in his head. He commanded his body to obey, to work, to just *move, dammit,* and his stone limbs gradually became muscle and sinew and tendons again.

He rushed to scoop the little girl into his arms.

"Daisy. Daisy, darlin'."

He said her name over and over, running his hands over her body, kissing her face and her pigtails and her head again and again. Her face was filthy. She was wearing the same nightgown that she had gone missing in, but she was real. She was here, and she squirmed and snuffled and grudgingly allowed him to kiss her. Relief filled the hole in his heart, but something new and dark lined the edges. He held her to him and glared at Rosemary.

"You had her the whole time?"

She looked confused.

"You sound angry. I thought you said you understood."

"You kidnapped a baby. A baby! Do you know how worried we've all been? We thought she was dead. They arrested a guy for her murder."

Whooping. Screaming. Mordachi peered through the slats on the window, saw the fire in the sky. He cursed.

"This town's gone to Hell, Rosemary, and it's your fault. They're gonna kill some guy out there, thinking he hurt this little girl. How could you do this?"

Rosemary looked like a ghost in the dimness of the room. "I didn't mean to hurt anybody. Cherry had two children. I didn't have any. It only seemed fair to share."

Mordachi felt the disgust displayed on his face. He didn't hold it back.

"We'll deal with it later. I need to get Daisy back to her mom, see if I can calm everything down. This town is eating itself alive because of you."

He turned to the door. Rosemary flew at him, grabbing his arm.

"No, don't take her! You said you wouldn't take her. You said she could be my family."

He shook her off. She grabbed him again and he pushed her away, hard. She stared at him with shocked betrayal.

"Don't touch her. She already has a family. Leave us be," he said and shut the door. The key was in the lock, and he turned it.

Rosemary slammed her hands against her side of the door. "Don't take her! Please don't take her, Mordachi. I need her."

Her words were muffled from the thick wood, but he could hear the tears in her voice. He closed his eyes and swallowed hard.

"I'll come back for you soon, Rosemary. Sit tight."

He kissed the little girl who clung to him like a monkey, her blue eyes wide and scared.

"Come on, baby girl. Let's get you home to Mama."

Daisy looked at him hopefully. "Mama?" she asked.

Her voice was like bells. Mordachi had never heard anything so sweet. His eyes burned with tears, and he wasn't the least bit ashamed.

"Yes, Mama. Oh, little one, she misses you so much."

He ran down the stairs and leaped into his truck. He buckled Daisy in and kissed her filthy hair one more time. He could see that several bonfires were going. Heard bullets. Heard screaming and cheering and shouting.

His truck kicked up gravel as he tore out of the driveway to Cherry's house.

# Chapter Sixty-Three

CHERRY TRIED TO stand, but Ephraim kicked her once in the stomach. She fell and wrapped around herself.

"Stay down, honey. You're gonna enjoy this."

He nodded to the men who held Azhar. They slipped a noose around his neck.

Cherry tried to cry out, but her breath was still knocked out of her. She struggled to her hands and knees, and E kicked her again. She collapsed.

"Look at this town," E said to the crowd. "Look at what happened since she came back. I don't know what she has against Darling, but this is what she does, don't you see? Causes problems. If only y'all knew what I had to deal with."

The mud. The fire. The sounds of Darling cannibalizing itself. Cherry turned her face to the mud and sobbed.

"Then she sluts around. The girl? The one that went missing? Not even mine."

E's eyes reflected the firelight in the unholiest of ways.

"Not even *mine*."

The crowd murmured. That Cherry LaRouche had always been trouble. Nothin' but.

"And to make it worse? She seduces my best friend. Pushes him from the window and tries to kill him."

Runner came forward, the bonfire at his back. His eyes were hard and cold and full of a darkness that made Cherry's mouth go dry. Darling had spread to him, infested him. It rode around in his bones like a malignancy.

E slapped Runner's back.

"Now, most men would be mad, but I don't blame him. She can be pretty convincin'. I fell for her myself years ago. And she does make a good little ride."

The men yanked Azhar to his feet. He met Cherry's eyes. His were beautiful and liquid. Full of sorrow and fear and sympathy.

"No," Cherry managed to breathe.

E nudged Runner, who slapped her so hard her lip split. She gasped and her eyes filled with tears. He backhanded her again.

"And then she brings a baby killer to Darling. I'm so sorry," E said and looked Monica square in the eyes. "I'm sorry for what she did."

Monica cried, covering her face with her hands. E screwed his face up into something that resembled pity.

"Your boy ain't never coming back, but at least we can have some justice."

He nodded, and the men yanked on the end of the rope. Azhar gagged and was lifted into the trees. His feet scrabbled uselessly in the air.

Cherry screamed and reached for him.

E mimicked her, cruelly.

"Stop! Cherry, I found her." Mordachi shouldered his way through, pushing past E and Runner. He yanked Cherry to her feet and held her protectively.

"Daisy," he said urgently. "I found Daisy." He raised his voice. "Let him down. I found the girl alive."

Cherry's head spun, but Mordachi held her steady.

"She's alive, Cherry. Do you hear that?" He turned to the crowd, supporting Cherry in his arms. "Cherry's little girl is alive! Right now!" The mob's faces twisted devilishly. "Let Azhar go. The Handsome Butcher isn't here at all."

Azhar kicked and jerked on his rope. His dark eyes bulged.

Monica pressed her way forward.

"But what about my grandson?"

Mordachi looked at her with so much sympathy that Monica had to look away.

"I'm sorry, Monica. Looks like a drowning to me. A horrible accident, but still an accident. We were just so caught up in the idea of a killer in Darling that maybe we read it wrong."

The men released the rope slightly. Azhar's toes touched the ground and he struggled for breath.

"M-Mordachi?"

Cherry's eyes were beginning to clear. Mordachi kissed her grimy face, two, three times.

"She's home. I brought her to your house. When the kid told me you were out here … Rosemary had her."

"Rosemary? Why would she …?"

"She was lonely, Cherry. Her mother's been dead for years by the look of her. She had her bones inside of the house. I've never seen anything like it."

"And Daisy?"

"Go home to her. Now."

The crowd had become a beating heart. The anger seethed and pulsed. Rosemary did this? A dead woman in the house? Stealing babies and corpses?

The heart became a mouth, became something twisted. The mouth opened, and the sounds that came out were unhallowed. Men surged forward with flaming branches. Women splashed gasoline on the wooden siding of the tottering old house. Rosemary's house started to burn, became the biggest bonfire of all.

"Run, Cherry! Go!" Mordachi screamed. "I have to help Rosemary. I locked her inside."

Cherry nodded and turned to flee. She slammed directly into something tall and hard.

Ephraim.

# Chapter Sixty-Four

CHERRY STRUGGLED TO push past him, but E caught her easily by her wild hair. He wrenched her head back, pulling her off balance and forcing her into the mud again. She floundered, trying to pull her nightgown down over her thighs. She used her filthy sleeve to wipe the mud and tears from her eyes, leaving her face more streaked than before.

The crowd shifted uneasily from foot to foot, murmuring. This was who they were doing this for. The mother of a victim. But things had suddenly changed.

Mordachi slammed his fist into Ephraim's jaw. Grabbed his fingers and bent them back until he untangled them from Cherry's hair. He swept her up from the mud and held her behind him.

Monica crept forward and put her arms protectively on Cherry's shoulders. Pulled her discreetly back.

"Shh, just be quiet," Monica whispered into her ear. "I've never seen Ephraim like this."

Cherry touched her tender cheek. "I have."

The brothers stared at each other in the light of the fires. In the distance, the whooping and screaming and pleas for help continued.

"You sure spend an awful lot of time with my wife," E said. His face was piggy, harsh.

Cherry's eyes flicked from one to the other.

Monica's hands held firm and steady on her shoulders.

"You gave up the right to call her that years ago."

"Gotta make her pay."

"And Runner, too, right? For touching your wife?"

E smirked. "You knew I pushed him, then?"

Mordachi shrugged, seeming casual, but Cherry could see his muscles bunching under his shirt.

"I knew you used to hang out on the roof when you were younger. After all, you're the one who showed me the best place to stay, right?"

"Best way to keep an eye on a slut, right? Dad taught me that."

He moved toward Cherry, but Mordachi blocked him.

"Let it go, brother. Let her get her kids and leave. She'll never bother you again."

E's eyes narrowed. "That's not good enough. She has to be *sorry*, you see? Cherry!" he screamed. "Are you sorry?"

"I know how to make her sorry."

Runner. His tall, lean frame. His mussed hair. His green eyes, cold and full of something so ugly her soul cried for her to look away. She couldn't. She was transfixed.

He took a step toward Azhar. Pulled out his pistol.

"No!" She surged forward. The crowd moved with her, in her way, warm bodies stopping her movement, her momentum, her goal.

Runner pointed the gun at Azhar's head. Right between his beautiful eyes. Those unearthly, loving, caring eyes locked with Cherry's, and the look in them made her want to cover her head and howl.

Runner fired.

"No! No!"

Azhar slumped against the rope before his body dropped.

Runner turned and pointed the gun at E.

Chaos. Shouting and yelling and screaming. The dark vines of Darling wrapped around them, pulling their souls into the soil one by one. Bullets sounded like fireworks. Knives flashed in the firelight. Monica's hands were torn from Cherry's shoulders, and she was lost in the crowd.

Mordachi lunged for Cherry. She held out her hand. The residents of Darling had turned into monsters, into demonic things, and they pushed and pulled her away from him.

"Mordachi!" Cherry struggled closer. She stretched out, her fingers just inches away.

He almost grabbed her, then his eyes went wide. A trickle of blood ran from his mouth. A torrent. Life, redness, a precious thing. Something meant to stay inside had come out. Cherry couldn't process what she saw.

He fell forward and Cherry screamed.

Her scream was swallowed up in everybody else's screams. The smell of slaughter. Blood pattering on the grass and dirt, mixing with the mud. Cherry crawled to Mordachi, pulled his head into her lap.

His eyes were open. Empty. They reflected the ash that rose into the air from the fires. The front of his shirt was stained with blood. Bullets that had met their mark, piercing the biggest, most beautiful heart she had ever known.

"Please," she said and pressed down on his wounds. Blood seeped from between her fingers. "Please," she repeated and shook him. If only he would blink, would take a deep breath, would show her that he was alive. She needed him. She wanted to say how grateful she was for everything, that she appreciated it even when she acted like a caged cat. He was her brother. He was her family.

She bent over him, sobbing, giving herself up in the grief of the only man who had ever really loved her, and the only man who had ever earned her trust.

"Cherry!"

Ephraim.

She froze, pressing against Mordachi's body like a baby rabbit in the bush. She didn't want to leave him, wanted to protect him from the bloodthirsty crowd. The idea of these heathens tripping over him and stepping on his body made her ill.

"Cherry. Don't you hide from me."

E's voice sounded like madness itself. His vocal cords had grown spines. He opened his mouth and the hate and sickness from Darling was what vomited out. The town had a spokesperson, a mouthpiece, and it was her husband. She remembered his fists. She remembered Mordachi's battered face when he told her Ephraim was back in town. She sobbed, then covered her own mouth to keep herself silent.

"When I find you, you ungrateful—"

The rest of his threat was lost in the shrieks of the crowd, the snarls of the terrain. But she knew what he said. He bared his teeth in the firelight, and Cherry had never seen anything wilder. He was the beast of her nightmares. The horror on the roof, the ghost in the walls. He was everything she had ever feared, and he was looking for her.

She leaned over and kissed Mordachi softly on his bloody cheek. Then she moved.

She scrambled away on hands and knees, keeping low so E wouldn't see her. She didn't realize she was breathing too hard and fast until she heard herself, felt herself get dizzy. She swallowed and tried to regulate her breathing.

"Nice and slow," Mordachi would have said. His Louisiana drawl wasn't the uneducated accent she had always been afraid of. It was a thing of beauty. Sweetness and stability in the long vowels, in the roundness of his 'o's. "That a girl, Cherry. Get away, nice and slow."

Her fingers landed in something wet. Automatically, almost against her will, she held her hand up to see. The firelight tricked her eyes, made her think she was seeing something slick and red, but of course, that couldn't be. Swallowing hard, she looked down.

Most of his face was missing, but he still had one perfect cheekbone. One dazzling green eye. Some of the white teeth that she had admired whenever he laughed.

Cherry screamed and scrambled backward, away from Runner's ruined face. She staggered to her feet and pushed everyone out of the way. This crowd echoed the cries of the other bonfires, the other groups that were maiming and murdering throughout Darling.

She ran, not caring about whether or not Ephraim had her in his sights. She had to get away from Mordachi's ravaged body, from Runner's gory corpse. She wiped her hand hysterically on her nightgown, leaving a smear of blood, bone, and brain matter behind.

She thought she heard Mordachi running beside her, his heavy work boots hitting the ground with a heaviness that was reassuring.

"Breathe, girl. Get your kids and get out. Nice and easy."

She was running so fast she stepped out of one of her rain boots, leaving it behind. Her gait was so awkward, so uneven, that she kicked the other one off as well. Bare feet. Roots and rocks, bones and rotting undergrowth. She didn't care.

Cherry was too stunned to cry. She just ran until she reached the house—her mama's house, that house of horrors. Until she burst through the door and startled the kid asleep on her couch.

"Where's Daisy?" she demanded. Muddied and panicked, barefoot and scratched, hair wild and eyes wilder. "Where's my daughter?"

"Up in the room. With your boy. Mordachi said to put her to bed. Did he find you?"

"Go home," she said. "Go home to your mama and don't come out again tonight. You won't live if you do."

He looked at her and then slipped out the door. It slammed behind him.

She raced up the stairs. The door to the bedroom was open. Cherry held her breath and burst inside.

Daisy and Jonah were snuggled up together. Daisy. Her eyelashes were dark atop her white cheeks. Tear stains under her eyes. She slept with her fingers in her mouth.

Cherry fell to her knees. Stared at her children. The way their hair fluttered in the breeze from the open window. The way their pulses beat in their necks. She held a hand out to them, afraid to touch. To destroy. To discover it was a dream. She'd had so many.

Two gunshots. Several more. The roar of a human gone inhuman. Cherry straightened.

"Come here, my darlings. Quickly, now, come downstairs with Mommy."

She covered Daisy's face with kisses, buried her nose in her hair. She smelled like filth and sunshine. She held her in her arms while she guided her bleary-eyed Jonah down the steps. He squawked half-heartedly.

"Just a little more, dear heart. Once you're in the car, you'll be all settled.

She buckled the children in. Bumped her forehead against Daisy's and let her tears fall briefly.

The fires were burning closer, the entire town of Darling seething and buckling. She saw E running toward her, silhouetted against the flames. He was waving the gun, screaming something she could barely make out over the sound of the fire.

"Sleep, little ones," she said and slammed Old Sal into reverse.

A gunshot, and her back window exploded. The cries of her children, the shattering of glass, and the roar of the flames all combined into an unbearable cacophony, a tornado of sound. Cherry looked over her shoulder, aiming her car carefully, and then she shut her eyes.

She stomped on the pedal as hard as she could.

"Please, God," she prayed. She hadn't prayed in years before coming back to this cesspit, this little village of Hell. Could prayers even be heard here in the devil's backyard? "God, please."

She hit Ephraim solidly. She heard the sickening sound of flesh and crunching of metal, and nothing had ever sounded so good. The force jarred her, and for a brief second she was terrified he was caught under her wheels. She put the car in drive and sped forward.

"Jonah. Daisy. Are you all right?"

She adjusted her rearview mirror to look at them. Jonah's fuzzy hair bobbed as he craned his neck to look around. Daisy leaned against her brother.

"Don't look out the window, darlings. We're going for a long ride. Just close your eyes."

She readjusted the mirror and saw Ephraim sprawled on the dirt road. He didn't seem to be moving.

She didn't really care.

As soon as she hit the main road, she punched the gas. Pushed her foot as far down on the pedal as she could go. She thought of Mordachi's warm brown eyes and quickly thought of something else. She saw a man in an officer's uniform swinging slowly from a tree, and she prayed that it wasn't kind Ian Bridger. A group on the left was savagely kicking a woman while she screamed. One of the men looked up and met Cherry's eyes while she passed. It was John Holfield, the lawyer who had brought her back to Darling in the first place. His eyes were dead. He had blood on his crisp work shirt. He was a monster, just as they were all monsters.

Hell House. Horror House. A pool of the dead in a town that was feeding on itself, its inhabitants. She had fled Darling once, years ago, and that was what had saved her. Now she was forced to do it again.

Ah, but with her children. With her precious little ones.

She looked at them again through the rearview mirror. Jonah looked around hazily, still trapped by sleep. Daisy's beautiful eyes were starting to flutter.

She had them. Both of them. In a few hours, she would pull the car over, crawl in the backseat with them, and hug them until the sun rose. She'd never let them go. Never.

She noticed the small, partially made Daisy doll sitting on the front seat. It had blue button eyes and pigtails like banners. Cherry rolled down her window and tossed it into the road. She never needed to see it again. The power of the dolls wasn't necessary anymore. Her babies were no longer lost.

The town burned behind her, but she didn't look back. All that she needed was sleeping in the backseat. It was enough. It was everything.

# Epilogue

*T*HE TOWN HAD devoured itself, but it was time to move on, anyway. Find new animals to care for, a new hunting ground, new dolls to play with.

He'd fed Mordachi's horses one last time and then turned them loose. He didn't know what had happened to the other ranch hands, but odds weren't good that they had survived. He'd barely crawled away from that crazy massacre himself. The animals would have a better chance of surviving if they were free rather than cooped up in the middle of nowhere without anyone taking care of them. Letting them starve would be cruelty.

"Be safe," he said to one and patted the horse on its neck. Then he tossed his dark hair out of his eyes.

"Ready?" he said to a child that wasn't there.

Sada nodded back. She reached out to take the Handsome Butcher's hand, and they walked down the dusty road together.

# Other books by Mercedes M. Yardley

PRETTY LITTLE DEAD GIRLS:
A NOVEL OF MURDER AND WHIMSY

APOCALYPTIC MONTESSA AND NUCLEAR LULU:
A TALE OF ATOMIC LOVE

BEAUTIFUL SORROWS

LITTLE DEAD RED

NAMELESS: THE DARKNESS COMES

BLACK MARIAH: LAS VEGAS, NV

ARTERIAL BLOOM (Editor)

# Acknowledgements

Special thanks to Chuck, Jericha, Kristyn, Michelle, and Nancy, who came running when I needed you. Hurry up and wait, indeed! I'm privileged to have you by my side.

Special thanks also to my son, Niko, who lives with Williams Syndrome and autism. You are special because you are simply you, and that is enough.

Thanks to Nina and Lilia who collectively had pigtails like banners. You're both so cute and our neighbors were creepy enough that we had to learn how to play The Quiet Game.

Thanks always to Luke, who puts up with a creative madhouse.

Thanks to my parents who support me even though I didn't go into physical therapy and don't write nice, Christian fiction.

Thanks to the Illiterati and Minna, who were and always will be my favorite first readers.

And for all those who raise children with disabilities, or children on their own, or children who are difficult, or don't raise children at all…I see you. You are in my heart.

# About the Author

Mercedes M. Yardley is a dark fantasist who wears red lipstick and poisonous flowers in her hair. She writes in a lush, lyrical style about current social issues and finding love and beauty in the darkness. She authored *Beautiful Sorrows, Apocalyptic Montessa and Nuclear Lulu: A Tale of Atomic Love, Pretty Little Dead Girls, Nameless, Little Dead Red,* and *Love is a Crematorium.* She won the Bram Stoker Award for *Little Dead Red* and was nominated for her short story "Loving You Darkly" and for her *Arterial Bloom* anthology. Mercedes lives and works in Las Vegas with her family and strange menagerie. You can find her at mercedesmyardley.com.